A PUBLISHER'S NOTE

To my dearest readers:

Triple Crown Publications provides you with the best reads in hip-hop fiction. Each novel is hand-selected in its purest form with you, the reader, in mind. *Let That Be the Reason*, an insta-classic, pioneered the hip-hop genre. Always innovative, you can count on Triple Crown's growth: manuscript notes — published books — audio — film.

Triple Crown has also gone international, with novels distributed around the globe. In Tokyo, the books have been translated into Japanese. Triple Crown's revolutionary brand has garnered attention from prominent news media, with features in ABC News, The New York Times, Newsweek, MTV, Publisher's Weekly, The Boston Globe, Vibe, Essence, Entrepreneur Magazine, Inc Magazine, Black Enterprise Magazine, The Washington Post, Millionaire Blueprints Magazine and Writer's Digest, just to name a few. I recently earned Ball State University's Ascent Award for Entrepreneurial Business Excellence and was named by Book Magazine as one of publishing's 50 most influential women. Those prestigious honors have taken me from street corner to boardroom accreditation.

Undisputedly, Triple Crown is the leader of the urban fiction renaissance, boasting more than one million sizzling books sold and counting...

Without you, our readers, there is no us,

Vickie Stringer
Publisher

Karma

BY SABRINA EUBANKS

Compilation and Introduction copyright © 2009 by
Triple Crown Publications
PO Box 247378
Columbus, Ohio 43224
www.TripleCrownPublications.com

Library of Congress Control Number: 2009935876
ISBN 13: 978-0-9820996-9-8
Author: Sabrina Eubanks
Graphics Design:
http://www.leapgraphics.com
Editor-in-Chief: Vickie Stringer
Editor: Alanna Boutin
Editorial Assistant: Christina Carter

First Trade Paperback Edition Printing 2009

10 9 8 7 6 5 4 3 2

Printed in the United States of America

Acknowledgements

It's an amazing feeling to finally touch down where you always wanted to land. Through God and my Lord and Savior Jesus Christ, I've discovered that anything is possible. All you have to do is believe in Him without question – and believe in yourself without arrogance. I am truly grateful to Him … and I'm *stayin'* grateful. Thanks go out to my wonderful parents, Mary and Julius Sr. I really, really wish you were here for this. I miss you guys so much.

With that said, let me give my shout outs: Thanks to my ultimate motivator – and the love of my life – my sweet little boy, D.J. Mama loves you. To Jay, my brother – thanks for holding me down like steel. Much love. My nephew Jayson (what up, Pookie!) and my beautiful, aspiring niece Joli' – love you guys. Thanks Aunt Kadie for all you do. All my aunts and uncles – love y'all! Hey, Uncle June! Much love, family. Derrick … Derrick … Derrick.

Thanks to my cousin Kimberly for letting me bounce this book off her, and for all our old good times. Winston, you were a Godsend. I'm gonna get back. Doug, you know I had to holla at you. Karyn, you know I think this is surreal, right? Love you much – peace, two fingers to Marley. Vera, thanks for holding me down and giving me confidence. Love ya, but you still gotta buy some damn shoes.

Desiree, Brenda, James, George, Chuck and Criag and dem … y'all some bad asssed kids, but I still love y'all. Craig, stay focused and do you. To all my old friends – forever friends – Barbara, Vickie, Billy, Larry and the rest of y'all, isn't it funny how you can always pick the thread back up? Much love. Mrs. Davis, you're a dream. Thanks for your faith. B.D. Lewin – you've been there more than you know – thanks.

Crazy love and respect to my T.A. family! Love y'all! You know who you are!

Lastly, thank you so much to Ms. Vickie Stringer for having enough faith in me to give me a chance. God bless you always. Christina Carter, you are an indispensable joy to work with. Really, this is the ultimate happy dance! Crazy love and mad respect. Alanna, you're the greatest. Thanks for all the kind words and encouragement. Much love. Thanks to everybody at TCP that helped get this book on the shelves. Y'all are the best.

Dedication

To my parents, Mary and Julius, wish you were here,
but I know you're along for the ride.

Chapter One

Justine

Justine stood in the vestibule of the church with her father. Looking handsome and proud in his tuxedo, he beamed at her. "I'm losing my little girl," he said through misty eyes.

Justine smiled at him. "I'm not going anywhere, Daddy. I'm just getting married."

He smiled back. "Seems like just yesterday I was playing with you, teaching you how to ride a bike, walking you to school …" he choked up and trailed off.

Justine put her hand on his arm. "Well, now you're going to be able to do it all again … with your grandkids. Don't be sad, Daddy. This is the happiest day of my life."

He kissed her cheek. "I know, baby."

The music started, and he held his arm out to her. She took it, and he kissed her cheek once more.

"Be happy," he whispered.

Justine nodded, not wanting to cry. "I will."

They stepped through the doors and started down the aisle.

There he was. Standing there, so solemn and handsome and strong, he was all she could see. At last. Their eyes met, and he smiled at her. The walk down the aisle seemed to take forever. Justine wanted to run into his arms, but she continued that long, slow walk. Somewhere, bells were ringing...

The sound of the doorbell snatched Justine from her pleasant dream. She checked the clock. At two in the morning, she could only assume Lucas had forgotten his key. She slid out of bed and made her way to the door, unlocking it without bothering to check who was there.

"What happened, baby? It's not like you to forget your key," she said as she pulled the door open.

Someone pushed hard from the other side, knocking her back into the wall. Startled and now fully awake, Justine moved away from the door. Panic froze her like a statue.

Simone stepped over the threshold, and Justine felt a rush of relief. She could deal with an angry Simone. She couldn't deal with a burglar or rapist. Simone quietly closed the door behind her.

"I don't have a key, baby," she said, mocking Justine's caring tone.

2

Karma

Justine put her hands on her hips. "What are you doing here, Simone?"

Simone took a long look at Justine. "I just came to have a word with an old friend."

Justine immediately noticed Simone's slurred speech.

"You're drunk, and we're no longer friends. Maybe you'll remember that when you sober up." Justine moved around her and held the door open. "You should leave, Simone. Now."

Simone laughed and pushed her out of the way, slamming the door shut.

Just then, Justine's phone rang in the background. Barging into her apartment drunk took a lot of nerve, and Justine was beyond pissed. Simone smiled sardonically and shrugged out of her coat.

Taking a step toward Simone, Justine said, "Uh-uh. Don't get comfortable. Did you not hear me? I said get out!"

Justine's phone stopped ringing. Simone was still looking at her with that smile still plastered to her face. A chill traveled up Justine's spine.

"I'm not going anywhere, Justine. Someone shot at me tonight. This shit is going to stop right now."

Oh, shit! Justine thought. She knew she had nothing to do with it. She was clear when she called everything off, right? It had to be Nine.

"I don't know what you're talking about," she said.

Simone shook her head. "I'm tired of hearing that from you. We both know it's you behind all this. Trying to make me believe it's Nine. He wouldn't do this to me. He loves me. You have every reason to do this, though. You've got a hell of a reason, don't you?"

Justine felt her anger boil up again. "You know what, Simone? You come in here, acting like I did something to you. I never did anything to you except try to be your friend. Look at what you've done to me. All you've ever done was try to destroy me. It didn't work. Lucas and I are going to be happy. You should get out and stay out of our lives."

Simone smirked. "You know what they say, whatever doesn't kill you makes you stronger. I'm tired of your sanctimonious bullshit. You always get your happy ending. Maybe this is the one time it's not going to go your way, Justine."

A ball of fear dropped in Justine's stomach.

Simone laughed. "Oh, you look worried now," she said.

Justine backed up, truly frightened. Simone kept laughing, a low, sinister rumble in her throat. She moved in closer. "Backing up won't help you." She walked up until she had Justine with her back against a wall. Justine's phone rang again in the background. Simone frowned for the first time since she entered the apartment.

Karma

"Who's that? Prince Charming? Too bad he can't help you now."

Justine shook her head. "Look, Simone ..." She started toward her, but Simone shoved her back.

"No! You look!" Simone shoved again. Hard.

Justine's head bounced off the wall. The sudden pain surprised her, and she threw up her hands defensively. "What's the matter with you? What did you come here for?"

The phone stopped ringing.

"How does it feel to be terrorized, Justine?"

Simone shoved Justine again and this time knocked her to the ground.

Okay, now Justine was really scared. She was not a fighter, and she knew it would be hard for her to win against Simone, who had six inches and 30 pounds on her. When Justine attempted to get on her feet, Simone struck her down again. Justine tried once more, and to her disbelief, Simone kicked her in the side as hard as she could. Justine heard her rib snap and sank to her knees, clutching her side.

"Are you crazy?" she wheezed.

Simone's laughter was a mix of hysteria and spite. "Oh, yeah. I'm crazy! I imagine people are following me. I dream up prank calls. Yeah, that's me, crazy. Call off your dogs, you little bitch!"

"It wasn't me, Simone."

Simone's grin disappeared. She reached down and grabbed a handful of Justine's hair, dragging her up to her feet. Justine was shocked. Was this really Simone? Had they ever been friends at all?

"It was you, you fucking liar!" Before Justine could say anything, Simone punched her in the jaw, sending her sprawling. "Get your little lying ass up!" Simone yelled. Justine attempted to rise, but Simone kicked her back down. "I changed my mind. It's good to see your ass down for once."

Justine looked up at her and asked the most important question. "Why? What did I do to you?"

Karma

Simone's smile crept back onto her face. "You offend me, Justine, you always have. Little Miss Perfect! You had everything handed to you on a silver platter, right down to Lucas. I'm sick of you and your perfect world."

Justine narrowed her eyes and quickly scrambled to her feet. "Is that what this is all about? Lucas? In case you haven't noticed, Lucas chose me. He doesn't want you! Get the fuck over it!"

Simone looked at her in mock surprise. She seemed amused. "Is that so? You think the day you saw us was the first time? I've got news for you, honey. I've had him on more than one occasion, so don't play yourself."

Justine's anger bubbled up so fast that she could hear the blood pulsing in her veins. She reached out and slapped Simone without even thinking. "You're a liar!" she screamed.

Simone's head snapped back with the force of the blow, but she was smiling maniacally when Justine turned around. "Am I?"

Justine had a sudden, intense desire to rip the smile off Simone's face. She couldn't believe what Simone just said. She didn't want to. "Bitch!" Justine screamed and launched herself at Simone. They went at each other with all the pent-up anger and resentment they had harbored for so many years. The women tore, scratched and punched. Simone was bigger than Justine, but Justine held her own until Simone tripped her up. Justine fell backward and an ominous crack sounded as her head hit the corner of the coffee table. Pain exploded inside her head like a white-hot bright light. Immediately, darkness seeped into her peripheral vision. Something had just gone terribly wrong. She knew it and started to panic. She was blacking out!

Simone took advantage of Justine's vulnerability and wrapped her hands around Justine's throat, squeezing with all her might. Justine clawed at Simone's face, but she couldn't quite control her hands. Something was wrong! That wasn't just a knock on the head. Simone kept squeezing with a look of deadly determination on her face.

"I hate you," Simone said so quietly that Justine barely heard her.

Justine dropped her hands to Simone's and tried to pry them from her throat. She couldn't breathe! This couldn't be happening! Simone was killing her. She was supposed to get married. Oh, God, no! She watched her own hands flutter helplessly and without the strength to remove Simone's.

The last thing she heard before everything faded completely was Lucas screaming, "What are you doing? What are you doing?"

A last thought crossed through her mind: Lucas! I love you! I'm so sorry. Help me.

Chapter Two

TWENTY-TWO MONTHS EARLIER ...

Lucas

Lucas Cain sat at the bar at Gideon's, sipping his single malt scotch, half listening to Noah talk shit. Most of his attention was focused on the door. He watched women as they came in, waiting for one to catch his eye. He turned around as he felt someone behind him.

"Hey, Lucas," a beautiful little light-skinned sister with a dusting of freckles across her nose offered brightly. He stared at her a moment, then flashed her a smile.

"Hey, you," he said just as brightly. They stared at each other another moment.

When he didn't add anything, she looked disappointed and a bit upset, but she recovered nicely. She patted him on the shoulder and looked from him to Noah. "You gentlemen have a nice evening."

Noah raised his glass to her, and Lucas kept smiling as she walked away. When she was out of earshot, Noah leaned back on his stool and laughed. "So ... who was that, man?"

Lucas sipped his drink and shrugged. "Some woman."

"Some woman? You tapped that?"

"Of course."

Noah looked at him slyly. "What's her name, man?"

Lucas looked surprised. "What kind of question is that?"

Noah laughed again. "C'mon, Luke. I'll give you $20 if you can tell me her name."

Lucas chuckled before he answered. "Rachel? Raychelle? Hell, Susan? Brother, keep your money."

"That's extremely fucked up, man. At least get the name straight. You hurt the bitch's feelings." Noah punched his friend lightly on the arm.

Lucas frowned. "I know your wife threw your ass out last year, but you had enough time to get over it. What's up with calling women 'bitches'?"

Karma

"Ouch! Damn, man. That stung a little," Noah had a serious look on his face as he leaned toward Lucas. "Bitches and hoes, that's how it goes."

Lucas shook his head and laughed. "That's real ghetto."

"Maybe so, but you're the pot callin' the kettle black."

"What's that supposed to mean?"

"It means — I might as well come right out and say it — hell, everybody knows how I get down. You just fuck 'em and shut 'em down, Luke. Hey, I'm a man. I admire the cold bastard in you, but a woman? Man, that shit's got to hurt."

Lucas finished his drink, as did Noah. He signaled the bartender for two more.

"You on my ass tonight, Noah?"

"I'm just saying, I know why I'm fucked up and angry. What happened to you?"

Lucas paid for the drinks. "Who says I'm fucked up or angry? I just don't want to settle down. I keep it movin'. Hit it and split."

"Nah, man. You do more than keep it movin'. When's the last time you saw a woman more than a week? Maybe two. You get 'em to give it up and treat 'em cold. They know exactly where you're comin' from. Ass, and that's it."

Lucas raised his eyebrows, amused. "Since when are you so concerned about it? You ain't exactly a prince, No."

"Never claimed to be. But I'm not talkin' 'bout me. I've known you a long time, and you've never been in a real relationship. Hit and run, then you freeze 'em out. There's something wrong with that, bro. I mean, it's like you don't even want to be decent and just say hello to somebody after you slept with 'em."

"I said hello."

Noah shook his head. "No, you didn't. You said, 'Hey, you.'"

"So?"

Noah stared at Lucas for a minute. "A'ight, Luke. I ain't fuckin' with you no more. I was just trying to see where you comin' from."

Lucas nodded. "Good, 'cause I was just about to tell your jealous ass off."

Noah gave him the screw face. "Jealous? Man, come on, I get as much ass as you."

Lucas had to agree. He looked at Noah. They both had tall, strong, athletic physiques, but that's where any similarity stopped. Noah was light-skinned. He had thick, dark curly hair and large, dreamy gray eyes. Lucas' complexion resembled a rich mahogany. His jet-black beard and moustache contrasted nicely against his dark skin and large, chocolate-brown eyes. In the precinct, they called them the Bible Brothers. Luke and Noah. They'd been partners, and friends, for seven years. Narcotics detectives were more like brothers than friends anyway. They also had women breaking their necks everywhere they went.

Karma

"That you do. Well … almost," Lucas finally conceded.

"Man, fuck you," Noah said, laughing. Lucas joined in on the laugh and they drained their drinks. Then Noah looked at Luke seriously for a moment. "Sorry, Luke. We cool?"

"Always."

"Good," Noah said, leaning toward the bartender. "My man, once again."

Lucas eyed his drink when it arrived. He pushed it away discreetly. He wasn't trying to be three sheets to the wind. He glanced at Noah, who was still sipping and had turned to chat up the woman to his left. Lucas turned his attention back to the door and put a stick of gum in his mouth. He watched the women entering the bar. Hoochie. Too skinny. Too fat. Ugly. Too loud. Chickenhead. He turned back toward Noah to see the woman he was talking to. Not bad. A little young, though. Lucas turned his gaze back to the door.

Three women walked in together, laughing and joking. Lucas straightened up. First one was pretty. Dark with Chinese eyes, long braids and bangs. Second, gorgeous red bone, lots of hair, tight clothes. Lucas licked his lips and took a long sip of his drink as he turned his attention to the third woman. His eyes widened. Caramel skin, huge, doe-like eyes, ebony hair falling softly over her shoulders. She removed her jacket and turned to talk to one of her friends. Body was banging. He stood up to get a better look and continued to watch her as she moved to a table with her girls.

Lucas placed a hand on his stomach and let out a nervous laugh. Shit! Butterflies? It had been a long time since he'd felt that. He watched her with her friends. She was lovely. Something about her seemed familiar to him. Lucas frowned. If he'd seen her before, he would have remembered. She laughed at something her friend said, and he admired the dimples in her cheeks and her perfect white teeth. Lucas was used to beautiful women, but there was something about her.

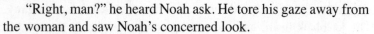

"Right, man?" he heard Noah ask. He tore his gaze away from the woman and saw Noah's concerned look.

"What?" Lucas asked.

"I asked if you were all right. You okay, dawg?"

Lucas shook his head as if to clear it. "Yeah, I'm fine."

Noah didn't buy it. "You drunk?"

Lucas looked insulted. "Hell, no. Do I look drunk to you?"

"I don't know," a grin crept onto Noah's face, "but you were lookin' pretty strange, starin' into space with your mouth hanging open."

The look of insult on Lucas' face was genuine. "My mouth wasn't hanging open, and I definitely wasn't staring into space." He discreetly pointed out the women at the table. "The one in the middle."

Noah appreciated Lucas' taste. "Damn, Luke, all three of them women are fine."

Lucas glanced at him, then back to the table. "The one in the middle ... isn't she famous or something?"

Noah looked a little closer. Recognition washed over his face. "That's that news reporter. Greer. It's something Greer."

Lucas pulled out his wallet and signaled the bartender. The bartender smiled when Lucas finished speaking, took the bill from

Lucas' hand and nodded.

"Oh, shit, player! Tell me I don't see this shit happening! You sendin' drinks? I been drinking with your ass for seven years, and I ain't never seen you send nobody a drink." Noah laughed in amazement.

"Shut up, Noah." Lucas straightened his tie and replaced the gum in his mouth with a breath mint. Then he carefully checked himself in the mirror that ran along the back of the bar.

The waitress delivered the drinks to the table. The three women all looked flattered, and when they looked toward the bar, Lucas stepped away and made eye contact with the woman in the middle. Her smiled never faltered. Her lips parted slightly, and she blushed. Lucas never broke the gaze. Without smiling, he picked up his drink and toasted her before taking a sip. He stared at her a moment longer. She blushed again, but did not look away. Lucas turned back to the bar.

Noah leaned over. "Play, playa! That was smooth."

"Yeah, well, let's just see if it works."

Noah frowned. "You're not going over there?"

Lucas shook his head. "No. She's going to come to me."

"That sure of yourself, huh?"

Karma

Lucas wasn't that sure. Instead of answering Noah's question, he finished his drink. He'd taken a chance. Either way, he wasn't leaving without meeting her.

Chapter Three

Justine

Justine dressed quickly, but carefully. Her girls would be here any minute. She slipped her feet into a pair of Jimmy Choo mules and adjusted her black silk skirt. Then she slid a spangly gold Dolce & Gabbana camisole over her shoulders to complete the outfit. With a little makeup, the look was complete. Just as she finished combing her hair, the intercom buzzed.

"Yes, Danny?"

"Miss Greer, you have Holly and Simone waiting for you."

Justine grinned. "Tell 'em I'll be right down." She went back to the mirror for one last look. The gold camisole accented her smooth, caramel skin. She smiled to herself. For a 33-year-old woman, she looked good. Hell, she'd never be tall, but she had her figure and there were no wrinkles around her eyes. She grabbed a short jacket from her closet and headed downstairs to see her two best friends.

When Justine made it to the lobby, her friends were already there waiting for her. Holly was a vision, subdued but glorious in a clingy sheath dress and cashmere shawl thrown haphazardly over her shoulders. Simone, on the other hand, was Simone. She wore a shockingly tight, orange satin dress, with ribbons barely crisscrossing the bodice. Justine could not imagine where she found them, but Simone was sporting a pair of 3-inch orange pumps with a spiderweb motif. The sparkle and glow of her honey-colored skin made it seem alive. Her brown, naturally curly hair bounced vibrantly, the blonde highlights shimmering with every shake of her head. When she saw Justine, Simone's light brown eyes lit up. All that, and a stripper's body. Justine smiled, secretly a little jealous. Simone might be a lot of things, but she was gorgeous. Beautiful, with a personality just as in-your-face as her looks.

"Simone, what is that you're wearing?" Justine asked.

Simone laughed, showing perfect teeth. "Shit, girl, come on! It's Halloween. It's just a little something I dreamed up."

"Dreamed up?" Holly asked. "You must have been somewhere between a nightmare and a wet one! You're wearin' a pair of FMPs with spiderwebs."

Simone winked at Holly. "Laugh all you want. You've got what we all want. I'm still trying to get it."

They all piled into Holly's BMW, laughing and teasing one another. A night out with the girls was a rare occasion. Holly was a book editor, married, with two kids. Simone was a stylist and enjoyed working with the rich and the famous in the hip-hop set. With nothing tying her down at home, she seemed to throw her rod into the stream at every opportunity.

"So, where are we headed?" Justine asked, settling into the backseat.

Simone turned around in her seat to answer Justine's question. "Gideon's. It's a jazz place uptown."

Justine wrinkled her nose. "Jazz?"

Holly stepped in. "C'mon, Justine. Jazz is good. Besides, Gideon's is more of a supper club. Sometimes it's jazz. You might get lucky and get R&B."

Justine still sat with her mouth turned down. "I don't know about jazz. I kinda wanted to dance."

Simone turned halfway around in her seat. "Let the jazz thing go. I doubt some fool will be up in there scatting. I've been there before. You can dance. Anyway, we have to go."

Justine leaned forward. "Why's that?"

"Because they have some fine-ass brothers in there, and girl, I'm tired of sleeping alone."

14

Karma

All three women burst out laughing. They high-fived and amened and kept the conversation light and breezy. The mood was pleasant, and they were ready to party.

It didn't take long to get there, and when they walked through the door, Justine was glad they'd come. The main floor was spacious, with a long bar and a dance floor. The décor was eclectic and bright. Upstairs had room to sit and eat and listen to live music. They sat at one of the tables that dotted the bar and ordered a round of mojitos.

"It's not what I expected," Justine said, taking a sip of her drink.

Holly brushed her bangs out of her eyes. "Glad you came?"

Before Justine could answer, Simone pointed along the bar. "Hell, yeah! That's why I wanted to be here. Just like I said. Look at all these brothers in here."

Justine scanned the place. Simone was right. There were some very decent-looking men there. They looked promising. No thugs, no hoodies, no boots. It had been a while since Justine had done any serious dating. She didn't come here for that, but she was open to it. Gideon's offered some very prime pickings.

15

Karma

"Almost makes me wish I was single again. Yummy!" Holly took a sip of her mojito.

Justine came right back at her. "Holly, please. You've got a good man at home. Don't even pretend you're looking."

"Damn, right," Simone put in. "Save some for us. I'm not leavin' here without somebody's number tonight. I hope more than that."

Holly smirked. "Taking someone home tonight, Simone?"

Simone fanned herself dramatically. "Girl, I'm tryin'."

Justine laughed and shook her head. "Simone, you better stop being out there like that before you catch something."

Simone frowned and gave her a playful shove. "Leave me alone. I'm a free spirit."

Holly laughed out loud. "Oh, shit! Is that what they're callin' it now?" Simone stuck her tongue out at her, and they all shared a laugh. "Do your thing, girl. Just make sure you wrap it up."

"Don't worry. Each and every time."

The waitress picked that moment to approach their table. She smiled and set a mojito in front of both Holly and Simone. They exchanged glances as she set a flute of champagne in front of Justine.

"Compliments of the gentleman at the bar," the waitress said with a wink.

Justine looked up as the most gorgeous man she ever laid eyes on toasted her with a drink of his own. She felt herself blushing. The world stopped as they looked at each other. Suddenly, the room seemed a touch too warm. The way he had her locked into his gaze was a little unnerving, but pleasantly so. Justine didn't feel like she was being undressed. She felt like he was looking into her. It almost felt like he was touching her. Before she could raise her glass to thank him for the drink, he turned back to the bar.

"Goddamn, who's that?" Holly exclaimed.

Simone squirmed in her seat. "Did you see the way he looked at you, Justine? Damn, he made me hot!"

"Yeah," Justine said, "I noticed."

Simone and Holly giggled, then Holly reached over and shoved Justine lightly. "Girl, you better get over there and thank the man for your drink."

Karma

Justine looked at Simone for confirmation. Simone sniffed loudly and sucked her teeth. "You better listen to Holly. If you don't want him, I'll gladly take him off your hands." She looked back in his direction. "With his chocolate ass," she added wistfully.

Justine looked at Simone, anger starting to rise. "I bet you would with your whorish self."

Simone pretended to be hurt. "God, Justine, I was just kidding."

"Right, Simone," Justine replied with a smirk.

Holly put up her hands up. "Ladies, ladies! Please, no fighting over men. Didn't y'all do that enough in college? You don't even know this man. You might not even like him."

Justine smiled knowingly. "Something tells me I will."

Simone looked as if she tasted something bad.

Holly frowned at her. "Simone, don't you ruin this," she said quietly. "I hardly ever get a night out with my friends. I won't have you trying to spoil it with your funky attitude."

"But I —" Simone started to explain, but Holly cut her off.

"I'm not havin' it, Simone. Damn, he sent you a drink, too. Drink it and be happy. If he wanted you, he would have sent you the champagne."

Justine ignored Simone's pouting and freshened her lipstick. "Do I look all right?" she asked Holly.

"Stunning! Good luck."

Simone looked away. "Happy trails," she muttered.

Justine smiled and picked up her champagne. "Thanks, Simone. I'm sure you really meant that." She turned on her heels and started toward the bar, ignoring everything but the chocolate stranger.

When she arrived, he was deep in conversation with a good-looking, light-skinned brother. Justine hung back and took advantage of the dark stranger's preoccupation to look at him more closely. He was taller than he seemed from across the room, about six-two, with rich cocoa-colored skin. His hair was thick and black, cut low, with just enough room to run your fingers through it. Nicely manicured beard and moustache surrounding full, sensuous lips. Justine sighed. She didn't want to be rude, so she lightly tapped the light-skinned man on the shoulder.

Karma

Chapter Four

Karma

Lucas

Lucas knew the second the woman left her table to approach him. He pretended to be completely engaged in what Noah was saying. Before he could interrupt Noah, the woman touched his shoulder.

"Excuse me," she said softly with a smile. Her voice made him quiver.

Noah turned and looked down at her, clearly startled. She had been standing behind him. "I'll be damned," he said and stepped aside, which left the woman face-to-face with Lucas.

They stared at each other for a moment without speaking. Then Lucas flashed her a smile. She returned it for a minute. The blush returned to her cheeks, and she looked down before catching his eye again.

"I … um … I came over to thank you for the drink."

Lucas nodded. "You're very welcome." He moved a bit closer and looked down at her. "Lucas Cain."

"Justine Greer." She set her champagne glass down and extended her hand. Lucas was amused and stepped about six inches into her personal space. He took her hand and instead of shaking it, he just held it and pulled her toward him. Her touch alone sent an electric shock up his arm. The air in the half a foot of space between them felt charged.

"So, the hard part is out of the way, Justine. We've met."

He felt her grip soften as his words and demeanor took effect. Even though she was still smiling at him, he could sense her doubt.

"Mr. Cain, are you trying to persuade me to be a notch on your belt?" she asked sweetly.

Lucas frowned, then laughed, a deep and mellow sound. "Not at all. And you can call me Lucas. Listen, I know you're here with your friends. I don't want to intrude on your evening. I just need a moment of your time. Is that okay?" He still held her hand in his, although he took a small step back. She glanced back at her table, which was empty.

"Yes, it's okay."

"Thank you. Excuse me." He touched Noah's shoulder to let him know he would be back in a few. Noah nodded and turned back to the bar. Lucas retrieved Justine's drink and led her to a table. They sat across from each other.

Karma

"So, Lucas, like you said, we've met. What now?" she asked, leaning across the table. He followed her lead and leaned in also.

"What now? Now we get to know each other. Gideon's really isn't the place for that. I was hoping you'd let me take you to dinner." He was hoping for a lot more than that, but he had a feeling he wouldn't mind taking his time.

She blushed at his direct approach.

"Am I making you nervous?"

Justine blushed even harder. "Just a little. Is it me, or is it hot in this place?"

Lucas looked thoughtful and tapped the table between them with his forefinger. "No. Just right here."

Justine sat back and fanned herself. "My, my, Mr. Cain. You're a very dangerous man. For all I know, I could go out with you, let you ply me with champagne, and wake up in a very compromising position."

He loved the way his name sounded on her tongue. She had no idea how much the scenario she described was distracting him. This was so unfamiliar. Lucas was used to being the one to catch a woman off guard, not the other way around. "Justine, I can promise you, I'll never take advantage of you. You can always feel safe with me."

Justine looked at him with amused skepticism. "You sure about that?"

"I can guarantee it." He took a leather case out of the inside of his breast pocket and handed her his business card.

"Detective Lucas Cain. Narcotics Division. Major Case Squad. Midtown South," she read aloud and looked sheepish. "I apologize. I didn't mean to insinuate that you were a masher or something. I feel safer already."

He smiled at her. "I'm glad. Does that mean you'll let me take you to dinner?"

"I'd be happy to join you for dinner. Thank you for inviting me."

"No, thank you. When's a good time?"

"Well, tomorrow's no good. I have a late taping."

A small grin touched his lips. "Taping?"

"Yes, taping, Lucas. Don't you watch the five o'clock news? I thought you knew." Justine smiled. "So, you wanted to meet me …" she trailed off.

Karma

Lucas recovered. "Justine, when you walked through that door, I had to meet you. I didn't want your autograph."

She blushed. His heart sped up each time that adorable pink colored her cheeks. "Had to, huh?"

Lucas touched her hand. "Absolutely."

They exchanged numbers and made plans for Friday.

"I guess I'd better let you get back to your friends." Lucas didn't want to let her leave his sight, but she was intoxicating his senses and he had to regain his bearings.

"I guess so. It's been a pleasure meeting you, Lucas. See you Friday?"

"Friday it is, but you'll be hearing from me way before then."

"Is that a fact?"

"That's a promise." She seemed reluctant to leave and lingered for a moment. He sighed. "See you, Justine. Go have some fun. Just not too much."

Chapter Five

Justine

Wednesday and Thursday seemed to stretch on forever. Lucas was as good as his word though. Justine had spoken to him twice, and she couldn't wait to see him again. She sat in a cab on her way to Le Bernardin and took out a small, gold compact. She checked herself for the fourth time, wondering again if she should have kept her hair down. She had it in a soft upsweep that showed off the small diamond studs in her ears. Her makeup was fine, no smudges. Justine quickly scanned her winter white pantsuit to make sure there were no smudges there either. Again, she did a quick debate in her mind. Should she have worn a dress? Too much cleavage? She sighed. There was nothing she could do about it now. The cab turned onto 51st Street and stopped in front of the restaurant. Justine's heart started to pound.

She opened the door and was about to pay the driver when Lucas appeared and tapped on the window. He inconspicuously paid the driver as Justine got out of the car. She watched him as he walked toward her. Navy blue pinstripe suit, cream-colored shirt, black trench. Justine wondered if he knew how strikingly handsome he was. No, scratch that. She was pretty sure he knew. He smiled down at her, and she smiled back nervously. Yes, he definitely knew. When he got to her, he stepped into her personal space again. Justine wanted to lean into him, he smelled so good.

Lucas bent forward a little and smiled playfully. "Hi, Justine," he said teasingly. She couldn't help it. She had to touch him.

"Hi, Lucas. Thanks for the cab." She reached out and put her hand on his chest. She could have touched his arm. She didn't know how her hand landed there. Lucas looked surprised, but he covered her hand with his. Justine could feel his heartbeat. It was just as fast as hers. She stepped back, knowing she'd been slightly forward. She didn't want to send the wrong message, but when she moved, he moved with her. Almost like they were dancing.

"Sorry ..." she managed.

"Don't be. It was nice." They stood that way for a long moment with him still holding her hand to his chest.

Justine cleared her throat. "Lucas, this is ..."

He smiled again. "I know. Let's go inside and talk about it." He took her elbow and led her inside the elegant restaurant. When they reached their table, Lucas pulled her chair out for her.

"So," he said, sitting down himself, "let's get to know each other, Justine." Justine glanced at him. He was looking at her attentively. She picked up the wine list to avoid his eyes. Lucas laughed quietly. "Justine, you know, you're beautiful when you blush like that. Am I still making you nervous?"

"Just a tiny bit." She put the wine list down and stared back at him. "So, you think I'm beautiful?"

He nodded. "Lovely."

She smiled and touched his hand. "You're not so bad yourself."

The waiter appeared then, and Lucas ordered a bottle of wine. Shortly, the waiter returned and uncorked the bottle, poured their glasses and left the table.

"All right," Lucas said, settling in, "let's begin at the beginning."

They talked all through the meal without any moments of awkward silence. The conversation flowed as if they had known each other for years. They both attended New York University. When he said he decided not to finish law school, Justine was surprised. She could not see him as a lawyer, although working as a narcotics detective certainly came with a lot of dangers. Justine wasn't interested in his job, though. She was interested in the man.

"What do you do when you're not working?" Justine asked.

"It seems like I'm always working. I do the usual stuff."

Justine smiled wickedly. "Ah, the things men do."

He laughed. "I'm not that bad."

She sipped her wine. "I'm going to ignore that." They shared a laugh. Then she placed her glass on the table. "You seeing anybody?"

Lucas looked pensive. "No. You?"

Justine shook her head. "No."

He gave her a pleased grin. "Good."

They kept the evening light and shared a lot of laughs. When the check came, Justine was disappointed that the night was coming to an end. Lucas helped her into her coat, and they stepped outside.

"I really enjoyed dinner," she said.

"So did I."

They stood there, both not wanting to leave. Lucas moved closer. "Let me drive you home, Justine. It's late. I don't want you to take a taxi."

Justine nodded. He took her hand and led her around the corner to his silver Lexus. "Wow, nice car," she teased.

Lucas smiled and helped her in. "Takes me where I want to go."

Justine continued to tease him. "Nice car, nice suit, nice restaurant. I'm quitting my job tomorrow. I want to be a narcotics detective."

He laughed at her. "Yeah, right. It's a good job, pays well. My grandfather was the head of cardiology at Harlem Hospital. He left me two brownstones in Carroll Gardens when he died."

"Wow, so you live in Brooklyn?"

He nodded, and she gave him her address. They weren't too far, so they arrived quickly. He parked, and they walked the short distance to her building.

"Walk you up?" he asked, looking down at her.

Justine nodded. She greeted the doorman, and they stepped into the elevator. She noticed Lucas stayed a respectable distance away from her. They got off on 10. Justine stopped in front of her door.

"This is me."

Lucas was looking at her with those mesmerizing eyes. "I had a nice time, Justine."

Justine leaned against the door and looked down. Don't look at him or he's coming in.

He put a finger under her chin and lifted her head as he looked her directly in the eyes. "I like you, Justine. Remember what I said about not taking advantage of you?"

Justine met his eyes. "It's not you I'm worried about."

A couple came out of their apartment, headed for the elevator. They looked at Justine and her companion with obvious interest. Justine unlocked the door and pulled Lucas inside before he could say anything. Then she looked out the peephole and watched until the couple went away. A moment later, she turned to Lucas who was standing there in her foyer looking amused. He rolled up on her. This time there was almost no space between them.

"You like me too, huh?" He touched her face, and her whole body seemed to turn into a tuning fork.

"This is scary."

Lucas moved in closer, looking serious. "It is."

"We just met."

Karma

Closer still. An inch of space left.

"We did."

"You're sweeping me off my feet," she breathed.

Lucas put his hands on her arms and pulled her to him. "That's the plan." He kissed her forehead.

Justine sighed. "Lucas ..." She didn't get to finish, because he kissed her and her knees went weak. She kissed him back. It was a soft, tender kiss, their mouths barely touching. Barely exploring. Justine was dizzy. She was well aware of how tall he was, how strong he felt and how good he smelled pressed against her like that. He kissed her harder, teasing her with his tongue, then gently stepped away.

"I think I should go," Lucas said.

Justine nodded. He ran his hand over his beard and looked at her sincerely. "I don't know where this is going, but I'm in it."

Justine nodded. "Me too."

He touched her face again. "Earlier, you said you weren't seeing anyone. I think you should be seeing me."

Justine nodded again. "Okay, Lucas."

He kissed her lightly on the lips. Then again.

"Good night, Justine."

"Good night, Lucas."

She let him out and slid down the wall until she hit the floor. She was falling, and there was nothing she could do about it.

Karma

Chapter Six

Simone

Simone strode briskly down Lexington Avenue, smiling to herself. She was on her way to meet Holly and Justine for lunch. They hadn't seen each other since that night at Gideon's and Simone was eager to see them and start making plans for Thanksgiving. They usually had Thanksgiving at Holly's house and Christmas with their families. Simone loved this time of the year. They got to spend more time together. They'd been her girls since college, and they were dear to her. Dearer than anybody else, anyway.

She frowned unconsciously — even though Justine got on her nerves. She had to admit to herself that there was a touch of jealousy there. She'd never say it out loud, though. She couldn't even say exactly why. Maybe it was because everything always seemed to fall right into Justine's lap. If she wanted something, it happened, as if by magic. Simone had to work hard for everything, but she'd made it. She was more than comfortable financially. Had a great job, nice place to live and she was good-looking. But sometimes she wished things had gone a little easier for her. Her past taught her to live in the moment. She shook her head to clear it of negative thoughts. A guy walking by smiled at her. Simone smiled back and walked into the bistro to meet her friends. They were already there waiting for her and smiled as she approached the table.

"You're late," Holly said, flipping her hair over her shoulder. Simone leaned over and kissed them both.

"Fashionably late. Y'all know my MO — I like to make an entrance." She took off her leather peacoat with a flourish, revealing really low-cut jeans and a fringy suede top that barely covered her back.

Holly shook her head and grinned. "Simone, you give new meaning to the phrase 'showing your ass.'"

"Yeah, aren't you cold? It's November," Justine added.

Simone made a face at them. "No, I'm not cold. How could I possibly be cold in a body this hot?"

Justine laughed. "Oooh, you are sooo conceited!"

"And an exhibitionist," Holly said dryly. The three of them burst out laughing.

30

Karma

"Guilty. How's the hubby and the kids, Holly?"

"Good. All driving me crazy."

"I know that's right." Simone turned to Justine and looked at her slyly. "Justine, how's that fine-ass Lucas?"

"His ass is fine."

They laughed together.

"No, seriously, how're things going? We haven't talked much. Catch me up."

Holly dug into her steak. "Girl, Justine is gone."

Simone raised her eyebrows. "Gone?"

"I think he put some serious mojo on our girl. Look at her sitting there glowing."

"Shut up, Holly," Justine said, blushing in spite of herself.

Simone sat back and looked at her. Look at this happy bitch. If she isn't in love, she's in something. "Look at you. Damn, it's only been three weeks. You're definitely looking a little open, Justine."

"Girl, I am, and I can't help it."

Simone frowned. "Well, did you fuck him yet?"

"Simone!" Holly hissed.

"Holly!" Simone hissed back.

Justine laughed. "It's okay, Holly. No, Simone, I didn't."

"Well, damn, it's been three weeks. What are you waiting for?"

Justine smirked. "Simone, you just said three weeks wasn't long enough to be catching feelings. Why would I have slept with him already?"

Simone smiled at her. Justine was the most naïve person when it came to men. She'd seen Lucas. She hoped Justine didn't think he'd taken a vow of celibacy just because Justine wanted to play nun and not open her legs.

"Justine, sweetie, don't get upset. I'm sorry. Things are going well between you two then?"

"Yeah. I'd like to see a little more of him, though."

Holly looked sympathetic. "What happened? Conflicting schedules?"

Justine nodded. "He's working undercover right now, and his hours aren't predictable."

"Is he feeling you, too?" Simone asked seriously.

"I think so. It's like we're … I don't know. It's weird, but it's nice. We have a good time together, you know, laughing, joking. But when it gets quiet, it's like we don't even have to talk. If he touches me, it's like he's really touching me. I don't know how to explain it."

31

Karma

Simone sucked her teeth. "I do. Hell, Justine, that's physical. Y'all need to hit the sheets and get it over with."

Holly looked exasperated. "Simone, get your mind out of the gutter. They're falling in love. I think it's sweet."

Justine's cell phone rang. She answered it and excused herself, walking toward the front of the bistro. Simone watched her go, grinning into the phone. She was almost fucking skipping.

"So, Simone, what's going on with you?" Holly asked. "Seeing anyone important?"

Simone looked away from Justine. She stuck her chest out and licked her lips. "Not yet."

Chapter Seven

Lucas

Lucas sat at his desk in the squad room staring out the window. He was tired. They'd made a major bust and had just finished the paperwork. He was glad this particular case was over. They'd been working on it for three months, and it was seriously cutting into his free time. Normally, that wouldn't have been a problem, but he had other things he wanted to do. He wanted to see Justine. The first time he saw her, she took his breath away. He'd never had a woman just take his breath away.

He thought about the way she touched his chest that first night. He shook his head. When he kissed her, she gave him butterflies. He was using incredible restraint to keep his libido in check. He didn't want to just jump into bed with her, but it was a bit difficult to keep his hands to himself. He wanted to touch her. She was so damn soft.

Lucas ran a hand over his face and stroked his beard. He'd been with more than his fair share of women in his life. But none of them made him feel the way Justine did. Noah was right. He was the fuck 'em and leave 'em specialist. He didn't let moss grow under his feet. He kept it moving. It wasn't that some woman had dogged him out. He just didn't want to get too emotionally involved. People you love leave you. He knew that to be true. So he tried to remain emotionally detached. Lucas frowned. Okay. Maybe one woman had dogged him out, but he didn't allow himself to think of his mother very often.

He straightened up in his chair. But Justine — he liked her. He liked her a lot. She was changing his philosophy. He didn't want to keep it moving. He wanted to stay for a while and see where this was heading. It felt good. It felt right.

"You all right, Luke?" Noah asked, entering the room and sitting in the chair next to Lucas' desk. Lucas turned away from the window.

"Yeah, man. I'm cool."

Noah grinned. "Good! Let's bounce up outta here and hit the titty bar."

Lucas laughed. He stood up and put his coat on, following Noah outside. It was windy and cold.

Noah dipped his head and pulled his collar up. "You comin', bro?"

Karma

Lucas shook his head. "Nah, man. Not tonight."

"Come on, we ain't hung out in a minute. Don't leave me stuck with Nelson and Morales."

"Nah, man. Gotta take a rain check."

Noah looked at him and smiled. "Justine?"

"Yeah, I thought I'd stop by."

Noah slapped him on the back. "Damn, son! You met your match? You gonna have to turn in your playa card."

Lucas laughed. "I don't know, Noah."

Noah looked at him earnestly. "I don't believe I'm watchin' this shit happen."

"Ain't nothing happening."

"Bullshit, homey. You goin' down."

"Fuck you, Noah," Lucas said with a smile.

Noah laughed at him. "Yeah, okay. You didn't deny it though. Shit, it's about time."

They gave each other dap and went their separate ways. Lucas got in his car and started it up. He looked at his watch. It was 11 p.m. on a Saturday night. He hoped Justine was home. He hoped she was alone. He was taking his chances. He wasn't calling first.

Lucas parked his car and went up to Justine's floor. He hesitated for just a moment before he rang the bell. What if she wasn't alone? What was he talking about? She wasn't that type of girl. Lucas smiled to himself. Confidence, Lucas. She's alone, if she's here at all. She wants you just as much as you want her. He summoned his courage from years of being a mack. Ring the doorbell, man. What's wrong with you? He almost laughed out loud at himself. He was nervous. He stood up straight and squared his shoulders. Fuck that, he was Lucas Cain. He rang the doorbell and leaned against the jamb. It took a moment.

"Who is this? Simone, that better not be you!" Justine threw her door open without waiting for a reply. When she saw Lucas standing there, she looked shocked, holding her phone to her ear.

"Oh, shit, Holly. I gotta go." She clicked off and stared at him. He stared back. She was wearing her pajamas, a pair of plaid, red flannel shorts and a red T-shirt. Her hair was up in a ponytail, and she wasn't wearing any makeup. Lucas smiled at her, and she smiled back, her dimples lighting up her face. She smelled like vanilla. She was gorgeous. He was glad he'd come.

"You know, you really shouldn't answer your door like that. Might not have been me." He didn't lose his smile. She didn't either. Justine beamed at him.

"Actually, I thought you were Simone. She's the only person that rings my doorbell this late."

"Not anymore." Lucas let his eyes wander over her. Her body was nice. Her breasts were round and firm, her waist was small, and he was trying not to cry looking at her ass. Justine blushed and folded her arms across her chest. Lucas licked his lips.

"Are you gonna let me in?"

Justine looked embarrassed. "Oh! I'm sorry, Lucas. Sure, come in." She held the door open, and he stepped inside.

"Take your coat?" she asked.

Lucas shrugged out of it and handed it to her. Justine's hand trembled when she took it, and she quickly turned and hung it in the closet, avoiding his flat-out stare. Lucas knew she was nervous, that she didn't quite trust herself with him. Hell, he didn't trust himself with her. But there was a time for everything, and he'd made up his mind that he was going to wait until it was right. That would be hard. She was standing there in nothing but her pj's. He let his eyes bounce back up to her face as she turned around. Too late. She'd caught him looking at her ass.

She smiled and shook her finger at him. "Bad boy. I saw that." He didn't apologize. He moved closer to her. Justine

35

Karma

cleared her throat. "Let's not stand here in the foyer. Come in. Get comfortable."

He followed her into the living room. Nice apartment. Cool, cream-colored walls, plush white furniture, lots of glass. Her flat screen television was tuned to "Sex and the City," and there was an open pint of Ben and Jerry's Cherry Garcia on the coffee table. Lucas laughed.

"Is this the way you spend your Saturday nights?"

Justine put her hand on her hip. "Well, I didn't have a date."

"You will until I have to work odd hours again."

Her face lit up. Her dimples were killing him. "Your case is over?"

"Yep."

"I'm glad."

"Me too."

She reached out and took his hand, pulling him toward the sofa. "Have a seat. Can I get you anything?"

Instead of sitting down, Lucas pulled her to him. "Yeah, you can get me something."

36

Karma

He kissed her softly, and she put her arms around his neck and leaned into him. He ran his hands up her sides, tracing the curve of her breasts with his thumbs. Justine shivered and kissed him harder and deeper. Her mouth was soft and sweet. He loved the taste of her. The smell of her. He was lightheaded, kissing her like that. Justine ran her fingers through his hair, lightly caressing his scalp with her fingernails. Lucas shuddered. Damn! He was fighting a losing battle to maintain control. He felt himself becoming aroused. His hands slipped to her hips.

He made an attempt to step back, but Justine hooked her fingers in his belt and pressed herself against him. She caught her breath, and Lucas moaned. He broke the kiss and gently moved away from her. Reaching under his sweater, he removed his holster from his belt and placed his gun on the coffee table. Lucas realized he'd just given her a little show. He looked at her as she looked up from his body. She was ready. If he pushed it, he could have her. He wasn't ready tonight. It was going to be special when it happened, and he wanted to remember it.

He sat down on the sofa and pulled her down beside him. They sat there, turned toward each other. Lucas took her hand. He turned it over and kissed her palm. "Sorry I didn't call first."

Justine smiled. "I'm glad you came, Lucas."

"I had to. I missed you."

"I missed you, too."

Lucas put his hand on her thigh, caressing her satiny skin. He kissed her neck. "I'm trying to be good, but I can't keep my hands off you."

Justine took his face in her hands. She looked him in the eye. "I know what you're doing, Lucas. I'm a grown woman. I can make up my own mind."

Lucas let her go and looked at her. He sighed and leaned back on the sofa as he ran his hand over his beard.

"I know. I don't want to rush this."

Justine was looking at him intently. "What's wrong?" she asked, slipping her hand into his.

He laughed. "Nothing's wrong. Nothing. Everything's right."

She raised her eyebrows. Lucas stood up and walked to the window. He took a deep breath and let it out slowly. "You don't know me, Justine," he said quietly.

She sat up. "What's that supposed to mean?"

Lucas dropped his head. "I've always been a certain way with women. I wasn't always nice." Justine was still looking at him, waiting for him to go on. "I don't want to be that way anymore."

Karma

Justine got up and put her hand on his arm. "Lucas ..."

He kissed her forehead. "I don't want to hurt you."

She looked confused. "What are you saying?"

"I'm saying that I don't know if I'm ready for this."

Justine stiffened and slid away from him, dropping his hands. She looked at the floor. "So ... you don't want to see me anymore?"

Lucas felt an instant surge of panic well up in him. Oh, shit! How'd she take it there? He was quick to clear it up. "No, baby. That's not what I meant."

"That's what you implied."

"No. Justine, look at me. You got me trippin'. I'm ... I don't know. I'm not used to this. I'm being honest. I'm used to being in control. I don't feel like I'm in control. I'm walking around daydreaming. Lately, you're all I think about. You think I don't want to see you?"

Justine dropped her stiff demeanor. "Lucas, I ..."

He stepped away from her again. "I don't want to mess this up."

Justine wrapped her arms around him. He returned her

embrace, holding her close to him. They stayed that way a long time, not moving, just holding each other.

"I'm scared, too," Justine said after a while.

Lucas opened his eyes. Nail right on the head. "Who said I was scared?"

"You did."

"Did not," he teased.

She giggled. "Did too."

He kissed her again. He liked kissing her. Lucas had never been a big kisser. It was too intimate. But he could just eat Justine up. His hands moved across her bottom. He couldn't wait, but he had to. Lucas wanted to take her clothes off and look at her, but he'd see her soon enough. His hands went back to her waist, all the while he was kissing her voraciously.

Then he slipped his hands under her T-shirt. He hadn't intended to, but he couldn't help himself. His fingers trailed a light path up her sides and found her bare breasts. They fit into his palms perfectly. Justine arched her back as his thumbs traced lazy circles around her nipples. She threw her head back and sighed with satisfaction. Lucas watched her face. She was beautiful. He'd been waiting for her.

"Justine?"

She bit her bottom lip and opened her eyes. "Yes?" She was breathless.

"It's just us now. Nobody else."

She nodded and reached for him. She seemed delighted with what she discovered. Justine looked at him like she was trying to gauge his reaction to her question. "That means I'm your woman." It didn't sound like a question. It was most certainly a statement.

Lucas kissed her long and hard. "What do you think?"

They moved to the sofa and made out like teenagers, kissing and feeling each other up. It seemed to go on for hours. Lucas was far from tired of her, but he decided to come up for air when he realized if he didn't stop soon, he was going in. Justine was straddling his lap. They were still kissing. Lucas had never kissed someone for so long. It was nice. He hadn't believed it was possible to be so aroused without seeking release or just exploding. They'd been doing this slow grind for a while, his hands planted firmly on her hips. He was proud of himself. Justine still had all of her clothes on. Lucas had lost his sweater and undershirt in the process, and was sitting there naked from the waist up. He lifted Justine up gently, so that they were no longer making contact. Then he gave her a peck on the lips.

"We gotta stop."

Justine gave him a sultry little smile. "Why? What's wrong?"

He returned her smile. "You know what's wrong."

She gave him another kiss and got up. Lucas watched her as she stretched, her shirt riding up, showing her flat stomach. She was killing him slowly, and he had a feeling she knew it. Lucas glanced at the coffee table.

"Your ice cream melted."

She looked surprised. "I forgot all about it." She scooped it up and headed for the kitchen. Lucas stood a bit stiffly and shook himself out. Down, boy. He was still looking for his sweater when Justine came back.

He picked his gun up and clipped it back to his belt. Their eyes met. Justine looked sad.

"Everything all right?" he asked.

"Yeah. I just don't want you to go."

Karma

Lucas walked to her and took her in his arms. "I don't want to, but I have to." He kissed the top of her head. "I'll be back tomorrow. I'll take you to dinner. Promise."

It didn't take him long to get home since traffic was light at that hour. Lucas let himself in and headed for the bedroom. He undressed quickly and hit the shower, turning the water on full blast and letting it wash over him. His thoughts went to Justine. She had called him on being afraid. He had to admit he was. He'd been macking so long, he wasn't quite sure he could change. He was doing pretty well so far. He hadn't been with anybody since he'd met Justine.

Lucas rinsed off and stepped out of the shower. Reaching over to the towel bar, he grabbed a towel and wiped the steam off the mirror as he stared at his reflection. He was open, and he hoped he didn't fuck it up.

Chapter Eight

Simone

Simone picked up a pair of jeans from the pile in front of her. They were perfect, just not in her client's size. She tossed them aside and continued her search.

"Uh-uh, boss lady, they don't have them in his size. We have to try something else," her assistant, Raphael, said over her shoulder, shaking his head. He laid a garment bag on top of the pile of jeans and unzipped it as he removed a silver dress cut to the navel in front and to the rear in back. It was a dangerous dress. Simone examined it carefully. She held it up to her body and looked in the mirror.

"Thanks, Raphael. You just found my party dress for New Year's Eve."

He sucked his teeth. "Bitch, I'll fight you for it."

"Raphael, it takes a real woman to fill out this dress."

Raphael tossed his curly hair over his shoulder and put his hand on his hip. "I can handle mine. What you want the dress for, chica?"

Simone smiled slyly. "I've got plans." She walked across the room and unzipped another garment bag. It contained a strapless red dress. It was simple, but the split up the back was deadly. Simone had tried it on. She could barely breathe in it. She'd decided to wear it for Thanksgiving. She knew it was over-the-top, but that was her style. Raphael came over and stood next to her, looking suspicious.

"What kinda plans you got, Simone?"

She gave him a devilish grin. "I'm not saying."

Raphael looked at the two dresses, then back at Simone. "Somebody's in trouble."

Simone laughed. "Damn right."

Karma

Chapter Nine

Lucas

Karma

Lucas parked his car in front of Holly's house. Although he wasn't big into holiday gatherings, Thanksgiving was important to Justine. He looked over at her, sitting there with a cake box on her lap, pulling on her gloves.

She smiled at him and touched his hand. "Thanks for coming with me, Lucas."

"Not a problem." He got out and helped her out of the car. He couldn't remember the last time he'd made a big deal out of a holiday. Lucas thought back to when he was a little kid. His parents made big productions out of the holidays. Those were memorable. He rang the doorbell.

A cute little guy who was losing his teeth opened the door. His face brightened when he saw Justine.

"Mommy! It's Aunt Justine!" He ran up to her and hugged her around the waist.

"Hey, baby! Happy Thanksgiving." She hugged him back and kissed his face. He turned to Lucas.

"Who's this?"

Justine beamed at him and took Lucas' hand. She looked up at him, smiling her beautiful smile. "This is Lucas Cain."

"Is he your boyfriend?"

Lucas bent down a touch to be more at his level. "Yes, I am. What's your name?"

The youngster grinned at Lucas and pointed to himself. "I'm James."

Lucas returned his smile and offered his hand. "Nice to meet you, James."

James nodded and returned the shake solemnly. Holly materialized, dazzling in raspberry silk, and threw the door open.

"Hey, girl!" She grabbed Justine like she hadn't seen her in years.

"Y'all, come in. I'm sorry my child forgot his manners. Let me take your coats." Holly took the cake box and handed it to James. "Take this into the kitchen and give it to Grandma." James disappeared down the hall, running with the cake. Holly's smile was contagious. Lucas found himself smiling back. Holly put her hand on her hip and looked at him astutely. "Mr. Cain?"

"That's me."

"I've been dying to meet you. I heard a lot about you."

"Same here."

Holly slipped her arm in his. "Come and meet my husband." She took Justine's hand and led them into the living room, where she made introductions all around.

"Robert, come meet Lucas!" Holly called out.

Justine had left Lucas' side to catch up with Holly's family. Robert grinned at Lucas and instantly gave him dap and the one-shoulder hug.

"Good to meet you, man. Heard a lot of good things about you. You smoke cigars?"

"Once in a while."

"Good. We're gonna leave the cooking to the women and go get our drink on. You down?"

"You know it." He followed Robert to the den. Holly's father and brother joined them.

"What you drinking, Lucas? Hennessy?"

"You wouldn't have single malt, would you?"

Robert grinned and reached behind the bar. "Glenlivet?"

"That's it."

Robert laughed. "My man! I don't usually drink this stuff.

Gets my head bad, but hell, we drinkin' it tonight, goddamn. Welcome, Lucas."

"Thanks, man."

They got acquainted, laughed, and joked and drank. Lucas was enjoying himself. He'd had a few misgivings about this type of function, but it seemed to be for nothing. Robert poured the third round as the doorbell rang.

"Drink up, fellas. I think that's Simone."

Lucas watched with some amusement as they looked at each other pointedly and took big gulps of their scotch.

"What's the deal?" Lucas asked.

Holly's brother grimaced as the scotch burned the back of his throat. "Man, you better drink up. Satan just rang the doorbell."

Lucas recalled the red bone in the tight clothes. He shrugged. "So?"

Robert looked amused, then turned to Lucas. "Bro, you know, I had a conversation with my wife not too long ago about Simone."

Lucas raised his eyebrows. "And?"

"And, Simone is gonna come in here half-dressed, tryin' to take everybody's man. I don't know why they stay friends with her. Shit, she even got a little live with Pops once. Tried to say she had too much to drink."

Karma

"One of the best days of my life," Holly's father said wistfully.

Lucas couldn't help straight-out laughing. "So, Simone's a flirt?"

Nobody said anything. Lucas looked at Robert. Robert looked back and finished his drink. "Steel yourself, bro."

Lucas straightened up and finished his drink too. "Shit, I can handle a flirt." He put his cigar out.

Holly's brother drained his glass. "Not when she's got her hand on your dick. 'Scuse me, Pops."

Lucas looked at them. It was almost funny. They were acting like they were afraid of her, actually afraid of a woman. These guys had to be kidding.

They left the den and walked into the living room. Justine was playing with the kids. She got up when they returned and drew Lucas aside.

"How was it?" she asked.

Lucas smiled. He was feeling the effects of three straight shots of Glenlivet, but he was good.

"It was fine."

Justine hugged him. "You smell like scotch."

Lucas laughed. "That's what I was drinking."

She gave him a kiss. Lucas looked at her standing there in a cobalt-blue wrap dress. He almost wanted to skip dinner. Holly emerged from the kitchen, Simone hot on her trail. They were bickering about the food. Simone was beautiful, but Lucas wasn't particularly impressed. The dress was impressive, red and strapless, with a deep slit. Big breasts, tiny waist, and a fat ass. He looked away. Simone poured a glass of white wine and walked over to them.

"Hey, Justine." She paused and gave Lucas the once-over as she smiled seductively at him and licked her lips. "You've got to be Lucas. I'm Simone." She touched his arm.

He felt her checking out his bicep. He frowned in surprise and stepped away from her. Damn! She just flirted with him like Justine wasn't even there. He glanced at Justine. She was glaring at Simone, who took a sip of her chardonnay as she smiled at him.

Karma

"Aren't you going to say hello?" She put her hand on her hip and leaned forward. He had an excellent view of her cleavage. Lucas couldn't help it. He laughed. Simone had to be on some shit! She was tripping. This had to be a joke. Simone cocked her head. "You think I'm funny?"

His laughter stopped as quickly as it came. He studied her with great offense. "No. I think you're disrespectful." He looked at Justine. She looked furious and mortified at the same time.

Justine finally stood up to her. "Simone, how could you just flirt with him like that? What's the matter with you?"

Simone giggled. "Don't be so serious, Justine. I was just having fun."

"Go away, Simone," Justine said. She was looking at the floor. Simone flashed Lucas a smile, then turned on her heel and walked away slowly, shaking her ass for him.

"Sorry about that," Justine apologized.

Lucas stared at her. "So, that's Simone?"

Justine looked uncomfortable. "That's Simone."

"I thought everybody was exaggerating."

"Nope. That's Simone."

Lucas continued to stare at her. "She's not your friend,

Justine."

Justine looked slightly annoyed. "Sure she is. She's just always been that way."

Lucas looked at her carefully. Justine wasn't trying to hear what he just said. He let it go.

"All right," Holly called everyone to dinner, and it turned out to be very pleasant.

Justine sat across from Simone. After a few frosty gazes, she started talking to Simone again. The meal was amazing, and conversation flowed. They were nice people. Lucas felt at home. After dinner, they all settled in the living room. They were talking about plans for New Year's Eve, apparently some big to-do. Lucas glanced at his watch. It was nine o'clock. They should be wrapping this up. He had an early morning. He said as much to Justine, and she nodded. When they stood up, Holly looked disappointed.

"Oh, no! Don't leave, it's too early."

"We have to. We've both got an early morning. Gotta get to bed." They said their good-byes while Robert retrieved their coats.

Holly grabbed both their hands and walked between them. She looked up at Lucas and smiled. "I like you, Lucas. I'm glad you met my friend."

Karma

He smiled back. "What a nice thing to say."

"I meant it." She gave them both a squeeze.

Robert patted Lucas' back. "A'ight, man, see you New Year's."

"I'll be there."

Robert nodded. "You better be. I'm not going through that shit by myself." They shared a laugh.

Simone rushed up to Justine. "I know you weren't going to leave and not say good-bye." She gave Justine a hug and a kiss, then she turned to Lucas. "Sorry about earlier. I think you might have taken me the wrong way."

"Did I?" He looked at her, then to Justine. Justine was watching him.

"Of course," Simone said, though he didn't believe one word she was saying.

Lucas was glad they were leaving. He ignored Simone and turned to Robert and Holly. "Thanks for a lovely evening. See you soon."

Chapter Ten

Simone

Simone let herself into her apartment and sat on the sofa in the dark. She threw her purse down and put her head in her hands. Fucking Lucas. Arrogant bastard. He laughed at her. She was humiliated. He thought she was stupid. He'd chastised her like a bad puppy. Said she was disrespectful. He ignored her. Simone was infuriated with him. She wasn't used to men turning her down. She stood up and took her coat off.

She hadn't seen him since that night at Gideon's. He caught her off guard. She'd known he was fine, but he was much more handsome than she remembered. Her game was off. Simone twirled a lock of her hair. He hurt her feelings. He didn't have to be so mean. She had to have Lucas. Justine never even crossed her mind.

Chapter Eleven

Justine

Karma

Justine sat on her living-room floor wrapping Christmas presents. It was the Saturday before Christmas. She was still in her bathrobe at one in the afternoon and contemplating the rest of the day when her tea kettle whistled.

She got up, made herself a cup of Earl Grey and looked out the window. The snow made her smile. She really wanted to see Lucas. They hadn't had a chance to spend a lot of time together. Their jobs were very demanding. The Major Case Squad was in the middle of a huge investigation. Lucas' hours were crazy. He didn't really talk about it much. She thought he could be in danger. Her phone rang, and Justine looked at her caller ID. She grinned. Lucas' cell.

"Lucas? Hi!"

"Hey. I'm outside. Thought I'd call first."

Justine ran a hand through her hair. "Sure, come on up."

The doorbell rang before she could hang the phone up. She smiled to herself. He didn't leave her a lot of time to get ready, calling from right outside her door like that. She opened the door, and Lucas stepped inside. He smelled so good. Before she could say anything, he was kissing her. He kissed her hard as he picked her up. Justine was breathless when he put her down.

"Get dressed. Spend the day with me."

She leaned back and looked at him. "Lucas, are you all right?"

"Never better. Get dressed."

"It'll take me a minute."

Lucas shrugged out of his leather jacket. "I'll be right here." When Justine was ready, Lucas stood up. "Let's go."

They walked down Fifth Avenue, pausing to admire the holiday windows.

"When I was a kid, my parents used to take me into the city around this time of the year. They'd show me the windows, the tree in Rockefeller Center, all that stuff. They made it real special for me," Justine reminisced. They were looking at a Nutcracker scene.

Lucas looked down at her. "You're an only child?"

She nodded.

"Spoiled?"

She grinned and nodded again. They laughed together.

"What about you?"

He smiled. "I'm not spoiled."

She swatted his arm playfully. "That's not what I meant."

His mood darkened visibly. "I have a brother. He lives in California. We're not close."

"Really? Why?"

Lucas looked back into the window like he was looking back into his life. "I never met him."

"Oh." Justine moved closer to him.

Lucas rarely talked about himself. Justine was surprised he was doing it now. He frowned. "He's maybe 10 years younger than me. My mother had him after she left us."

"You're parents are divorced?"

"No. Far as I know, they were still married when my father died."

Justine didn't know what to say. "Let's go get something to eat."

They walked to Serendipity and got a corner booth. Then they ordered a totally fattening meal of chili dogs and fries with frozen hot chocolates.

Karma

Lucas reached across the table and took her hand. "Justine, I've been in love with you from the moment I saw you. Don't tell me you didn't know that."

Justine thought her heart was going to stop. She felt tears well up in her eyes. Lucas lifted his hand and brushed her tears away. "I know, I'm happy. I love you, too, Lucas."

He smiled. "I know."

They stared at each other. Justine was ecstatic, but she also felt the heat growing in the air between them. She could tell he felt it too. Lucas was looking at her in that intense way, making her blush. Making her want him. Bad. Lucas called the waiter over without breaking eye contact with her.

"Check, please."

They left the restaurant, almost running back to Justine's apartment. They were both breathless when they reached the elevator. Lucas pressed her against the wall before the doors even closed. She felt his tongue before she felt his lips. Her knees buckled. Lucas kept her steady. His lips were cold, but his mouth was hot. They stumbled out of the elevator and made their way to her door, still kissing each other. They stopped only long enough to unlock the door and get inside. Then Justine took her coat off. Lucas removed his, and he moved toward her and touched her hair.

Karma

"Let's slow down. Just a little," he said.

"Okay."

He touched her face. "I don't want to rush through this. I'm taking my time."

"Okay," Justine repeated in a whisper. She felt dreamy, like he was hypnotizing her. She had never wanted anyone as much as she wanted Lucas. She knew she never would. He put his hands in her hair and kissed her gently.

"We've been waiting a long time for this. Let's make it last."

Justine nodded. She couldn't even speak. Lucas stepped away from her and took his sweater off. He tossed it on the sofa. Justine approached him. She put her arms around his waist and tucked her hands beneath his undershirt, slowly running them upwards, feeling the strength of the muscles in his back. Slowly she helped him out of his shirt.

Lucas was looking down at her. Justine ran her hands over his stomach, tracing each muscle. His body was chiseled. His stomach was perfection. His chest was hard and well-formed.

She kissed him at its center, letting her fingers dance across the light, downy hair there. Finally she looked up at him. He was still looking at her.

"Lucas …" He silenced her with a kiss. Justine braced herself. There was nothing left to say anyway. She took his hand and led him to her bedroom. Her body was humming. She had been waiting a long time for this moment. She smiled seductively.

Justine reached down and pulled her sweater over her head and tossed it over her shoulder. Her bra followed. Then she kicked her boots off and unbuttoned her jeans. She looked at Lucas. He was watching her with the tiniest of smiles. Before she could make her next move, he was on his knees in front of her. Justine put her hands on his shoulders as he used his teeth to pull her zipper down. He eased her jeans over her hips, and she stepped out of them. Justine felt his warm breath on her, and her nipples stiffened as she waited for his next move.

Lucas circled her navel with his tongue while his fingertips drifted up lightly, over her calves, to her thighs, his fingers found the round curve of her bottom. He moaned, then he hooked his thumbs through the sides of her panties and slid them off, gently easing her onto the bed. Justine caught her breath as Lucas put his mouth on her, his beard tickled her thighs. True to his word, he took his time with her. Lucas stayed there until she arched her back and screamed his name. She was still trembling when she felt him leave her.

Karma

Justine watched him as he undressed and smiled. He was a beautiful man. She closed her eyes and felt his hands on her skin again. His mouth worked miracles on her breasts, teasing her nipples until she couldn't take it anymore. She put her hands on him and raised her hips. They gasped in unison as he slid home, remaining still for a moment, savoring the impact. The next moment, they fell into a rhythm. They moved leisurely, as if they had all the time in the world, rocking together and making slow circles. Justine could have stayed that way forever. They did stay that way for a long time.

Then Lucas turned slightly and picked up the pace. Justine's toes curled, and she came instantly. Lucas kissed her deeply and lifted her leg. She saw stars as she exploded again. Suddenly, her eyes flew open. Lucas was watching her face closely.

"One more time," he said. He turned his body as he went deeper. Justine felt the wave hit her again. She put her hands on his hips and pulled him in, forcing him to follow her. They came hard and long. Justine had never felt this satisfied in her life. Lucas rolled over on his back. She put her head on his chest. She loved him. She blushed. Lucas looked amused.

"Too late for that."

She laughed, rising up on one elbow as she looked at him. "I love you, Lucas."

"Love you, too." He was falling asleep. He turned onto his side. Justine started to move over, but Lucas reached out and pulled her to him. Then he snuggled against her back and put his hand on her hip, all while kissing her neck. "Mmmm ... love you." He kissed her shoulder, and they fell asleep.

They slept straight through the night. Justine woke at seven in the morning. Lucas was still asleep, on his back, with his arm over his head. He was snoring softly. Justine watched him sleep. She wanted him again. He was the perfect man for her. And he was hers. He was so handsome. She stifled a laugh. He even had nice feet. She slipped into her bathrobe and quietly left the room.

Justine went into the kitchen and started breakfast. She was still chopping green peppers for the omelets when Lucas walked in wearing his boxers and yawning.

Justine couldn't keep the smile off her face.

"What?" Lucas asked.

"Look at you sitting up in my kitchen in your underwear. This is a Kodak moment."

He laughed. "Want me to get dressed?"

Justine shook her head quickly. "After last night, I don't ever want you to get dressed again."

Lucas leaned back in his chair and gave her a cocky little smile. "Oh, you liked that, huh?" he asked with a nod.

Justine sipped her coffee. "Oh, I loved it. You're a very talented man, Mr. Cain."

"I try."

Justine put her mug down. "You succeed."

Lucas looked her in the eye. "Keep talkin', sweetheart, I'll be succeeding again."

Justine tossed her head and crossed her legs. She toyed with the belt to her robe. Lucas was drinking his coffee and watching her. Normally, Justine was modest. But she didn't feel like that with Lucas. He liked looking at her, and she wanted him to. She pulled on the belt, and her robe fell open. Lucas licked his lips and

Karma

put his cup down. He challenged her.

"Go ahead. Take it off."

She got up and walked around the table to face him. Then she shrugged out of her robe, and it slipped to the floor. Lucas leaned back like he had the wind knocked out of him.

"Damn, girl."

Justine beckoned him with her finger, and obediently, he got up and followed her back through the bedroom and to the master bath. She stepped into the shower and turned it on. Lucas was right behind her. When she turned around, they were all over each other. The warm water was raining down on them and made their bodies pleasantly slippery. Justine pressed her body against his and brought her leg up. She was amazed at how fast he had her up in the air, her legs around his waist. He inhaled sharply through his teeth when he went in. He handled her like she didn't weigh anything.

"Oh, God!" Justine cried out as Lucas bounced her, his hands cupping her and holding her to him.

56

Karma

Lucas put his face against hers. His beard scratched her face lightly. Justine gently bit his bottom lip. Lucas moaned, and they dipped as his knees went weak. Quickly, he caught himself and laughed. "Don't make me drop you."

He never stopped his pace. Justine opened her eyes, her brows knitting. Lucas was looking at her. His tongue darted into her mouth.

"Go. Go, baby." He ground into her, and she detonated. Lucas got her back against the wall, bent his knees, then came back up. Justine's leg kicked out reflexively. She came again. "Lucas!" she moaned her delight.

He put his mouth to her ear. "Say it again," he whispered. His lips found hers as he ground into her once more.

This time, Justine screamed his name and lost control as her body shook and trembled. She tightened around him and grabbed his ass, pulling him in as far as he could go. She smiled as he came violently. He was pumping hard, pressing her back into the wall and growling. Then he shuddered and was still. He started to let her down gently, still inside. Then he shook again and ground into her, breathing hard. Reluctantly, he put her back on her feet, and they parted. Tenderly, Lucas took her face into his hands. Justine looked up at him.

He started to smile, but it faltered. "Justine …"

She watched him. He put his forehead against hers. "Love you," he said very quietly. Justine could barely hear him over the running water.

"I love you, too."

They kissed for a long time, then began to wash each other. Justine loved the way he was so gentle with her. She truly believed they were meant to be together. She had waited her whole life for him. She was in love with him. They rinsed off and dried each other, making little jokes and memorizing each other's bodies. Justine was disappointed when Lucas started to put his clothes on.

"Do you really have to leave?"

He kissed her tenderly. "I really have to. We got a buy and bust."

Justine looked serious. "Please be careful."

He stood up. "I'm always careful. Besides, Noah's got my back."

Justine stood, too. "Noah, huh? When will I get the chance to really meet him?"

Lucas clipped his gun on. "When do you want to meet him?"

"Bring him New Year's."

"I might be able to do that."

She followed him into the living room, where he retrieved his sweater from the sofa and pulled it on. Then she handed him his jacket. "Have a good day."

"I'll try. I'll call you tonight." He kissed her sweetly and went to work.

57

Karma

Chapter Twelve

Lucas

Lucas stepped out of his brownstone and walked to his car. It was cold out, but he wasn't. He had dressed carefully. Black tux, crisp white shirt, French cuffs, black cashmere overcoat. He'd been to the barber. Formal wear was pretty rare for him, but he knew he cleaned up very nicely. He hadn't seen Justine in three days, and he was anxious. He smiled to himself as he put his coat over the driver's seat and got in to pick up Noah.

Lucas hit the highway. Justine. He was always smiling when he thought of her. She had spent Christmas with her parents while he spent it working. Lucas tucked his hand into his jacket and touched the inside pocket where he placed the present that he hoped she would like. Hell, he knew she'd like it. Noah had been with him when he purchased it. Noah was still on his "bitter divorce" campaign. Lucas laughed as he remembered how Noah had carried on.

"Don't get her that, man! What's wrong with you? That shit costs almost three paychecks! What the fuck you gonna do? Marry her ass?" Noah didn't realize the thought had crossed his mind.

Lucas was shook. He thought maybe after he'd slept with her things would change. Maybe he'd just had a crush. But it was real. He was astonished. He hadn't thought he was capable of feeling this way about someone after being shut down for so long. Maybe he finally found that one right person. Yeah, he loved her. He smiled. He pulled up in front of Noah's house and got out.

Noah stepped outside with his date, a pretty Dominican girl in a nice magenta dress. She didn't wait for Noah to introduce her. She offered Lucas her hand.

"Hi, I'm Lissette Maldonado. You've gotta be Lucas."

Lucas smiled. Very pretty. A little young. He shook her hand. Noah's women were always a little young.

"I am. Nice to meet you."

Noah grabbed Lissette's hand and moved toward the car. "All right, Lucas, let's go get your woman."

They made good time getting to Justine's. Lucas' excitement and nerves made time go slowly as they rode up the elevator. He felt his breath leave his body when she opened the door. Justine was wearing a gold evening dress. It flowed over her body like liquid, as if it were painted on, and she was showing some serious cleavage. She had her hair down the way he liked it, and she smelled like flowers. Her smile dazzled him as she threw her arms around his neck. Damn! She was fine.

Karma

"Hi, baby," she said in his ear.

Lucas wanted to take her directly to the bedroom, but there'd be plenty of time for that. He kissed her neck. "I missed you."

She hugged him tighter. "I missed you, too."

They were the only two people in the world until Noah cleared his throat. "Can we come in, or is this a private party?"

Lissette giggled.

Lucas smiled and looked over his shoulder. "Private party. Get lost."

Noah laughed and pushed him.

"Man, get your ass outta the way and let me meet Justine."

They all stepped inside, laughing. Lucas put his arm around her. "Justine, this is Lissette, and this charming asshole is Noah."

Justine exchanges hellos with Lissette before turning to Noah. "Noah, I'm so glad to finally meet you. I feel like I know you already."

Noah bent and kissed her cheek. "You kinda do. I was standing next to him at the bar. The pleasure's all mine, Justine. Now I can really see why my boy's head is turned so hard."

Lissette was looking at Justine curiously. Her eyes opened wide as recognition set in. "Oh! I know you! You're Justine Greer from the news! Wow, Lucas, your girlfriend is Justine Greer from the news!"

"Yeah, she is." Lucas couldn't help himself. He stifled a laugh and added, "Justine Greer from the news."

Justine jabbed him with her elbow. "That's just my job; I'm just me."

Lissette was a bit starstruck. She had to say it one more time. "Wow, Justine Greer from the news."

Lucas looked at Noah. They both started laughing.

Justine scolded them. "Stop, you two. Don't laugh."

Lissette blushed. "I'm sorry, it's just that I watch you all the time."

"Okay, enough of that," Noah said. He poked Justine on the arm with his finger. "See? She's a real, regular person."

Lissette looked annoyed. "I know that, Noah. Lucas, I bet you did the same thing when you met her."

Before he could answer, Noah grabbed the back of his neck.

"Actually, his jaw hit the floor, and he was standin' there with his eyes popped out of his head, droolin' on the bar. Did I paint a pretty accurate picture?"

Justine touched Lucas' hand. "Is that a fact?"

Lucas peeled Noah's hand off him. "Well, maybe. Look, man, you gonna do me like this all night?"

Noah looked at him and smiled, mischievously. "Yes, sir. That is my intention."

Lucas rolled his eyes.

Lissette laughed. "It's gonna be a long night for you, Lucas."

"So it seems." He turned to Justine. "I need to borrow you for a moment."

She nodded. "Could you two make yourselves at home? We'll be back in a second." Lucas followed her to the bedroom. She closed the door behind her and turned to face him.

"God, you look good in that tux."

He smiled and stood very close to her. "You're not so bad yourself."

Justine ran her fingers over his chest, smoothing his lapels. "You make me not want to go."

He took her in his arms and kissed her. "So, let's stay here."

61

Karma

She giggled. "We can't. Besides, Noah's in the living room."

"He'll leave if we don't come back out."

They stared at each other. Finally Lucas broke the silence. "I have something for you."

Justine smiled up at him. "I bet you do."

They laughed.

"Yeah, I got that, too, but you're gonna have to wait on it. You don't have to wait for this." He gave her the box from his pocket.

She was surprised. "Lucas, what's this?"

"Open it and see."

Justine opened it and gasped. Her eyes went wide. "Lucas, oh, no, you didn't. Oh, I love it!"

It was the reaction he'd been looking for. He put the platinum diamond tennis bracelet on her wrist. "Sorry I couldn't find a corsage to go with your dress."

Justine put her arms around his neck. "I love you, Lucas."

"I love you, too."

"You've got a really big thank you coming up."

"Can't wait."

The four of them laughed and talked in Lucas' Lexus on the short trip to the club. Lucas circled the block twice, looking for a parking space. His patience was wearing thin.

Noah leaned over the seat. "Yo, Luke, man, I know you're tryin' to be nice 'cause you got your girl in the car, but I'm gettin' motion sickness goin' in circles like this. Flex the credentials and park this shit."

Lucas nodded. "You read my mind."

He made a tire-screeching U-turn and reached into the glove compartment, pulling out his police placard. Lucas stuck it in the window and parked in front of the club, just beyond the velvet rope, behind a limo. Sure enough, a bald-headed brother, not too tall but with a lot of muscles, rolled up on the car. Lucas looked at Noah in the rearview. They got out at the same time.

"Come on, fellas! Come on. Y'all know you can't park here."

They took their badges out.

"Yeah, we can," Noah said.

The guy nodded truculently. "A'ight. Y'all better have your shit in the window."

"It's there," Lucas said.

They watched him walk away.

"Fuckin' five-oh, rollin' up, flexin'," he muttered under his breath.

Lucas opened his door, reached for his coat and put it on, then helped Justine out of the car. Noah did the same for Lissette.

"Everything okay?" Justine asked.

"Perfect."

They walked inside. The club was almost at capacity. Everyone was laughing and dancing and having a good time. It was an upscale club, with regular folks mixing with a peppering of celebrities. Lucas noticed Robert dodging the crowd to get to them. Justine saw him, too. They met in the middle of the floor, and he greeted them.

"What's up, y'all? Happy New Year! Come on upstairs; we're in the VIP room."

They followed Robert upstairs, and the atmosphere instantly changed. Things were pretty exclusive up here. Big round tables surrounded by velvet chairs. Bottles of Dom and Cristal. Huge glass dance floor. Balloons covered by netting were close to the ceiling waiting to be released. They checked their coats and went to their table. Holly got up when she saw them and walked around the table to get her hugs and kisses.

Karma

"Happy New Year! Boy, y'all are looking good." She kissed Justine then Lucas. He introduced her to Noah and Lissette. She greeted them warmly, and they all sat down.

"We drinkin' that single malt tonight?" Robert asked, looking from Lucas to Noah. Lucas nodded.

"That's about all I drink, bro," Noah said.

Robert grinned and turned to Holly. He gave her the car keys. "That makes you the driver, baby."

Holly made a face at him. "Damn that. We'll catch a cab. It's New Year's."

They all laughed at them. Noah ordered a bottle of GlenlivetGl.

"Where's Simone?" Justine asked.

"Girl, you know Simone likes to make an entrance," Holly said, and turned to Noah. "Glad you decided to come hang out with us, Noah."

Noah looked around at the pretentious surroundings. "No problem. I felt like slumming."

Robert laughed. "Man after my own heart. I'd rather be home watchin' 'Dick Clark.' The women want this."

Lucas put his arm over the back of Justine's chair. She instinctively leaned toward him.

Lissette said, "Why are y'all complaining? Do you see Lucas complaining?"

Lucas smiled and picked up his drink. "Uh-uh. Don't put me in it."

Noah turned to Robert. "His ass is whipped," he whispered loudly. Robert nodded.

Lucas started to protest, but thought better of it. He ignored them

Holly looked at Justine's wrist and said, "I love your bracelet. Is it new?"

Justine couldn't keep the smile off her face. "Thank you. Lucas gave it to me tonight."

Holly looked at Robert. Robert shook his head. "Don't even try it, baby. Look at that rock on your finger." He took the wind out of her sails, and Lucas smiled.

Robert looked over Justine's shoulder and put his drink down.

"Here comes Hurricane Simone." He averted his eyes quickly.

Noah looked over his shoulder and let out a low whistle. "Goddamn!"

Lissette looked insulted and swatted his arm. Lucas actually smelled her before she arrived. An exotic, gingery, citrus fragrance. He felt her hand touch the back of his chair. She put the other one on Noah's.

"Happy New Year, everyone! The party can start now. I'm here." She paused and leaned over to Noah. "I don't believe I know you."

Holly cleared her throat. "That's Noah and Lissette. They're our new friends. Come sit down."

Simone shook hands with Noah and ignored Lissette. "Pleasure to meet you," she purred.

Lucas hadn't acknowledged her presence. He had his arm across the back of Justine's chair. He reached for his drink with his left hand so he could move away from her without being obvious and drank half of it. Then she put her hand on his shoulder. When he turned his head, he was eye level with her crotch. He looked up at her face. She smiled at him.

"Hey, Lucas. Aren't you going to speak to me?"

Lucas sat up straight. "Hello, Simone." Now, sit your ass down, he thought to himself.

Justine was giving him the "Pleassse, for me," look. Lucas shook his head and looked at her. She needed to be giving Simone that look. He saw what Robert meant. He couldn't understand why they were friends. Simone was trying to seduce him right in front of Justine's face. Justine put her hand on his thigh and whispered in his ear, "For me, okay?"

He nodded and kissed her. Simone sat next to Justine. She looked over Justine's shoulder at him and smirked. Lucas looked around the table. Everyone seemed to be missing this shit but him. Maybe it was his imagination. He turned and looked at Noah. Noah was looking at him square in the eye. Nope, it wasn't his imagination.

"Shut her ass down, Luke," he said quietly and poured them both another drink.

"I got this," Lucas replied.

Justine was laughing at something Simone had said and talking with the other women. She couldn't be that oblivious. He knew she wasn't. Maybe she expected him to handle this situation with Simone and cool her out.

Karma

"I know what," Simone started, looking at her watch, "We only have an hour and a half left in this year. Ladies, we're doing Patron shots." She signaled the waiter and got a bottle and setups. Lucas looked at Robert, who shook his head.

"Come on, y'all, drink up," Simone said, pouring tequila.

Holly laughed and took her shot glass. Simone pushed a glass at Justine. "Here you go, girl, drink up." Lucas knew for a fact Justine was not a big drinker. Two or three of those and she'd be asleep.

Simone raised a toast. "Out with the old, in with the new." She tossed hers back like an expert and poured another one right away. Holly did the same. Lissette and Justine were a bit more reserved. Lissette drank half of hers; Justine sipped.

"Oh, come on, Justine. This ain't whiskey! Knock it back."

Justine drank a little more. "Girl, this stuff is strong. I'm not trying to get drunk. My man is here."

Simone sucked her teeth. "Justine, please. Lucas will make sure you get home. It's New Year's Eve. He understands. Isn't that right, Lucas?"

Lucas stared at her. He wasn't feeling her at all. He gave

Justine a little smile. "Do what you want. You know I got your back. Have fun." He knew she'd only go so far.

Justine stood up. "I'm going to the ladies' room," she announced.

Lissette also stood up. "Me, too."

Holly pushed her chair back. "I might as well go, too. I don't want to go by myself later. You coming, Simone?"

"I'm good," she said.

"Lucas, baby, I'll be right back," Justine said.

Lucas nodded and watched her walk away. He loved watching her walk away. She had the sweetest ass he'd ever seen. Simone turned to face him. He had to admit, she was gorgeous. She would have been beautiful if she weren't so slutty.

"So, Lucas, are you having a good time?"

He shrugged. "Why are you talking to me?"

Simone licked her lips. Lucas sipped his drink.

"You don't want me to talk to you, Lucas?"

He noticed that Robert and Noah were blatantly silent. Lucas put his drink to his lips. "I'd prefer you didn't."

Karma

Simone was wearing a very short silver dress. It was so low in the front he could see her navel. She leaned back in her chair. "You afraid of me, Lucas?" Simone flashed him. She opened her legs wide and crossed them slowly. Lucas couldn't help it. He was a man. He looked. A glimpse of pink through gossamer silver panties, the bottom of her ass.

He heard Noah behind him. "Oh, shit! Damn!"

Lucas threw back the rest of his drink and stood up. He couldn't believe she'd done that shit! This was a fucked-up situation. Lucas put his glass back on the table and walked out of the club. He didn't even look at her. It was cold, and he'd left his coat inside. The Glenlivet did a little to warm him up. He was angry and wanted to leave. He really didn't need this shit. Noah stepped out of the club and handed him his coat. Robert was right behind him.

"You all right, Luke?" Noah asked.

Lucas put his coat on. "You got a cigarette?" he asked.

Noah took a pack of Dunhills out of his pocket and gave him one. He lit one himself and gave Lucas a light. Robert looked concerned.

"What happened?" Robert asked. He had been sitting on the other side of the table and missed Simone's little peep show.

Lucas shook his head. "She flashed me."

Robert looked appalled. "Say what? Are you serious?"

Noah inhaled. "Yep. She flashed him. Opened her legs up wide and showed him the goods, Rob."

Robert shook his head slowly in disbelief.

"She didn't seem to mind if I had a look, too," Noah said. He continued shaking his head.

"Lucas, man, I tried to tell you about Simone. I guess you thought we were just trippin'."

Lucas turned and looked at him. "Yeah, I did. What the fuck is wrong with her?"

Noah answered him. "She wants to take you from Justine. Maybe she's hatin' and just wants to ruin your relationship. Shit, at the very least, she just wants you to give it to her. Hard."

Lucas stared at the sidewalk. He inhaled deeply from the Dunhill and let it out slowly. Now he felt lightheaded. He didn't say anything until he finished it and flicked it in the street. "I don't believe this shit," he said angrily.

Robert looked at his watch. "We should go back in. They're gonna wonder where we are."

Noah put his hand on Lucas' shoulder. "Come on, Luke. I know this is fuckin' with you, but let's go back inside. You the man. Handle yours and cut her horny ass down."

Lucas really didn't want to go back in there. He didn't want to deal with this crap. Noah still had his hand on his shoulder.

"Pop your collar, Luke. Put the bitch in her place. Don't worry about what Justine will say."

Noah was right. That's what he was worried about. Justine. Lucas nodded, and they went back inside. By now, the ladies were back at the table.

"Where'd you guys go?" Lissette asked.

"Just out for a smoke," Noah answered her, sitting back down.

Lucas glanced at his watch. Not too much longer. He'd give it a half hour after the New Year came in, then he would roll out. He didn't want to be around Simone a moment longer than he had to. She was dangerous. He tried to clear his mind. Justine and the other women were engrossed in a conversation about fashion. Lucas kept his eyes down.

"You want another drink, dawg?" Noah offered.

Lucas shook his head. "I'm straight."

Robert and Noah got into a chat about football. Lucas remained silent, sitting close to Justine. After a while, she leaned back and regarded him curiously. "Why so quiet?"

He smiled at her. "No reason. Just admiring your dress."

Justine touched his face. "You're sweet. Let's dance."

Lucas led her to the floor. They started to dance. Alicia Keys faded to Luther Vandross. Lucas felt better. He felt like he could breathe over here. Justine peered up at him. "Let's not stay after the year comes in."

Lucas was surprised, but glad to hear it. "You don't want to stay?"

She put her head on his chest. "No. I want you to take me home and help me out of this dress."

He looked pleased. "Really?"

"Yes. Then you know what I want?"

"What's that?"

She put her arms around his neck and looked deep into his eyes. "Then I want you to make love to me until we're both exhausted and we just can't do it anymore."

"Not a problem."

Karma

They finished their dance. Lucas couldn't wait to get her home. He planned to make good on her request. They went back to the table, and Justine sat on his lap with his arms around her. They laughed and talked with the others. Simone didn't single him out again, although she did throw him a few amorous looks. Lucas pretended she wasn't there. The DJ called everyone to the floor at 11:58, where they all counted down and rang in the New Year together. Lucas kissed Justine, Holly, and Lissette. He gave Robert the one-shoulder hug. Noah hugged him like a brother, which he was.

Then Lucas was ready to bounce. He excused himself and went to the bathroom. There was only one other guy in there, and he left as Lucas came in. He walked to a urinal and relieved himself. He'd just tucked himself back in when he heard the door open and close. He flushed the urinal and zipped his pants. Lucas was about to turn around when he smelled that gingery, citrus aroma. Oh, hell, no! He turned around. Sure as shit, there was Simone, standing with her legs apart, hands on her hips.

"Why'd you put it away, Lucas? We could have had some fun."

He walked to the sink to wash his hands and looked at her in the mirror. "Get out, Simone. I don't want you."

Simone smiled smugly. She used her thumbs to move her dress to the side and popped her breasts out. Then she fondled them herself. They were perfect. Her nipples were like drops of dark sweet chocolate on her honey-colored skin.

"That's bullshit," she said shrewdly. She reached out with lightning speed and grabbed his manhood before he could step away. He was instantly hard as stone. Lucas shoved her roughly away from him.

"What the hell's the matter with you? Calm your ass down!"

She laughed and looked him in the eye. She was almost as tall as he was.

"That's cool, Lucas. I kinda figured you'd give it to me rough." Simone was quick. She locked her arms around his waist. She was strong, too. She ground her hips against his and grabbed his ass. He grunted and ground back impulsively. He couldn't believe this shit was happening. He didn't want to, but he couldn't stop himself from reacting to her. Simone sank to her knees and started to unzip his pants. He pulled her up, violently, by the hair.

"Get your ass up!" He threw her face-first against the wall. She stuck her ass out. Lucas felt his common sense leave him like a door slamming shut. He reached under her dress, stuck his hand in her panties and slid his fingers inside of her. Simone squealed with delight. Lucas pushed against her. He was way beyond furious with Simone, but he was also primitively aroused by her. His fingers stroked her intimately, but rudely. Simone gasped and cried out again. Lucas grabbed her hair and pulled her head back.

Karma

"Shut up! Is this what you want? Huh? You want me to touch you, you slut?" His hand was soaking wet. He pulled it out suddenly, and she turned around. He grabbed her face with his wet hand and forced her back into the wall. He spoke very close to her ear.

"Leave me alone. Stay away from me. I am not fucking around with you. Do you understand?"

She grinned and maneuvered his thumb into her mouth. She sucked it like she was going down on him. Lucas' eyes widened. What kind of freaky bitch was this? Her face was covered with her own juices. Lucas felt like she was mesmerizing him. His hand tightened on her face. She put her hands on him again. He was incensed with himself for just wanting to bend her over and take her like an animal. If she didn't stop, they both knew he would do it. He sunk his fingers into her face harder and mashed her head back into the wall.

"Get yourself together, then get the fuck out of here before I hurt you," he said quietly.

Simone moved away from him. She went to the sink and splashed water on her face, dried off quickly, and smoothed her dress, tucking her breasts back in. Then she turned back to face him. "Why are you fighting me, Lucas? Just do it and get it over with. We both know how this is going to end. You won't win. You won't be able to resist me, no matter how hard you try. I won't let you."

Lucas put his hands in his pockets and didn't look up. "Just get the hell out of here."

"If you're worried about Justine, don't. She's had enough tequila. She's probably asleep."

The muscle in Lucas' jaw tensed angrily. He stared at her darkly. "You've got two seconds to get out that door." He removed his hands from his pockets and clenched his fists. A trace of alarm crossed Simone's face, and she slipped out the door. Lucas stepped into a stall. He willed himself down. That was no easy feat. Then he heard the door open and close again.

"Lucas?" Noah called in a quiet voice.

Lucas came out of the stall and walked to the sink, where he washed his hands vigorously. He knew Noah was watching him.

"I saw Simone come out of here," he stated flatly. Lucas splashed water on his face. Noah handed him a towel. They looked at each other in the mirror.

"Noah, that woman is crazy."

Noah nodded. "I agree. She's got pretty big balls, too."

Lucas checked his clothes for anything incriminating. He sniffed his jacket for that loud-ass perfume she was wearing. Then he washed his hands again. He felt Noah's eyes on him. Lucas turned to face him, exasperated. "What, man? What?"

Noah folded his arms across his chest. "What did you do, Luke?"

Lucas looked away. "Nothin'."

Noah looked skeptical. "Then why you scrubbin' so hard, checkin' your clothes?"

They stared at each other. Lucas let out a deep breath and studied his feet. "I didn't fuck her, man."

Noah shook his head. "I didn't say you did."

"I thought about it."

Noah nodded. "I know you did."

"I thought I'd changed."

"You did."

"No, I didn't. For about five seconds, I could've thrown everything away, just to see what she felt like."

Noah smiled encouragingly. "Yeah, dawg, but you didn't. You changed. A few months ago, you woulda been comin' outta here whistling with a smile on your face."

Lucas shrugged. "Maybe. I didn't do as much as I could've done, but I still wasn't a prince, Noah."

Noah put a hand on his shoulder. "Look, bro, I know it's hard to resist a woman like Simone. Especially when she's throwin' herself at you. I know I probably couldn't. Probably wouldn't even want to. Shit, Simone might be a bitch and a ho, but she's also one of the finest motherfuckers I've ever seen, and she knows it."

Lucas felt terrible. For all he knew, Simone could be out there right now, telling her version of what happened. Guilt was making his skin crawl. Noah was observing him closely.

"You really love Justine, don't you?"

A touch of astonishment tinged his voice. "Yeah, I do." He went to the door. "Noah, I'm gonna fuck this up. I know it."

"No, you won't. Everything's gonna be fine."

Lucas didn't think he sounded too sure. He opened the door. "Let's get outta here."

"Anything you say, Luke."

They returned to the table. Lucas stood behind Justine's chair. She was laughing at something Simone had said.

"Hey, Lucas! Where've you been?" Simone yelled out.

He looked at her with mild aversion and glanced at Noah, whose face looked like he wanted to shake the shit out of her. Simone stared back and bit her lower lip, sexily. Lucas didn't believe in beating women, but he was ready to knock her ass out. He touched Justine's hair.

"Let's go, sweetheart."

They made their good-byes and wished everyone a Happy New Year.

Lucas dropped Noah and Lissette off. He didn't feel like driving all the way back to Manhattan, so he took Justine back to his place. He fulfilled her request by first helping her out of her dress and then making love to her until they were both exhausted.

71

Karma

He knew he'd been a little rough with her. She seemed surprised at first, but then she let herself go. He doubted he had hurt her. He'd been seeking release from that crap Simone had put him through.

Now Lucas lay on his back with his arm behind his head. The other one was around Justine, who had her leg thrown over his hip and her head on his chest. He was staring at the ceiling. His mind drifted, and he closed his eyes. As he was falling asleep, he saw a glimpse of pink through transparent silver panties, the bottom of her ass. Lucas' eyes popped open. He tried in earnest to blink the image out of his mind. He silently fought against the recollection of how wet his hand was when he pulled it out of her.

"Lucas?"

Justine startled him, and he jumped apprehensively. He thought she was asleep.

"Yes?"

She turned so she could look up at his face. Justine was frowning slightly. "Are you okay?"

He averted his eyes and rubbed her back. "Yeah, I'm fine."

"Are you mad at me?"

He looked at her. "Justine, no. Why would I be mad at you?"

"You just seemed angry earlier when we were making love."

"I'm sorry. I got a little carried away. I didn't hurt you, did I?"

She kissed his chest. "No. You didn't hurt me."

He continued to stroke her back.

"I love you, Justine." And he did. He was just afraid he wasn't as strong as he needed to be.

Karma

Chapter Thirteen

Simone

Simone was getting pissed off. She'd sent slow-assed Raphael out to pick up lunch, and he wasn't back yet. He knew she couldn't work on an empty stomach.

She couldn't concentrate, so she walked across the room and looked out the window. She ran her hand through her hair absently. It wasn't just hunger that had her on edge. Well, maybe it was, but it was a hunger of a different sort. She rubbed her thighs. Her thoughts went back to New Year's. She'd almost had his ass. Fine bastard. She thought about how he felt in her hand. He was packing, sure enough. She ran her hands over her body and relived the moment he'd slipped his fingers inside of her. She closed her eyes and rubbed her thighs together. She had come at once when he did that. Simone threw her hands over her head. Lucas Cain! She had to have his ass.

"Damn, chica! Are you having an orgasm or what?"

Simone's eyes flew open when she realized she wasn't alone. She winked at him. Raphael winked back.

"You sneaking up on me, girlfriend?" she asked, stepping

away from the window.

Raphael put her lunch on her desk. "Hardly. But I'll tell you, if I wasn't so gay, I would want you sooo bad right now with your sexy ass."

Simone laughed and sat down. "It's funny, I can make a gay man want me, but I can't get the man I want into my bed."

Raphael hung his coat up. "Why not?"

"He's taken."

Raphael's eyebrow shot up. "And what man is that?"

Simone opened her Cobb salad. "Wouldn't you like to know?"

"I'm dying to." He sat across from her. He'd gotten a salad, too.

Simone wrinkled her nose. "I can't tell you. I've been a bad girl."

Raphael sniffed. "What else is new?"

Simone slapped his hand playfully. "Don't talk about me, Raphael. Remember, I pay your salary."

"How could I forget? Come on, boss lady, tell me who it is."

Simone licked her lips and opened her salad dressing. "It's Lucas."

Karma

Raphael opened his Pellegrino. "Lucas? Isn't that Justine's boyfriend? Let me see the picture again, chica."

Simone opened the top drawer of her desk and gave it to him. It was a picture of all of them at the table in the VIP room New Year's Eve. Everybody got one. Raphael studied it and pursed his lips.

"Damn, he is fine. I wonder if he's got a down low side. I could definitely get with him."

Simone looked amused. "Raphael, I seriously doubt that Lucas has a gay bone in his body. No offense."

Raphael ran a hand through his newly short, newly platinum hair. "That's not a problem. I took a so-called straight man from his wife."

Simone nodded and picked up a forkful of salad. "I remember that."

Raphael laughed. "So does his ex-wife!"

They ate in a comfortable silence for a while.

"So, that's why you wanted those dresses. They both were a little over-the-top — even for you."

Simone grinned wickedly. "Precisely. Those dresses were

icebreakers. The silver one broke the surface. It let me know the pond's not totally frozen."

"For real? Then what's the problem?"

"The problem is I never see him without Justine. He's always right up under her tight ass. I had to jump him in the bathroom just to get him to touch me."

"Damn, girl. You're serious, huh?"

"Very. It's like I've gotta have him. I've got to figure out a way to get him alone. Without Justine."

Raphael took a sip of water. "Do you know where he works?"

Simone shook her head. "I do, but I would think twice about going there. He's a detective."

"You're right. No humping at the precinct."

That was true, but she'd wanted him from the moment she saw him. He didn't know what he needed. He needed her. Besides, their relationship was still new enough for Justine to get over him. In other words, Simone didn't care. She didn't feel particularly guilty about it. She didn't want to take him from Justine just yet. She wanted to satisfy her curiosity. If he was good in bed, then he was the total package. Maybe after she found the answer to that, her plans would change.

75

Karma

Chapter Fourteen

Justine

Justine sat in the news van sipping her coffee. She had the shakes. She hated covering stories like this one. She looked at the medical examiner's van parked on the other side of the street.

Things had gone wrong in a routine buy and bust. The perp, a 15-year-old kid, had gotten nervous, pulled a gun and landed a fatal shot in the temple of the first cop as well as hitting his partner in the neck. Justine shivered. What good was a vest when they aimed for the head?

She was scared to death. This was the Major Case Squad. She hoped to God that hadn't been Lucas and Noah. Her cameraman, Darius, stuck his head in the van.

"Live in two," he said.

Justine put her coffee down and got out. Quickly, she smoothed her coat, took the mike and waited to be cued.

"This is Justine Greer, live, with breaking news. Two police officers have been shot, one fatally, at a buy and bust gone tragically wrong …" Justine told the sad story and waited to be cued out. Then Darius walked over and put his hand on her shoulder.

"You okay, Justine?"

She shook her head. "No. I'm scared."

There was some commotion in the alley where the shooting occurred. The forensic team was removing the body. Justine clasped her hands together to keep them from shaking so bad.

"It's just, this guy I'm seeing, he's a narcotics detective with the Major Case Squad, and I can't get in touch with him."

Darius was quiet. She didn't know which part of what she said had caused the silence. "Oh," was his only reply.

They watched silently as the body was brought out of the alley and put in the back of the ME's van. Solemn detectives and a few uniformed officers drifted out with the forensic team. Justine's heart was in overdrive. She should assume Lucas was okay, but she'd feel better if he'd answered his phone. She tried him again and still got his voicemail.

"Why won't you answer your phone? Goddammit!"

Darius grabbed her shoulders. "Look, honey, you need to calm down. He's probably not even here. Maybe he was off today."

"I talked to him earlier, Darius. He said he had a buy and bust. Now I can't find him."

Karma

Darius looked at her a long moment. He took her in his arms and kissed the top of her head. "I'll bet he's fine. You love him, don't you?"

Justine nodded. "Yes. Very much."

"Lucky him," Darius said softly. He stood there holding her a moment longer, then abruptly let her go.

"Looks like maybe he's okay. Is that him?"

Justine turned to follow Darius' gaze. Lucas was walking toward her, Noah was right behind him. They were dressed down in boots and jeans, but they had their badges prominently displayed. She wanted to run to him, but she didn't want to appear unprofessional, more for his sake than hers. When he reached her, he took her hand.

"We're all right."

She was relieved and couldn't stop smiling. "Boy, am I glad to see you. You, too, Noah."

"Hey, Justine, nice to see ya." Noah was eyeing Darius.

Justine introduced them quickly. "Lucas, Noah, this is Darius. We work together. He's a videographer. Darius, my boyfriend, Lucas, and his partner, Noah." Justine didn't realize Lucas was pissed until he shook Darius' hand. He looked him coolly up and down.

"Darius," he acknowledged him, giving him a small, tight, smile.

Darius returned it. "Lucas." He shook Noah's hand and got a better response. Darius excused himself and walked back to the van. Lucas watched him go.

Noah cleared his throat. "I'm gonna head back over and see if Internal Affairs is done with us. See ya, Justine." He kissed her cheek and walked away.

"Lucas, I was really worried. I'm so glad you two are all right."

"Plans changed at the last minute; that could've been us." He paused for a second and looked in Darius' direction. Justine looked up at him expectantly, waiting for the hammer to fall. Still, she couldn't help but smile at him. He stood there scowling at her with a toothpick sticking out of his mouth. Then he took it out and pointed toward Darius with it. "Old boyfriend?" He was jealous. It was a huge compliment. Justine kept smiling.

"Something like that."

"He still likes you."

"You think so?"

Karma

Lucas scowled at her and threw his toothpick away. "I'm not laughing. I had a really bad day."

"I know."

"Then why are you smiling?"

She put her arms around his waist. To hell with professionalism. "Because you're okay. So go ahead. Be jealous for no reason. Be mad at me. Be anything you want. I'm so glad you can just be alive, Lucas. I thought something real bad happened to you. I love you so much."

The anger fell away from his face, and he hugged her back. "Thanks. I needed that." He kissed her softly, then he stepped away and looked over his shoulder.

"I can't stay. I'll call you later." He turned and walked away. Justine watched Noah wave him over to an unmarked police car. He got in, and they sped away.

Darius reappeared out of thin air. "You know the cop that was shot in the neck?" he said over her shoulder. She looked at him and nodded.

"Just died. He bled out. We have to update."

It was a long night. Justine was exhausted when she got home.

She let herself in and made a cup of chamomile tea while she ran a hot bath, then got into the tub. She thought about Lucas. If anything happened to him, it would kill her. She loved him that much. She loved everything about him. He was in her soul.

The door to the bathroom opened, and Justine sat up. Lucas walked in and closed the door behind him. It hadn't been long, but Justine hadn't hesitated to give him a key. He undressed and slipped into the tub behind her. She leaned back against his chest. He was so warm.

"Thought you'd be asleep," he spoke into her ear.

She smiled and lifted his hands to her breasts. "I thought I'd wait up for you." Justine felt him harden against her as he toyed with her breasts.

"Sorry."

Justine slid her hands over his thighs. "You don't have anything to be sorry about. You had a horrible experience today. I understand. And you don't have anything to worry about. I belong to you, Lucas." She turned to face him, and he slid down.

"I love you, Justine." He eased into her, and they made love in the soapy water. Justine had never felt so close to any man in her life. They came together, the water sloshing out on the floor. Eventually, they moved to the shower and washed each other. They ended up making love again. Lucas carried her to the bed, and they did it one last time before they fell asleep. Justine was glad he was here. Glad he was whole. She wanted to love him forever.

Karma

Chapter Fifteen

Simone

Simone was surprised when Holly popped into her office. She was putting the finishing touches on an outfit she'd designed herself. Raphael was out running an errand. She looked up when Holly came in.

"Hey, girl," she said, getting up to greet her. "What brings you downtown? Take your coat off. Stay awhile."

Holly walked over and sat across from her. "That's okay. I won't be here long."

Simone looked up from what she was doing. Holly was so angry, she barely contained it.

"What's the matter?"

Holly put her purse on Simone's desk. "What's the matter? Simone, I should slide across this desk and choke the shit out of your whorish ass."

Simone looked at her blankly. "What are you talking about?"

Holly leaned toward her. "What was up with that slutty little stunt you pulled on New Year's Eve?"

Simone continued to look blank. "What stunt?" Simone

wondered whether she was talking about what happened at the table or in the bathroom. Holly stood up. Simone stood up with her. She knew how Holly got down. No way was she going to try to whip her ass in her own office. She really did look as if she were about to choke her.

"I'm talking about you sitting like a whore at our table and showing your entire ass to Lucas and Noah. Don't you have any respect? Not even for yourself?"

"I don't appreciate you rolling up in my office like you want to beat my ass. Especially over some shit dumb-ass Robert obviously told you. You need to calm down."

Holly took off her earrings and stepped out of her shoes. "I know you didn't just call my husband out of his name. You need somebody to beat your ass for you? I'm the one. I did it before, I'll do it again."

Simone moved away from her. "You're crazy, Holly. You need to back up. This is my place of business. I wouldn't do this to you."

82

Karma

Holly laughed. "How do I know what you wouldn't do to me when you gap your ass open like that? If you'd do that to Justine, fucking me over is right around the corner."

Simone folded her arms across her chest. "All I did was cross my legs. My dress was too short. That's all." Simone couldn't keep the smirk off her face. Holly was tripping. Now Holly took her coat off.

"Are you laughing? Then it must be true. You know, for years we tried to give you the benefit of the doubt. 'Everyone makes mistakes.' 'That's our girl.' 'Friendship is stronger than that.' Well, we were wasting our time. You'll never change, Simone. You were a worthless slut back then, and you're one now. Why do you keep doing this? Do you hate Justine? Why? Are you really that much of a bitch? Are you?"

"Are you done? 'Cause if you are, this conversation is over. Try not to let the door slam on your way out." Simone sat back in her chair. This wasn't about Lady Justine. This was about Simone for once. She had a right to what she wanted, too. It was unfortunate that Lucas had seen Justine first. He fell in love with her, sure, but he wanted Simone. She knew he did. More importantly, she wanted him. Fuck unrequited love.

Holly watched her face. She put her coat back on, stepped back into her shoes and put her earrings in her purse. "I'm serious,

Simone."

Simone didn't say anything. She looked at the floor.

Holly cocked her head to the side. "Did you do anything else?"

Simone continued to stare at the floor. She crossed her legs at the ankles. "Did Robert say anything else?"

Holly didn't answer her.

"Then I guess I didn't, according to Robert."

"He wasn't lying on you, Simone. I'll bet my last money you did more than that. Maybe I should talk to Lucas."

Simone shrugged. "Go ahead, but do you really think he'd tell you the truth?"

Holly frowned. "So, something else did happen."

Simone laughed. "Ask Lucas."

Holly picked her purse up and walked out.

Simone stood up and put her coat on. She called Raphael on his cell phone and told him to take the rest of the day off. Then she put her bag over her shoulder, locked up and went outside to hail a cab. She rode up to the garment district to find some fabric for one of her designs. She didn't really want to lose Holly's friendship. Justine's either. She also didn't want to give up her pursuit of Lucas. She knew she was becoming obsessed with him. Just like Michael back in college. She hadn't meant for things to go as far as they did. She just wanted a sample.

Michael Baldwin had been Justine's high-school sweetheart. Their life would probably have been a fairy tale if it weren't for her. Simone had met them and Holly at NYU. They went through a lot of things together, both good times and bad. Back then, they'd held each other down like steel.

Watching Justine's perfect life play out started to leave a sour taste in Simone's mouth. Nothing ever came that easily for her. When she was a teenager, she'd had an affair with her step father. After her mother made her get an abortion and testify against her step father, she just wasn't the same. Nothing was ever good enough. And meeting Justine, who lived in a perfect bubble, only made her want to knock her down a peg or two. Simone had never been in love, especially like Justine was with Michael.

Michael didn't even cross Simone's mind until Justine put too much of her business out there. They all used to talk about their men and their sex lives freely back then. Simone never kept a steady man for more than a few months. She was between men at the time that Justine made her comment. Simone couldn't even remember what it was. Something about oral sex.

That disclosure had turned Simone's head, and she'd started to look at Michael differently. She remembered how she'd be talking to him and staring at his mouth, wanting him to try his tricks on her. She always thought he was fine, but now, he was gorgeous. She'd find herself staring at his crotch. He noticed. Michael was no angel. He stepped to her pretty quickly. They hooked up quicker. It was on and poppin' after that. They turned each other out. They had sex every chance they got. They went on like that for four months. Then one day, Justine walked in on her riding Michael like he was a racehorse. She was devastated. She ran to Holly, hysterical. Holly, who could still revert back to being ghetto, was really ghetto back then. She jumped Simone in Washington Square Park. Simone had to admit, Holly did beat her ass. She even knocked her front teeth out.

Michael's ass was to the curb at once, and they stopped speaking to Simone. In fact, they didn't speak for a year, then they ran into each other at a show at the Beacon and started hanging out again. They'd gotten close once more, but things between her and Justine were never quite the same. She never did that again. They promised each other.

Simone put down the fabric she'd been looking at and sighed. Her mind fell on Lucas' sexy ass. Some promises were made to be broken. She left the shop and walked around the corner toward another store she knew. It was starting to get late, and she wanted to get home and rev up her sewing machine. This outfit had to be ready in two days. Just as she reached for the handle of the shop door, someone grabbed her purse. Simone reflexively grabbed it back. The guy was shorter than her, but he was thick. He knocked her down.

"Run your bag, bitch!" He wrenched the bag off her arm and punched her in the face. Then he started running, and Simone took flight after him, yelling, "He stole my bag! He stole my bag!"

Chapter Sixteen

Lucas

Lucas followed Noah into the squad room. He sat down at his desk and loosened his tie. Noah sat across from him at his desk and did the same. They'd spent all day at Internal Affairs being interviewed because IA wanted to make sure proper protocol was followed the night the two detectives were murdered. It had been a long, depressing day.

Lucas and Noah had been in the academy with one of the detectives. They'd known the other for years. Both murdered detectives had left behind wives and children. Lucas felt terrible. He knew Noah did, too. They had been across the street and down the block in an unmarked car when they heard all five shots. By the time they got there, no more than two minutes later, the shooter was scaling the fence. They dragged the perp's ass down and made the collar. The other team made the 911 call. The second perp fled, but the shooter ratted him out. They had to rehash everything about 12 times.

"You ready to get outta here?" Noah asked.

"Hell, yeah."

"You hangin' out tonight?"

"I could use a beer."

They stood up and started putting their overcoats on. Noah nodded at him. "You look tired, man."

Lucas laughed. "It's been a long day. So do you."

They started out of the huge room, passing criminals in different stages of arrest and paperwork and made their way into the hallway. Noah popped him lightly on the arm. "Oh, shit! I'll be damned." He pointed straight ahead.

Simone was waiting for the elevator, looking disheveled and holding her face.

"Oh, shit!" Lucas repeated Noah's words. "What the hell is she doing here?"

Noah shrugged. "Let's go find out." He started to move, but Lucas held him back.

"Nah, let her get on the elevator."

"No, Luke. Come on, let's see what she's here for. Maybe somebody kicked her ass."

Against his better judgment, Lucas followed Noah down the hall. Simone turned before they got to her and immediately started toward them.

"Somebody definitely kicked her ass," Noah said. She was sporting a black eye and a bruised cheek.

"Lucas! I'm so glad you're here." She approached him like she was his wife. She threw her arms around his neck and started to cry. Lucas had his overcoat on, but he could still feel her body pressing against him. He grabbed her shoulders and peeled her off him, then stepped away from her.

"What truck hit you?" Noah asked.

She looked at Lucas; he looked away. She started to cry harder, and Lucas rolled his eyes.

"I was assaulted and robbed."

Noah raised an eyebrow. Simone started shaking. Noah put his arm around her.

"Did you file a report yet?"

She nodded. "I just finished."

Noah went into police mode. "Did recover your possessions?"

"No, he got away."

"Are you all right? Do you need to go to the hospital?"

"Noah, do I look like I'm all right? But, no, thanks. I don't

Karma

want to go to the hospital." She looked at Lucas. He looked at the floor.

"Do you want us to take you home?"

Lucas looked at Noah like he'd lost his mind.

"Could you? I would appreciate it. I'm still a little shaken up."

"Sure, we'll take you."

Lucas shook his head and walked away. He couldn't believe this shit. He heard Noah tell Simone to hold on a second. Lucas rang for the elevator. Noah caught up with him.

"Luke, man, I know how you feel. Try to show some compassion. Look at her."

Simone was still crying and shaking. Lucas could almost hear the violins playing.

"She's a good actress, Noah. How are you just gonna volunteer us to take her home? I'm not responsible for her. Hell, you take her."

Noah was looking at him as if he'd lost his humanity card. "Come on, Lucas. Don't be like that. She's in trouble."

Noah's cell phone suddenly rang. Lucas listened to the one-sided conversation.

87

Karma

"Talk to me. Hey. Whoa, slow down, Nadine. What? Where are you? Okay, I'll be right there." He hung up.

"What's wrong?"

Nadine was Noah's ex-wife. Something was wrong if she was callin' Noah.

"Little Noah broke his arm. I gotta run."

"Handle your business. Let me know if he's all right." Lucas was Noah's son's godfather.

Noah looked back at Simone. "Be a gentleman." He waved Simone over. Lucas looked resigned.

"I'm gonna get you back for this shit, Noah."

Noah seemed unaffected. "No problem. Just be nice and take her home."

Lucas rang for the elevator for a second time. Simone stepped in with them.

"Listen, sweetheart, Lucas is going to take you home. My kid just broke his arm."

"Is he all right?" Simone asked.

"I'm sure he will be." Noah looked at her candidly. "Simone, Lucas is doin' me a favor. Be nice."

Simone nodded. They trailed Noah outside and parted company. Simone walked behind Lucas to his car. He got in without opening the door for her. She slid into the passenger seat as he started the car.

"Nice car," she said.

Lucas didn't respond. He put on his turn signal to pull out.

"Aren't you going to talk to me? You didn't even say hello.".

Lucas looked straight ahead. "Where do you live?"

Simone smiled and winced through the pain. "Oh, you can talk." She gave him her address, and he pulled out. Lucas was watching her out of the corner of his eye. She leaned into the seat and lightly touched her bruised face. She was looking out the window.

"Why don't you like me, Lucas? I mean, I may be a bit bruised up right now, but don't you think —"

He cut her off. "Uh-uh. None of that."

The perfume she wore, that gingery, citrus smell, was invading his nostrils. Lucas let his window down.

"You know, it is still winter. I'm freezing with that window down."

He shrugged. "Sorry."

Simone laughed. "No, you're not."

Lucas kept his eyes on the road.

"Do you mind stopping by my office?"

"Yes, I do."

Simone became whiny. "Come on, Lucas, please? I've got a client that I've got to have done. I'm already working against the clock. Please, Lucas."

He looked at her quickly and didn't answer.

"We're almost there. Please stop." She was getting on his nerves.

"All right, but I'm not babysitting you all night. In and out, okay?"

Simone touched his arm. "I love it when you talk dirty."

He ignored her. She told him where her office was, and he pulled up and shut off the ignition. When she didn't move, Lucas turned and looked at her. "What are you waiting for? Go."

Simone started looking upset again. "Would you please come with me?"

Lucas started laughing. He shook his head. "Don't think so."

"Lucas, please. That guy took my purse. All my information

is in that bag. Who's to say he isn't lurking around somewhere. Come on, Lucas. I'm really scared. Please, come with me."

Lucas was quiet. And aggravated. He wanted to get away from her.

"You're a cop. You're supposed to protect people, you know," Simone pouted. There it was. She played that card. Digging at the bottom of the barrel.

Lucas laughed without mirth and shook his head. "You are unbelievable." He opened his door and got out. He seriously doubted there was anyone lurking around. He just wanted to be rid of her. They rode the elevator up to her floor. He was thinking of ways to get Noah back for this. The elevator opened, and he followed her down the hall. Simone took her keys out of her pocket and let them in. She put on the lights and looked at him gratefully.

"Thanks for this, Lucas."

He retreated to a space just inside the door. "Just hurry up."

Simone took her coat off. She was wearing a pair of ultra-low jeans and a filmy black blouse. You could see her intricately lacey bra through it. Noah was right. Simone might be a lot of things, but she was undeniably stunning. Even with the bruised face. She was shuffling through some papers on her desk. Then she dropped a manila envelope, a calculated move, and bent over to pick it up. Lucas couldn't stop himself from looking at her. Simone grinned and wiggled her ass at him.

Karma

"Is that why you're so quiet? Do you like what you see?" She straightened up and turned around.

Justine's face popped into his head. "Let's go," he said.

Simone came closer. "I didn't get what I came here for."

Everything became sparkling clear to Lucas at that moment. He should never have put himself in this situation. Simone was the type of woman that, if she decided she wanted to give it to you, you'd either have to be gay or an invalid not to take it. And Lucas did want her. He felt weak. If he didn't get out right away, he was going to lose everything, and he couldn't. He loved Justine.

Simone smiled at him and kicked off her shoes. She removed her blouse. Lucas' feet were rooted to the spot. He couldn't look away. That feeling of being hypnotized returned. Simone peeled her jeans off and put them over the back of her chair. Lucas bit his bottom lip. She stood there in her frilly black bra and thong, looking like every man's wet dream. Slowly and enticingly, she took her bra off and flung it across the room. The thong was next. Her body was flawless. She beckoned him with her finger.

"Come on, Lucas. Come and get it. You know you want it." That broke his paralysis. He couldn't believe her brazenness. Lucas turned to walk out. He had to get out. He was breathing hard. He genuinely didn't trust himself. But Simone slipped between him and the door. Lucas pushed her out of the way, forcibly. She laughed and pushed him back. Lucas was surprised, but he recovered quickly, grabbing her by the shoulders and deliberately moving her aside. Simone was fast. She spun around swiftly and blocked the door again.

"Let me outta here. Move!" Lucas was angry now. She was a woman, and he didn't want to hurt her, but she was going to move. He tried to pull her, but she used leverage and wouldn't budge. The only way to move her was probably going to hurt. He took a deep breath and took her down like a criminal. She didn't go down easy, or alone.

Karma

Simone twisted her body and stuck her leg between his. They tumbled to the floor together. Lucas took the brunt of it, hitting the back of his head on the floor. Simone landed on top of him, falling into his diaphragm, cutting off his air supply. He was about to sit up, when Simone pushed him back. She put her mouth on his and kissed him deeply. Her mouth was soft and surprisingly delectable. Lucas kissed her back. Without thinking, he reached for her breasts. They were soft but firm, her skin was like fine silk. Her hand dropped to his belt. She worked it open. Simone unzipped his pants and broke the kiss.

"You taste so good, Lucas. I knew you would. I've been dying to put my mouth on you."

Fuck it! He'd gone this far, if she wanted a piece of him, she was going to get it. That was all she was getting. Just a piece. As angry as he was with himself — and Simone — he had to do it. He realized he was so hard he could barely walk as he got up and took off his overcoat and suit jacket. He undressed to his shirt. Yes, he was going to give her what she wanted, and he wasn't going to be nice about it. He wanted her, but he also wanted her to leave him alone. He sat in the chair and leaned back.

"This is what you wanted, right? You been dyin' to put your mouth on me? Go ahead, you fuckin' lunatic."

Simone crawled over to him. "Don't think for a moment you just hurt my feelings. You didn't." She grabbed him and gave him a lick. Lucas shuddered.

"Boy, do I love chocolate."

Lucas grimaced with gratification. He put his hands in her hair and pushed her head down. "Don't talk. Get to work," he said nastily.

Simone wrapped her hand around his rod. It was warm and soft. Lucas entwined his hands in her hair, forcing her head down until he was fully in her mouth. He moaned shakily. Simone was looking up at him, her head bobbing up and down. He stared back. She did a little trick, swirling her tongue. He gasped involuntarily and trembled. She kept it up.

Lucas grunted and twisted his hands in her hair. She could never say she'd never done this before. By far, it was the best job he'd ever had, and he'd had many. She lasted for a long time, long after most women would have quit. Lucas wasn't nice. He cursed her out the whole time. She loved it. When he came, he held her head down and yelled at her.

"That's what you wanted? Take it! Take all of it, you fuckin' slut!" He didn't let her up until he was empty and her mouth was full. The second he was done, he pushed her off him.

Simone sat back on her heels, still staring at him. Her mouth was full, all right. A little liquid seeped out of the corner. She wiped it with her pinky and licked it off. Then she swallowed. She smiled lewdly at him and winked. "Good to the last drop."

Lucas started dressing. He was totally disgusted with himself. He stood quickly and dressed. Simone was sitting in her chair with her legs crossed.

"Don't be mad, Lucas. It was good."

"It was wrong, Simone. Don't talk to me."

She stood up and sashayed over to him. Lucas backed up. He didn't want her to touch him.

"You didn't actually fuck me, you know."

"No. I fucked your mouth." He took his wallet out and extracted five twenties and stuck them in her face.

Simone looked offended. "What's that for?"

He glared at her. "Get yourself home. You don't have a ride."

"I don't need your money, Lucas."

He raised an eyebrow. "Why not? You earned it." He threw it at her and walked away.

Simone grabbed his arm. He shook her off. "Don't touch me. Move."

91

Karma

Simone looked as if she were going to cry, but she didn't fight him. She let him leave.

When he got to his car, Lucas put his head in his hands. He felt terrible. He was scared. He didn't want to lose his woman. He'd made a stupendous mistake. Simone was just crazy enough to be on the phone with Justine right now, telling all the sordid details of what happened. He hoped to God that wasn't true.

He started the car and turned on the radio. Aretha Franklin was singing about a no-good, heartbreaking, lying, cheating, bastard of a man. He turned it off. That was the last thing he needed to hear. He felt bad enough. Lucas' plan had been to end the night in Justine's bed. He drove to Brooklyn instead, beating himself up all the way. The phone was ringing when he walked through the door. He picked it up.

"Hello?" He looked at the caller ID. It was Justine.

"Hi, baby. What are you doing at home? I thought you were coming here."

Lucas smiled even though he felt a tight ball of fear in his stomach. "Hey, sweetheart. I wasn't feeling too well. I just came home, I didn't want to make you sick, too," he lied. It tasted sour in his mouth.

"I miss you. Do you need me?"

What an odd question. Lucas kept smiling. "I miss you, too, and, of course, I need you."

Justine paused. "I just talked to Simone. She told me what happened."

Lucas felt his heart lurch in his chest. His mouth fell open.

"Oh, yeah, she told me about the robbery and how the guy assaulted her. I thought it was very sweet of you and Noah to see her home. She really appreciated it, and so do I. I know she's not your favorite person, but she said you went out of your way to be good to her tonight. Thank you, Lucas."

Lucas was quiet for a moment, trying to form words around the sudden lump in his throat. "You're welcome," he mumbled.

"You okay, baby?"

Lucas shook his head. "Not really. I think it's the flu or something. I just want to get into bed."

"Well, try to get something to eat, or at least have some tea before you do that."

He smiled in spite of himself. "Yes, Mother."

Justine laughed. "Very funny. Feel better, sweetie. I love

you."

"Love you, too."

Lucas' smile faded as soon as he hung up the phone. He felt so guilty. He loved Justine. Hell, he wanted to marry Justine. Why is it that as soon as he fell for a woman, someone like Simone showed up, hell-bent on getting him in bed? He poured a glass of single malt and drained it. Refilling his glass, Lucas could only hope that he was strong enough to keep the only woman he ever loved in his life.

Karma

Chapter Seventeen

Justine

Justine couldn't keep the smile off her face. She followed Lucas and the bellboy outside to their bungalow. They'd flown down to Ocho Rios for a few days. Lucas had surprised her. Several days ago, she'd mentioned they'd been together six months. Lucas admitted he hadn't been keeping track, and she'd been disappointed. He promised to make it up to her. Now, here they were.

Justine was excited. They'd never been away together, and she had him all to herself for four days. The bellboy opened the door and let them in. Lucas tipped him, and he left discreetly. The bungalow was decorated beautifully. It was rustic with a lot of bleached wood and bright splashes of color. She loved it. She was about to say so when Lucas picked her up. He carried her to the bedroom and gently put her on the bed. He hovered over her, a knee on either side of her hips. He looked so serious as he began to undress her, staring into her eyes. Her blouse came off, then her bra. Justine smiled at him.

"Do you love me?" she asked in a whisper.

Lucas smiled, too, and whispered back, "I could eat you up. And I think I will." He proceeded to do just that. He took his time and made slow, long, leisurely love to her. She never wanted him to stop. Lucas was all she could have wanted in a lover. Patient, skilled and gracious. Also, a master at multiple orgasms. Unlike other lovers, she'd never faked one with Lucas. They had all been real. Mind-blowing. Earth-shattering.

Justine felt the familiar warm wave that spread up from her toes. Her body trembled. She was lying on her stomach, with a pillow beneath her. Lucas was on top of her, his breath was warm against her face. He went all the way in as Justine arched her back. She came so hard, she saw colors. Lucas was on his way, caught up in the tail end of her orgasm. She joined him, screaming his name. Lucas put his arms around her waist and brought her down with him. They lay spooning, breathing hard. Justine laughed.

Lucas rose up and looked at her. "What's so funny?"

"I'm starving."

"So am I."

Karma

They had dinner at a nearby seafood place. The food was great. They danced a little at a local club, and then they went for a walk on the beach. It was night, and the moon was full and bright. They were walking along the edge of the water when Lucas stopped and put his hands in her hair. He caressed the sides of her face and kissed her softly. A gentle breeze blew off the warm water.

"Thank you," he said, hugging her to him.

Justine put her head on his chest and hugged him back. "For what?"

"For accepting that glass of champagne."

She smiled. "There was no way I could have turned you down."

He kissed the top of her head and laughed. "I know. I just wanted to thank you."

She leaned back and swatted at him playfully. "Oh, you wanna play?"

He grabbed her behind, and she jumped away from him, laughing. He chased her back to the bungalow. Lucas caught her at the door. He wasn't even breathing hard. He backed her up against the door and put his arms around her waist. Justine reached up and wrapped her arms around his neck. They stared into each other's eyes. She thought he was the most handsome man she'd ever seen. And he was good to her. He was romantic, and sweet and kind.

She loved him more than she could articulate.

"Let's go inside," he said, unlocking the door.

When Justine walked in, she was speechless. There were candles and rose petals everywhere. He led her out to the little patio with the gorgeous view of the ocean. It was a fantastically beautiful setting. On a table sat a bottle of champagne on ice and lit candles.

"Be right back." He disappeared for a moment and quickly returned. Justine smiled as Brian McKnight started singing "Love of My Life."

"Dance with me." Lucas folded her into his arms. They swayed to the music. Justine was in heaven. She ran her fingers through his hair, moving his head down, then she gently kissed his lips.

"You're wonderful," she said.

Lucas smiled at her. "Think so?"

She nodded with contentment. "Know so."

They finished their dance, and Lucas popped the cork off the champagne. She noticed he didn't pour it. Justine sat at the table and watched him. He stood a moment longer, staring down at her. He rubbed the back of his neck and sat down across from her, leaning back in his chair. Once again, he looked so serious. He let his eyes drift over her.

97

Karma

"I need to ask you something."

Justine felt a little uneasy suddenly. "Okay."

A rose petal had fallen into her lap. She was glad. It gave her a reason to drop her eyes. She picked it up and rolled it around in her fingers. It was a deep shade of fuchsia. Sometimes Lucas unnerved her when he looked at her like that. It was like he was looking through her. Looking into her.

"I'm making you nervous."

"A little." She looked up.

Lucas smiled at her. "Don't be. I've seen you naked."

Justine laughed. "You're silly."

He reached out to her and took her hand. "I want you to answer a question for me," he began again. "I want you to be honest. Don't hold back. Tell me everything."

Justine looked alarmed. What the hell was he talking about? Lucas leaned back in his seat again and continued. "I need to know, in no uncertain terms, exactly what it is you want from me. Tell me."

Justine blushed. Lucas smiled. She frowned.

"What I want from you?"

"Yes. Exactly."

Justine took a deep breath. She shook her head. "I can't tell you that."

Lucas looked amused. "Why not?"

Justine was blushing furiously. The more she blushed, the more he looked amused.

"Because, Lucas, it would make me seem like I'm jumping the gun. You'd think I was crazy."

"Try me." He still had that look on his face.

She wondered what he was up to. "All right. I'll tell you. In no uncertain terms, Lucas, I want you to love me, and only me, forever. I want us to have a big house somewhere nice. I want two boys and two girls. I want to see your hair turn gray. I want us to always have what we have right now. This same fire, the same passion. That's what I want."

He was looking at her steadily. "Is that all?" he asked.

Justine was fighting to keep the heat out of her face. Maybe she'd said too much. She stuck her chin out defiantly. "Yes, that's all. You can run away now."

Karma

Lucas looked genuinely surprised. He laughed. "Run away? Not a chance, my love." He picked up the champagne and poured it. Justine's heart was doing somersaults. She was holding her breath.

Lucas leaned toward her. "Justine, I'll always give you what you want." He stood and produced a small blue velvet box in front of her. "Now give me something I want. Marry me."

Justine's mouth dropped open, and she put her hand over her heart. She sat there stunned, like a statue, until Lucas picked the box up and took the ring out, pulling her to her feet. She managed to close her mouth, but she started crying. Lucas took her left hand and kissed her palm. He slipped the ring on her finger and held her hand to his face. It was perfect. A three-carat, princess cut diamond in a platinum band. Lucas wiped her tears away. He was smiling.

"Don't cry, baby. Say yes. Be my wife." Lucas had a way of changing her life, and he was never subtle. Justine loved him for it.

"Yes, Lucas. Yes. I'd love to."

He took her back inside and made love to her again. This time it was deeper and more poignant. They had committed themselves to each other, and they were expressing their love for each other. It was sweet. When they were done, Justine lay with her head on his shoulder. She smiled and looked at her ring. It really was perfect.

"You like it?" he asked.

Justine kissed his chest. "I love it. It's beautiful."

"It was my grandmother's."

Justine sat up and looked at him. The sentiment behind the gesture touched her. "Wow, Lucas."

He smiled and sat up with her. "Wow, Justine."

"I know how special your grandparents are to you. This is precious."

He kissed her forehead. "Now you know how special you are to me."

Justine felt the urge to cry again, but choked it back. Instead, she got up and straddled his lap, facing him.

"I love you." She kissed him.

"I love you, too. When do you want to do this?"

"When do you?" she countered.

"We could do it now, before we leave."

Justine shook her head and smiled. "Negative, Lucas. My parents would kill me."

Lucas smiled at her distractedly. Her breasts had stolen his attention. He deftly traced her nipples with his thumbs.

"Yeah, they want the wedding." Justine looked at him slyly. He was ready again. Insatiable.

"Don't you?" she asked.

Lucas maneuvered himself until he was back inside. They both gasped.

"I don't care. All I want is you."

Karma

Chapter Eighteen

Simone

Simone looked at her watch; she was fashionably late. She'd be the last one there if she timed it right. Her thoughts drifted to Lucas. She hadn't seen him since that day at her office, even though they'd all gotten together since then. If he knew she'd be there, he wasn't coming. Justine always said he had to work. Simone could not think of another soul that worked as much as Lucas claimed he did. He avoided her like the plague. Holly had picked up on it and made some derogatory statement about it. Simone didn't care. She knew sooner or later Justine would drag his stubborn ass out. He couldn't let her go everywhere by herself forever. In any case, he would be at Holly's today. Simone called Justine last night to ask, cautiously. Justine confirmed, then had gone on and on about some little impromptu trip the two of them took. Simone tuned her out after the first sentence. So what? Lucky bitch.

Simone could hear the party. She followed the flagstone path to the backyard. The pool was filled with kids. Some of the older folks were seated in the shade, ladies in gossipy clusters, men playing dominoes. Holly and Justine were at a table with Holly's sister and sister-in-law, playing bid whist. Lissette was there, too. Simone smiled, because that meant Noah must be there. She liked him. She thought he was handsome. The grill was on the other side of the house. That was most likely where she'd find the men. Simone sighed and made the prerequisite stop with Holly and Justine. She was actually itching to see Lucas.

"Hey, ladies!"

They all greeted her.

"I thought you weren't going to make it," Holly said, studying her cards.

"You know me and my entrances. Gotta be the last one here. Justine, you look good. You must have really needed that trip."

Justine smiled at her. Or rather, glowed at her. She did look marvelous. Simone squinted at her. Holly was grinning from ear to ear.

"Yeah, I really did. Check it out, Simone." Justine raised her left hand.

Simone looked at the ring. She felt like a lead weight had just dropped into her stomach. "What the hell is that?"

Justine's smile faltered, but she rebounded. "It's my engagement ring."

"Engagement ring?" Simone thought she was joking. They're engaged?

Holly put her cards down. "Lucas asked Justine to marry him last week. Isn't it wonderful news?"

Holly was looking at her like she wasn't above jumping across the table to kick her ass. Lissette looked like she would help. Simone reached down and hugged Justine with an enthusiasm that wasn't there.

"I'm sorry. Sure! It's great news, Justine. I'm so happy for you. Let me see." Justine hugged her back and thanked her. Simone took her hand and inspected her ring. It was very nice. "It's beautiful. Very classy," she said truthfully.

Miss Perfect couldn't stop grinning. "Thanks, Simone."

Simone kissed her cheek. "You're welcome. I know I'm in the wedding, right?"

Justine laughed. "Of course, you are."

Simone straightened up. "Let me go congratulate the groom. I'll be right back." Her eyes touched Holly's. She seemed darkly amused.

Simone went into the house. She had to get herself together.

First, she went into the bathroom and leaned against the sink, surprised at her own reaction. She was so caught up in her own lust, she didn't even realize when she'd started to catch feelings. Simone freshened her lip gloss and went back outside, walking around to the far side of the house.

Robert was working the grill. Lucas and Noah were there with him, drinking beer and talking shit. They all fell silent when they saw her. Simone looked at Lucas. He turned completely away from her and drank his beer. She smirked. He was so stupid. He didn't realize she wasn't finished with his ass. She smiled brightly.

"Hey, fellas! Happy Fourth of July."

They gave a collective greeting. Lucas didn't open his mouth, although he did turn back around. He was looking at her like she'd better not start anything. She walked over to Noah. He always looked as if he were about to laugh. Gently, she touched his arm. He smiled crookedly and looked at her hand, then back at her. She didn't remove it.

"What's up, girl?" he said quietly.

"Not a thing. It's nice to see you."

"You were a bad girl, Simone."

"So I've been told. Excuse me." She stepped to Lucas. She would have gone to him first, but she didn't want to be completely obvious.

103

Karma

"Hey, Lucas. Heard you're getting married."

"Uh-huh," he said cautiously.

"I just wanted to tell you that I'm happy for you and Justine."

Lucas actually snorted. He laughed. "Okay. Thanks," he said with mock sincerity.

"I'm serious, Lucas."

He looked at her and shrugged. "Okay. Whatever you say."

Simone put her hands on her hips. "So you've taken yourself off the market, huh?"

Lucas laughed mirthlessly. "I've been off the market for a minute, in case you didn't notice."

She smiled at him and licked her lips. "I didn't."

"Leave him alone," Noah said over her shoulder in a low voice. He startled her.

"What?"

Noah took her by the elbow and escorted her out of earshot of Robert. "I said, leave him alone. Let it go."

Simone smiled at him. "Noah, I don't know what you're talking about."

Noah smiled back. His eyes changed, became a little lighter, a little steelier. "Yeah, you do. Haven't you done enough?"

She shrugged. "I obviously didn't do enough."

Noah frowned. "You tryin' to bust them up, or do you just want to sleep with him? Who's this about? Lucas or Justine?"

Simone stared at him. "I don't have to talk to you about this."

"Yeah, you're right, you don't, but you need to find somebody else to sink your claws into."

She moved closer and stuck her chest out. "Got anybody in mind?"

Noah looked at her appreciatively and took a sip of his beer. "Not a soul. You're a beautiful woman. I'm sure you can find a nice guy."

Simone reached out and touched his hair. "What about you? You're a handsome man."

Noah laughed out loud and shook his head. "Definitely. But I said find a nice guy. Not me. Thanks for the compliment, though."

"You sure?"

Noah looked at her with amused disbelief. "Yes, indeed. Damn, girl! I don't believe you're tryin' to get your flirt on with me. Is that how you're livin'?"

Simone laughed. "Am I scaring you?"

"I don't scare easy. I was just thinkin', you got balls like a man."

She looked at him, lewdly. "I do. You wanna see?"

Noah's smile widened, but his already-steely eyes glinted at her like a warning. He laughed again. "I'm not fuckin' with you, Simone. Leave Lucas alone. Good luck." He walked away from her, and she turned and watched him go.

Simone decided she'd had about enough of this little shindig. She couldn't believe they were engaged. She wasn't just disappointed, she was so angry she could smack that smile right off Justine's face. Justine always got everything she wanted, and just like everything else she desired, Lucas had fallen right into her lap. She had to be the luckiest bitch she'd ever seen. Simone's cell phone started ringing. She picked up on the third ring.

"Simone."

104

Karma

"Talk to me, boo. It's Nine."

She giggled into the phone. "Oh, I know who it is. What are you doing? Are you busy?"

"Well, hopefully, I'll be doin' you later. I'm at a barbeque."

Simone sighed. "Me too. I want to leave. I'm bored."

"We can't have you bored, boo. Want me to come get you?"

"I'd love it." She gave him the address and hung up. Simone usually didn't get involved with her clients, but she found Nine irresistible. Tall and brown with piercing green eyes and dark curly hair. He was nice to look at and great in bed. He also seemed to have a serious thing for her. Nine was the rapper of the moment. His first CD had just gone platinum. Everything he was touching was turning to gold, but he hadn't totally extracted himself from his first job. Nine and his family allegedly owned a nice piece of the drug trade in New York City. That part of his life made her nervous, but it also gave her a small thrill. She didn't know if it were true or not.

She started to make her way back to where everyone was seated. Maybe she shouldn't have told Nine to come here and get her; after all, there were two narcotics detectives here, not to mention all the kids. He may not feel like signing autographs. She didn't think anything would happen, though. She was more nervous about Lucas and Noah being there. Simone sat down between Holly and Justine.

Karma

"Are you all right?" Justine asked.

"I'm getting a headache."

Holly looked up. "You want an aspirin?"

"No, I'm going home. I'm just waiting for my ride."

Holly frowned. "Why are you leaving? Go inside and lie down."

"That's okay. My ride's on his way."

"His way? Who's he?" Justine asked.

"Yeah," Holly added, "we didn't know you were seeing anyone. Who is it?"

Simone reached for a soda. "Nine."

Justine looked surprised. "The rapper? Really?"

Simone noticed Lucas and Noah exchange a look. They both stood up.

"He's coming here?" Lucas asked.

"He's just picking me up."

"You might wanna think about not being in his company,"

Noah said.

Simone sat back in her chair and eyed him warily. "Why?" Nine's involvement in the drug trade, Simone thought, was probably hearsay. She liked to think it was, like with a lot of rappers, a strategically planted rumor that gave him street cred. Sure, he had a gun, but a lot of rappers did.

Noah looked at Lucas.

"Well?" Simone prodded.

Lucas gave her a blank stare. "Well, what?"

"Are you guys investigating him or what?"

Noah chuckled. "We didn't say that. Just choose your friends wisely."

Justine turned to Lucas. "Where are you two off to?"

He smiled at her. "Nowhere. We're just gonna check Rob out for a while." He and Noah disappeared, returning to the grill. The blind side of the house.

It took Nine about an hour to get there. Lucas and Noah stayed gone. Simone felt a small tremor of fear when she slipped into the Hummer next to him. Maybe they knew more than she did. Maybe it was true. She shook her head to clear her thoughts. Then again, maybe they were wrong. She dismissed this mode of thinking by smiling and putting her hand on Nine's thigh. She let it slide up to his crotch. He was hard already. Her smile expanded. She wasn't ready to let him go. Not yet. She hadn't given up on bedding Lucas. She'd break him sooner or later. In the meantime, there was Nine, and he filled the hole quite well.

Karma

Chapter Nineteen

Lucas

Lucas sat in the unmarked police car with Noah. Noah was drinking coffee and smoking a Dunhill. Lucas drummed his fingers on the steering wheel. They had one of Nine's minions under surveillance. A woman walked by in a very short halter dress. It was painted on, and she was shaking it. Her breasts were high and firm, butt tight and round. Legs for days. She tossed her head and looked over her shoulder at them, then winked. The face matched the body.

"Have mercy," Noah said, exhaling smoke. They watched her walk away.

"I agree," Lucas said.

Noah laughed. "You better cut that shit out. Justine'll mess you up for that."

Lucas laughed. "Don't think so."

Noah put his cigarette out. "How's the wedding plans going? You guys set a date?"

"I'm letting her do her thing. I already told her I'd marry her tomorrow if she wanted me to. I think she wants to do it in

February."

Noah looked at him jovially. "Damn, bro, that's soon."

Lucas stared out the window. He cracked a smile. "Not soon enough."

Noah shook his head. "I still can't believe it."

Lucas glanced at him. "You have to. You're the best man."

"I better be." Noah lit another Dunhill.

They were quiet for several minutes.

"Can you believe Simone is involved with this guy?"

Lucas nodded. "Yeah, I can."

"You think she'll take our advice and stop seeing him?"

"No, and neither do you." Lucas resumed drumming his fingers. He avoided thinking about Simone. As a matter of fact, he had effectively pushed her from his mind. It had been months since that brief interlude in her office, and he'd managed not to be around her until the Fourth of July.

Karma

He'd had a couple of dreams about her, though. Vivid dreams. Raw, hot, steamy, freaky dreams. His hands all over her perfect body. Whenever he did think about her, he envisioned her naked. He flashed back to her in her office, on her knees. Yeah, it had been good, but the guilt he felt made it not worth it. The word almost floated through his mind, like the devil leaning over his shoulder. He pushed it back with strength of mind.

He replaced thoughts of Simone with Justine. She still gave him butterflies. He couldn't wait to marry her. He was surprised at how fast things had gone, but Justine had his heart. He'd do anything for her. And he knew she loved him just as much. Somewhere in the back of his mind, though, he was waiting for things to start falling apart. Everything was too perfect. Something was bound to fuck it up.

Noah looked at his watch. "Not much longer," he said. As soon as the statement left his mouth, the doors to the apartment building swung open and out stepped Michael LaRoque aka Dirty Mike. They had intel that Dirty Mike was very high up on Nine's chain of command. Right after Papi aka Hector de La Cruz. In his pre-rap days, you could find Dirty Mike slinging everything from weed to heroin. He was also thought to have popped more than a few people. Post-rap, you can find him onstage. Part of the entourage backing Nine up. And still dealing, still enforcing.

"He's moving," Lucas said.

Noah groaned. "He would get his ass in gear now. Shit!"

"Yeah, we almost made it."

They only had half an hour left before they were due back at the precinct. They watched Dirty Mike walk down the street and get into a black BMW. They exchanged glances. That wasn't the car he arrived in. That would be the white Navigator down the block.

"Not a big deal," Noah said.

"Nah." Lucas started the car. Dirty Mike spent about five minutes on his cell phone before pulling off. They followed him down to the Lower East Side. He got out carrying a Banana Republic shopping bag.

Dirty Mike disappeared into one of the buildings. He came back 10 minutes later, still toting the bag. He looked around quickly and put it in his trunk. Lucas and Noah watched his movements until he hopped into his car and sped away.

"I wonder what was in the bag," Noah said, rubbing his chin.

Lucas pulled into traffic. "I don't think it was a sweater."

They drove back to the precinct and reported to their captain.

Captain Myers wasted no time. "What's up, fellas? Whatcha got?"

Karma

They sat down across from him. "Not much," Noah replied.

"He stayed put all day. He didn't start moving 'til late," Lucas added.

They went over his movements and spoke about the questionable contents of the shopping bag. They had established an undeniable connection between Nine, Papi, and Dirty Mike.

Captain Myers rubbed his hands together. "All right. We're progressing. We're going to take this slow. No mistakes. When this asshole goes down, he stays down."

They nodded.

"We want to run a few buy and busts down on Henry next week. You know, routine thing. Cain, I need the beard gone. Down to a goatee, at least."

Lucas' mouth fell open. His hand went instinctively to his face. "What? What's wrong with my beard?"

Captain Myers turned to him. "You gotta fit in with the rest of the unit. You guys are too used to being suits. We want you thugged out. This guy's a rapper. If we decide to put you in his environment, you gotta look and act the part. This isn't just a buy and bust."

"Shit," Lucas said under his breath.

Captain Myers was studying them both. Noah shrugged and stood up. "A'ight, even though we both hate to stop being grown-ass men."

Myers laughed. "Come on, guys, it won't be forever. We'd appreciate the adjustment."

Lucas stood. He was pissed. He was going to look like a kid, and it was going to take forever to grow it back right. He looked at the captain. "Is that it?"

The captain nodded and leaned back in his chair, still smiling. "Yeah, that's it. Don't look so glum, Cain. It'll grow back."

Lucas ignored him. He looked at Noah. "Let's go."

"See ya later, guys."

Lucas let the door close a little harder than he should have.

"Don't slam my door, Cain," Myers called from inside.

Noah laughed. They walked outside.

"You hanging out, or you goin' home?" Noah asked.

Lucas touched his beard. "Guess I'm going to the barbershop. What about you?"

"Maybe I'll take my kid to the movies." He stuck a Dunhill in his mouth.

Lucas laughed. "Myers is gonna make you switch to Newports."

Noah winced. "Probably. Maybe I'll just stop."

"Good idea. I'm out."

Lucas got his hair cut low, and his beard shaved down. He looked in the mirror. He looked younger. It wasn't a bad look for him. He'd just have to get used to it. He made his way to Justine's and let himself in. They had dinner plans. He was meeting her parents tonight. Lucas hopped in the shower and bathed quickly. He put on the suit he'd brought by the night before and was tying his tie when he heard Justine come in.

"Lucas?" she called out. He smiled. She was going to be shocked when she saw him.

"I'm in here," he answered. Justine walked in a moment later.

"Good, you're dressed. I'm just going to —" She stopped talking and looked surprised.

Lucas laughed. "How does it look?"

She smiled and touched his face. His beard wasn't totally gone. He still had a goatee. "Actually, it looks very nice. Very sexy."

She put her arms around his neck and kissed him. He kissed her back. What started out innocently enough became hot and steamy pretty fast. Lucas unbuttoned Justine's blouse and reached behind her, unhooking her bra.

"Lucas, we don't have time for this. We're going to be late," Justine said, as she slid his zipper down and eased her hand inside his pants.

"I'll take the blame," he said in her ear.

Justine surprised him and took the lead. She didn't seem interested in foreplay, either. She pushed his pants and underwear down in one swift move. Lucas laughed softly and picked them up. He put them over the back of a chair and sat down on the bed. Justine cocked her head to the side. She smiled as she took her blouse and bra off.

"Are you laughing at me?" she asked coyly. She raised her skirt and slipped her panties off. She kept her skirt on, but hiked it up so he could look at her. Lucas smiled. Very nice.

"Not at all. I like it."

Justine walked to the bed and straddled him. She pushed him down on the bed and slipped him inside of her. Lucas put his hands on her waist, but he let Justine set the pace. They made love fast and hard. Then he stood up with her and flipped her over. He got on his knees and pulled her to him. Justine arched her back and threw her legs over his shoulders. Lucas slowed down a little and leaned back. He felt her tighten up. She called his name. He went a little faster. There she went, like a bomb going off. He watched her face as she came. She was the most beautiful woman in the world to him. He let himself go and moaned and kissed her as she grabbed him and pulled him in. They climaxed together, and it was sweet.

"Wow! I'm marrying you!" Justine exclaimed, smiling.

He smiled back. "You better."

They jumped into the shower and dressed quickly. It was a long drive to Justine's parents' house out on Long Island, but they got there pretty fast. Despite the typical interrogation from Justine's father, the evening went off without a hitch. Lucas had never been interested in meeting her parents before, but this meant a lot to him. They were friendly, and they seemed to like him well enough. Lucas pulled away from the house and took Justine's hand. He was surprised to find she was shaking.

"Something wrong?"

She gave him a small smile. "Nothing. I was just a little nervous, I guess."

He laughed. "You? What about me?"

She smiled again. "They like you, Lucas."

He laughed. "Thank God."

She laid her head on his shoulder. "We're really getting married."

"Yeah, we are."

Karma

Chapter Twenty

Simone

Simone sat across from Nine and watched him talk on his cell phone. He was speaking so quietly, she couldn't even hear what he was saying. She picked at her salad and waited for him to hang up. It took another 10 minutes for him to get off the phone.

"Sorry, boo," he said, flashing a smile at her.

Simone was annoyed. She didn't like being ignored. "That was rude, Eric."

He laughed. "What's wrong? You pissed off?"

Simone picked up her fork. "Yeah, I am."

"I said I was sorry. What? You think that was some other woman?"

"I don't know who it was, Eric."

He laughed again. "Look at you, all pissed, callin' me by my government name." Eric Dillard was Nine's real name. Simone felt silly calling him Nine. They were a bit more intimate than that.

"I don't think it's funny."

He smiled at her. "That was business. I had to take the call.

Even when I'm with you, I still gotta get my paper."

Simone looked at him. He was so handsome, almost pretty. Almost. But there was nothing feminine about him. He stared back at her with those forest-green eyes.

"Let me make it up to you," he said in a low voice. The electricity between them was almost visible.

Simone leaned forward and gave him a magnificent view of her cleavage. She pouted prettily. "All I wanted was a little attention."

Nine looked at her like she was a seven-course meal. "You gonna get more than a little with your fine ass."

She pushed her plate away. "Let's go. You can talk shit later."

He grinned at her wickedly. They left the restaurant and drove to Simone's apartment. She was unlocking the door when Nine put his hand under her skirt and slipped it into her panties. Her mouth popped open as she was hit with a serious case of déjà vu. She felt like she was back in the bathroom with Lucas. Simone closed her eyes and unlocked her door. She gently removed his hand.

"Not in the hallway. I do have neighbors."

They went inside. Nine was all over her in two seconds. Tongue in her mouth, pushing her panties down. Simone stepped out of them and sat on the sofa. She shrugged out of her blouse as Eric dropped his pants. He slid a condom on and knelt in front of her. Simone slid down to meet him. He put his hands behind her knees and pushed her legs up. Then he went in all the way, slowly. Simone moaned and closed her eyes. She heard him laugh softly as he started moving real slow and hitting corners. Simone put her hands under the small of her back and lifted herself up, grinding with him. When she opened her eyes, they grinned at each other.

"This enough attention?" Nine asked.

Simone laughed. "Not quite." She wriggled away from him and pushed him backward. He looked startled and a little angry when he hit the floor. But she quickly got on top with her back to him and tilted forward. Simone was totally aware of the view she was giving him. She started her ride with Nine's hands on her hips.

"Yeah, girl. That's dirty. I like that."

She sped up and slowed down, gripping him until he was screaming. Simone looked over her shoulder at him. She smiled. "Is it that good?"

Eric started laughing. "Hell, yes! Please, believe me! You ain't runnin' this show, though." He flipped her over on her stomach.

Simone laughed. "That's it, Daddy. Finish me off."

"Oh, I'm goin' to." He plunged into her and briskly broke her down until this time, they were both screaming, coming so hard it almost hurt. Breathless and laughing, they collapsed on the floor in each other's arms.

"That was off the chain," Nine said, running his hands over her body. "You got me wantin' your freaky ass all the time."

Simone grinned at him. "What a cool way to tell me you like me."

He looked at her seriously. "Hell, yeah, I like you."

She sat up. He sat up, too.

"What's up, Eric? Are you catching feelings?"

He tilted his head. "Could be. Why? You wanna be my woman or somethin'?"

"Are you asking?"

He reached out and touched her face. "You want me to?"

Simone thought about it. Lucas flashed through her mind. It had been a long time since she'd been someone's actual woman. She also knew one thing to be true. If the opportunity ever presented itself with Lucas, she was taking it. She looked at Eric, sitting there waiting for her to say something. Hell, she could do a lot worse than him. He was fine as hell, a good lover and at the top of his game. She couldn't ask for anything more. Except maybe … Lucas. She shook her head. She could almost taste him again, after all this time. She looked back at Eric.

"Why not?" she said.

Karma

He laughed, green eyes sparkling, teeth flashing, curly hair shining. Oh, yeah, he was fine. And maybe she was catching a few feelings herself.

"Okay, then, that's what it is."

"I thought you were going to ask me, not just say it."

Eric kissed her, still smiling. He smiled more than any man she'd ever seen. It was cute, though. It hadn't started to work her nerves yet. Besides, it was refreshing next to serious-ass Lucas.

"I did."

Simone giggled. What the hell? "Okay, I will."

He kissed her again and stood up, pulling her up with him.

"I gotta go to the studio. You wanna come?"

Simone licked her lips and looked at him lewdly. "I

just did."

"If you don't put some clothes on, you will again."

Simone traced the outline of his name tattooed on his arm. "That would be nice."

He put his hands on her waist and his forehead to hers. "I'd love to, but I'm already late. I'll come back tonight to tighten you up."

She watched Eric get dressed. She had to admit he was almost perfect for her. Except for that iffy drug thing, and she really did like him a lot more than she cared to think about. Maybe it was time to get over Mr. Cain. Simone smiled to herself. He was, literally, a tough nut to crack.

Nine finished dressing. Simone walked over to kiss him good-bye. Surprisingly, he kissed her very tenderly, then kissed the tip of her nose.

"A'ight, boo. See you later." He gave her another kiss, and she let him out. Simone picked up her energy drink. She smiled very smugly. If he didn't love her already, he didn't have very far to fall.

Karma

Chapter Twenty-One

Justine

Justine sat at her desk daydreaming. She should have been prepping for a story she was working on for tomorrow's broadcast, but her mind kept drifting. Her mother called constantly, relentless about the planning of the wedding. Justine smiled. Lucas was funny. He'd deftly excused himself by getting totally wrapped up in a case. He suggested since she'd insisted on a wedding, going back to the islands and getting married on the beach. Justine's mother had quickly vetoed that idea. Her baby was getting married in a church. Before God. Not the ocean. At that point, Lucas quietly stepped back and relinquished control. He told her to just let him know what to show up for and when. He also gave her an out. They could always go to city hall and elope.

Even though her mother had her at her wit's end at times, deep in her heart, Justine really wanted a wedding. In the end, however, the church or the beach was fine with her, as long as Lucas was there.

A knock at the door snapped her out of her reverie. Justine hastily shuffled the papers on her desk to look busy.

"Come in," she said.

Darius entered her office and promptly sat on her desk. He had a smirk on his face. Justine sat back in her chair and laced her fingers across her stomach. They stared at each other a moment. She braced herself. She'd been expecting him.

"Hey, Darius."

He looked pointedly at her left hand. "Nice ring."

"Thank you."

He looked at her wistfully. "It's a lot bigger than the one I got you."

Justine didn't say anything. Her heart had never let her get that serious with Darius. Her head hadn't either. The lies he'd told had effectively sealed his fate with her.

He stood up. Justine stood, too. But she kept the desk between them.

"Yes, Darius. You have to let it go. Things didn't work out between us. I'm sorry. I know you're sorry, too, but you have to move on. Take the relationship for what it was."

He frowned and looked at the floor. "How can you marry him instead of me?"

Justine was blunt. "Because I love him."

Darius moved toward her. Justine took a step back and folded her arms across her chest.

"You were supposed to love me."

She looked at him incredulously. "I never said that, Darius. How could I?"

He was squinting at her. "What do you mean, 'how could I?'"

Justine was exasperated. "What I mean is I didn't have the freedom to have feelings like that for you. I wasn't putting my heart out there for you like that. It's not my fault you fell in love with me. That's not where our relationship was supposed to go, and you know it."

"No, I don't know it. Obviously, we weren't on the same wave length."

Justine nodded vigorously. "Yeah, Darius, we weren't. You were married."

"I left my wife for you."

She looked at him sadly. "No. You left your wife for you. Don't put that on me. I'm not going to live with that. We never should have gotten involved with each other. You didn't even tell

118

Karma

me you were married until after we slept together."

"You sayin' I tricked you, Justine?" He actually had the nerve to look hurt.

"I'm saying you didn't tell me." She talked to him like she was speaking to a slow child. He walked over to her, and Justine dropped her arms.

"Darius, we're friends. Don't mess that up."

His eyes softened as he looked at her. "I'm always right here, Justine."

She hugged him, and he hugged her back.

"I know you are. Just be my friend."

There was another brief knock at the door. Darius and Justine were just stepping away from each other when the door swung open.

"Hey, Justine, look who I found." Lucy, Justine's intern, entered the room. Lucas was right behind her.

Justine looked up and over Darius' shoulder. Her eyes widened, and she moved completely away from Darius. She felt guilty, even though she hadn't done anything. Darius had thrown her off, and she'd forgotten that she and Lucas had a four o'clock appointment to sample menus with her mother.

Karma

Lucy looked at her apologetically, moving speedily past Lucas and out the door. Lucas was looking at Darius. A frown creased his brow. He closed the door behind him. Justine put on her best smile and walked over to him. She wanted to nip this in the bud before Lucas jumped to conclusions. He seemed well on his way.

"Hi, baby. You remember Darius, right?"

Lucas didn't acknowledge her. Instead, he stepped to Darius. "What's up, man?" he asked. He looked like he wanted to kick Darius' ass.

Darius met his stare with his own. "Hello, Lucas. Nice to see you again."

"Am I missing something?" Lucas asked him quietly.

Darius shrugged. "I don't know what you mean."

Lucas took a step closer. He was about three inches taller than Darius. He leaned over him. Just a little. "Why is it every time I see you, you got your hands all over Justine? What's up with that?"

Justine looked at Lucas' face. He was livid. Darius laughed and rubbed his chin. He looked at Lucas cockily. Justine swallowed hard. Bad move, Darius.

"Why you always flexin' on me, man? I ain't scared of you."

Lucas gave him a tight smile. "You should be."

Darius laughed again, but also took a step back. "You threatening me?"

Lucas advanced on him. "I don't make threats."

"What's your problem? You need to ease up off me. I didn't do nothin' to —"

Lucas cut him off. Justine watched his hand curl into a fist. A muscle flickered angrily in his jaw. "Ease up off you?" The angrier Lucas became, the lower his voice got, like he was consciously not yelling. Darius was the opposite. He got louder and more belligerent.

"You come up in here flexin', tryin' to punk me out? You ain't no big deal. Who you think you are?"

Lucas stared at him for a second, then he smirked. "I'm the guy she's marrying. Who the hell are you?" he said condescendingly.

Darius lost it. Just as he finished closing the distance between the two of them, Justine jumped in the middle. She held her hands up to Darius with her back against Lucas' chest.

Karma

"Who am I? Who you talkin' to? We can take this shit outside. I ain't got a problem with that!" Darius did not realize he did not stand a chance against Lucas.

"All right!" Justine said. "That's enough. What's the matter with you two? Stop this nonsense right now! Cut it out!" She put her hand on Darius' arm to restrain him.

Darius looked at Justine. "I'm leavin' for you, okay?"

Justine nodded almost imperceptibly. Darius walked toward the door, pausing when he got to Lucas. They stared at each other. Darius looked like he wanted to say something but thought better of it. He walked out, and Lucas closed the door behind him.

Then he turned and looked at Justine like he was expecting some sort of explanation. She returned his gaze. Justine was upset with his overreaction. There was nothing going on between her and Darius. Sure, he'd witnessed the tail end of that hug, and he had seen Darius hug her before, but that was all. She resented the fact that Lucas' look implied he didn't trust her. As she shook her head slowly and took her bag out of her desk drawer, she felt Lucas watching her. Justine took out her compact and freshened up her lipstick.

"Justine." He said her name, not quite asking for her attention. She looked at him with displeasure.

"What is it, Lucas?" she asked flatly. His head snapped back like she'd slapped him. He looked at her a moment longer and dropped his eyes. She couldn't believe the way those two had acted. Part of her was flattered, but she was mostly pissed. She made sure the issue was definitely not up for discussion. "Come on, we're going to be late."

Lucas dutifully held the door open for her and followed her out of the building. They drove to meet her mother in silence. Lucas was being childish. He refused to even look at her. He wouldn't even turn the radio on. She guessed he figured he'd kill her with quiet. She knew he was upset, but so was she. This was their first fight. Justine sighed. It was turning into a battle of wills.

When they got to the restaurant, Lucas was perfectly charming to her mother. He wasn't himself with her, though. He didn't really look at her. He spoke to her minimally, and when she asked his opinion, it was "Whatever you want." That was pissing her off, too. She'd never been this angry with him before. Her mother picked up on the tension between them and asked her if it was anything serious. Justine told her not to worry. They were just having a little spat, and Lucas was acting like a baby.

Lucas drove all the way back to Justine's place the same way. No talk, no radio. He parked and went upstairs with her. She opened the door, and he followed her inside. Justine put her bag down and faced him. He looked at the floor. She moved closer to him.

"Are you staying tonight?"

Lucas looked at her and shrugged. "I don't know. Do you want me to?"

Justine studied his face. He looked sad and a tad remorseful. But she could also detect the slow simmer of anger just below the surface. Justine arched an eyebrow. "Oh, so you are talking to me. I thought you'd lost your voice."

He didn't come back at her. He was waiting for an answer to his question.

"I wouldn't mind if you did," she said.

His posture didn't relax, and he continued looking at her. "I need to know what's going on between you and that guy at your office."

"Nothing. He's my friend, and we work together."

He looked down at her. "So he is an old lover?"

Justine frowned at him. She went into the bedroom and started

121

Karma

to take her clothes off. Lucas slowly trailed her.

"I'm going to take a shower. Do you want to join me?" she asked.

He watched her undress. "I want you to answer my question, Justine."

Justine picked up her hairbrush and pulled her hair into a ponytail. She wasn't going there. She wasn't discussing Darius with Lucas. End of story. One had nothing to do with the other.

Lucas wasn't going to just drop it though. "You're not gonna answer me?"

"Let it go, Lucas." That was the second time she'd said that today. She was tired of saying it. "Really, honey, it's not the big deal you're making it out to be."

Lucas turned around and walked away. Justine went after him. "Where are you going?"

He unlocked the front door. "Home," he said over his shoulder.

She touched his arm. "Come on, Lucas. Don't be like that."

Lucas turned back to her. "Like what?" He asked in that same quiet tone he'd used with Darius. Justine knew he was angry and probably hurt, too, but her mind was set. She didn't want to talk to Lucas about Darius. She refused to. She was sure there were things Lucas didn't want to talk to her about either.

"Never mind."

"Justine?"

"Yes, Lucas?"

"Don't do this."

She didn't answer him. They stared at each other.

"I'm going home. Tomorrow, we'll start over."

Before she could say anything, he walked out the door and closed it softly behind him. Justine went into the bedroom and sat down. She really did not want to talk to Lucas about Darius, but she definitely did not want to be fighting with Lucas either. After her shower, she settled in for a night of dreamless sleep.

Karma

Chapter Twenty-Two

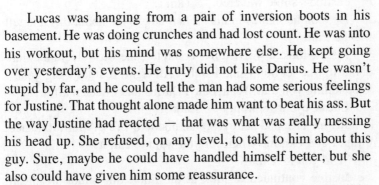

Lucas

Lucas was hanging from a pair of inversion boots in his basement. He was doing crunches and had lost count. He was into his workout, but his mind was somewhere else. He kept going over yesterday's events. He truly did not like Darius. He wasn't stupid by far, and he could tell the man had some serious feelings for Justine. That thought alone made him want to beat his ass. But the way Justine had reacted — that was what was really messing his head up. She refused, on any level, to talk to him about this guy. Sure, maybe he could have handled himself better, but she also could have given him some reassurance.

Lucas didn't stop his crunches until he got a stitch in his side. Then he stopped and went upstairs for a shower. He was just stepping out when his doorbell rang. Annoyed, he threw his robe on and went to answer it. He opened the door without asking who it was. Justine was standing there, looking very enticing in a short white sundress. Lucas was surprised. She had a key to his place, but she hardly came to Brooklyn.

"Hi," she said, looking at him timidly.

"Hi," he answered. He moved back and let her in, pushing the door closed behind her. They studied each other. Lucas cleared his throat. "What brings you all the way out here?"

"Lucas, you wouldn't pick up your phone. Your home phone or your cell. Why is that? Don't you want to talk to me?"

Lucas looked at her. She wasn't trying to argue. She was just asking a question.

"I needed to be alone for a minute."

Justine looked at him thoughtfully. "Do you still feel that way?"

Lucas put his hands in his pockets. He frowned at her. She wasn't getting off that easily.

"Should I?" he asked in a low voice.

Justine shook her head. "I don't like this, Lucas. I don't like fighting with you."

Lucas didn't like it either, but they had to talk about this. He wasn't resting until she did. Justine moved closer to him; he took a step toward her. They were almost touching. He looked down at her. He decided not to be cold to her.

"I love you, Justine."

She gave him a small smile. "I love you, too."

Lucas didn't smile back. "I'm serious."

Justine's smile wavered. "So am I."

He took her hands in his. "Then talk to me about this and tell me the truth."

Justine looked worried. He could tell she was reluctant to talk about it. She let out a small sigh. "All right. It's not a big deal. I keep telling you that. Yeah, okay. Darius and I had an affair."

Lucas' eyebrow went up. "Affair?"

Justine dropped her eyes. She nodded. "Yes. Affair, romance, thing. I don't know. Whatever you want to call it."

"Did you love him?"

Justine continued to look at the floor. She shook her head. "No. Not like that."

Lucas put his hand under her chin and lifted her head so he could look at her. "Well, he loved you. You know he still does, don't you?"

"I know."

Lucas dropped his hand. They kept staring at each other.

"What are you going to do about it?"

Justine frowned. "There's nothing for me to do about it,

Chapter Twenty-Three

Simone

Simone and Raphael were sharing a cab ride to a photo shoot. They'd spent all day picking up a couple of outfits for clients. Simone had made a special stop at a celebrity jeweler that catered to the hip-hop set to pick up a diamond-encrusted chain and bracelet. They were on loan to her for Nine's photo shoot. Raphael yawned and stretched luxuriously.

"Girl, I sure am tired. I'll be glad when Nine's shoot is over. I need some sleep."

Simone smiled. "Up late last night?"

Raphael smiled back lewdly. "No sleep for me last night, chica. I had work to do."

Simone laughed. "Oh, it was like that? Anyone I know?"

Raphael leaned toward her conspiratorially. "Let's just say you're not the only one that's got her own rapper to play with."

Simone's eyes went wide. "Are you serious?"

"As cancer, darling."

"Who is it? You better tell me!"

Raphael giggled and whispered in her ear.

Simone grabbed his arm. "Stop playin'! Get outta here! I had no idea he was gay!"

Raphael snickered. "Shit, I don't think he did either."

They high-fived each other and fell into a cascade of giggles. The driver looked at them disapprovingly in the rearview mirror.

"Mind your business, papi. Just drive," Raphael said rudely, rolling his eyes.

Simone laughed. "You know you need to stop, Raphael. You are so bad."

He shrugged. "And I'm gonna be worse tonight!"

The driver pulled up to their destination, and Simone tipped him generously as an apology for their raucous behavior. Then she and Raphael went upstairs to prepare Nine for his shoot. When they entered the room, Simone stopped, had a brief conversation with Nine's publicist, and made her way over to him. He stood when he saw her coming and ended his call. Simone took the jewelry box out of her bag and handed Raphael the garment bag with the outfit.

Karma

Nine smiled and some of his curly locks fell into his gorgeous eyes. "Hey, baby. Raphael, what's goin' on?"

Raphael smiled brightly. "Everything's coming up roses," he answered.

Raphael's homosexuality was not an issue with Nine, unlike other members of his posse.

"Glad to hear it. What y'all got for me?"

Simone showed him the outfit and slipped the chain over his neck. "You like it?" she asked.

Nine looked at her, undressing her with his eyes. He licked his lips. "You know I do. Come help me get dressed."

Simone gave him a knowing smile and turned to Raphael. "I'm going to help him get dressed, then I'll treat you to dinner, okay?"

Raphael nodded. "Thanks. Please don't leave me out here with these gay bashers too long. They might try to make me straight. Especially that Dirty Mike." He sat down prissily, watching Dirty Mike out of the corner of his eye.

Simone disappeared into a small dressing chamber with Nine. He grabbed her from behind, and they had a quickie before he got dressed, leaving him grinning as he put his clothes on.

"Simone, I definitely gotta keep you. This shit is too good."

She smiled. He was right. It was good. He was also keeping

her mind occupied. She found herself thinking of him at odd moments. She knew she was falling. Against her will, of course. Love had never been her thing, but she knew she was catching feelings for Nine. Even though he didn't exactly stir up the same things in her that Lucas did, she liked him a lot.

"You better keep me."

He looked at her seriously and advanced on her. Then he kissed her softly, wrapping his arms around her. Simone put her hand on his chest and gently pushed him away. "Why so serious?" she asked him.

He shook his head and laughed. "Nothin', boo."

She fiddled around with his outfit. He fell silent, watching her. Simone adjusted his belt buckle. She felt his eyes on her and looked up. Those green eyes hit her like a hammer. "What, Eric?"

"Not a thing, Simone. You're just not ready."

Simone frowned. "Ready for what?"

He smiled his megawatt smile. "Ready for me. But that's okay. I'm a patient man. I'll wait you out."

"Eric …"

He held his hand up. "No, no. It's okay. I got my mind made up."

Simone smirked. "Made up about what? Me?"

He put his forehead to hers. "Yeah, you. I'm gonna tame your wild ass. Well, at least slow you down."

Simone stepped away from him and put her hands on her hips. "I'd like to see you try," she said with a smile.

"I already have. It's workin', but it's workin' slow. You're a hard woman to break, Simone, but I'm the man to do it."

"Why are you trying to break me?"

He put his hands around her waist. "'Cause I need more from you."

Simone looked defiant. She lifted her chin. "I don't have it to give."

He gave her a peck on the lips. "Yeah, you do."

Simone was saved from this serious conversation by a knock on the door. It was his publicist.

"Nine, we need you in makeup ASAP."

"Be right out."

Simone fastened the bracelet on his wrist.

"I'll see you later, right?"

Simone smiled, a hint of mischief in her eyes. "Call me." She slipped out the door without looking back at him.

Trina was standing just outside, popping her gum. She looked at Simone icily. "Chop, chop. Let's go, mama. You holdin' up progress in there fuckin' my brother."

Simone started to ask her if she wanted to fuck him instead. But she thought better of it and said nothing. She'd speak to Eric about it later. Simone made her way back to Raphael, who'd caught a hint of Trina's attitude.

"Oooh, she ain't feelin' your ass, honey."

Simone made a face. "Good. I ain't feelin' her ass either."

Raphael put a finger to his lips. "Don't say it too loud. She might shoot you."

Simone shoved him lightly. "Shut up. Let's go get dinner."

Karma

Chapter Twenty-Four

Lucas

"You want us to do what?" Noah sat staring at Captain Myers in disbelief.

Lucas shook his head. He didn't think it was a good idea either.

Myers leaned back in his chair and folded his hands across his stomach. "We got a rare opportunity. We got a snitch right in the heart of Nine's crew. Close. Close enough to let us know Nine is looking for new security. You two can infiltrate easily and let us know every move this guy makes until we take him down."

Noah stared out the window. Lucas stared at his feet. Myers sat up.

"Everything is set up. You guys got any questions?"

Lucas looked up. "Who's the snitch?"

Myers sighed. "Michael LaRoque. Dirty Mike."

He stopped and let things sink in. Lucas and Noah exchanged glances. It didn't escape Myers' attention. He frowned with concern.

"What's the problem, Cain?"

Lucas sat back in his chair and passed a hand over his goatee. "I think we've got a conflict of interest."

"We know Nine's girlfriend," Noah added.

Myers' frown deepened. "How well?"

"Well enough," Lucas said.

"And you both know her?"

Noah nodded. "Yup."

Myers tapped his fingers together. He looked pensive and calculating. "What's she like?"

Noah laughed out loud. Lucas answered Myers. "Unstable, volatile, irrational ..." He trailed off and Noah picked up.

"Selfish, bitchy, loose cannon ..."

Lucas picked back up again. "Exhibitionist, disloyal ..."

Myers put his hand up. "Enough, already. God, don't you have anything nice to say about her?"

Lucas shrugged. "Not really."

"What are the chances, you think, of her blowing this sting out of the water?"

Lucas shook his head. "I can't honestly answer that, Cap."

Karma

Myers stood and stretched. "All right. Get her ass in here. I guess I have to give her the old 'aiding and abetting' song and dance. Not to mention obstructing justice. Bring her in."

Lucas and Noah looked at each other again. Lucas shrugged once more.

"What now?" Myers asked.

Noah winced; Lucas' eyes had returned to the floor.

"Let us talk to her. I think that would be better than draggin' her in here or havin' a uniform haul her in like a criminal," Noah said.

Myers nodded and rubbed the back of his neck. He looked at Lucas. "That all right with you, Cain?"

Even though he was a bit pissed with Noah for volunteering him for some more bullshit with Simone, they always kept a united front when it came to the captain.

"Fine."

Myers clapped his hands. "Good. This show gets on the road tomorrow morning. Ten o'clock sharp. You'll be meeting Michael LaRoque at the Tick Tock Diner on Eighth Avenue. He's gonna introduce you to Nine. Talk to this girl tonight. I mean tonight. Check in, let me know it's done. If it's not, she'll be sitting in my office tomorrow morning in her pajamas."

Lucas and Noah stood up.

"Is that it?" Lucas asked.

"Not quite. Listen, you were the guys I wanted for this operation. I know you won't disappoint me. When it's over, there's a couple of promotions in it for you."

Noah rubbed his hands together greedily. "Really? And was that a compliment?"

Myers smiled. "Shut your pie hole. You guys get the hell outta here. Good luck to you both." He shook their hands, and they walked out into the early evening air.

It was September, but it was still warm. They stood on the steps of the precinct facing each other. Noah lit a cigarette as Lucas took out his cell phone.

"We might as well get this shit over with," he said.

Noah nodded. Lucas got Justine on speed dial.

"Hey, baby. I'm good, you? Good. Listen, I need to get in touch with Simone. Long story. It's very important. Noah and I need to see her tonight. Even better. Thanks. See you soon." He clicked off. Noah was looking at him expectantly.

Karma

"Very convenient, No. They are meeting for dinner. Justine said be at her place in half an hour."

"Cool," Noah said. "It's better this way, Luke."

"Probably."

They got into Lucas' car and drove to Justine's. She wasn't there when they arrived. Lucas gave Noah a bottle of water, and they waited in virtual silence. Justine came in 15 minutes later with Simone. Justine greeted Lucas with a kiss and said hello to Noah. Simone looked perplexed from the sidelines.

"What's going on?" Justine asked, settling in next to Lucas.

"We need to talk to Simone."

Simone looked first at Lucas then at Noah. "What do you want with me?"

Noah patted the spot next to him on the love seat. "Come sit down."

Simone reluctantly obeyed. She looked at Lucas. "What did I do?"

Lucas moved to the edge of his seat. "Nothing. We need your cooperation."

Simone looked from one to the other again. She crossed her legs. "My cooperation?"

Noah inclined his head toward her. "Yeah, your cooperation.

Listen, it's like this. We're going deep undercover, and we don't need you to blow this."

Simone stood up and stamped her foot like a child. "What? What are you talking about? I'm not doing anything illegal!"

Lucas looked at her grimly. "Maybe not, but your boyfriend is. Sit down."

Simone's mouth popped open. She sat back down uneasily. "Lucas, what are you talking about?"

"Your boyfriend is under investigation for illegal drug trafficking, sale of illegal drugs, money laundering. I could go on, the list is long. The main thing is, we have to go in, and we don't need our cover blown. You have to cooperate."

Simone frowned. "Eric is my boyfriend."

Noah put his water down. "We know he's your boyfriend, Simone. But he is going down. You need to extricate yourself now or cooperate."

Simone was visibly upset. She was turning red. She looked at Noah sharply. Lucas stood and folded his arms across his chest. She stared at Noah insolently.

Karma

"Or else what?" she asked.

Noah took a moment to stare back at her. "Or else your ass is going to jail," he replied, taking a sip of his water, but keeping his eyes on her.

"Going to jail? For what?"

Lucas smiled at her tightly. "Aiding and abetting, obstruction of justice, a few other things."

Simone looked panicked. She looked at Justine. "What the fuck are they talking about?"

Justine looked grave and shook her head. "This is the first I've heard. I think you'd better listen to them. It sounds like you've got a big problem."

Simone let everything sink in. She sat back and looked at the three of them for a long time. "So, you want me to help set Eric up?"

Lucas turned to her. "No. We want you to be oblivious. Just let us do our job. Don't blow our cover. Better yet, you could just stop seeing him."

Simone shook her head. "I don't want to do this. You guys are forcing me to do something I don't want to do."

Noah looked at her. "Listen, Simone, it's a difficult decision, but it's one you gotta make. If you don't, tomorrow morning, you'll be talkin' to our captain. I'm sure he's got a nice warm cell, just for you."

Simone was silent. Noah looked at his watch. "We need an answer, Simone. This ain't gonna wait."

Simone jumped up and grabbed her handbag. "Fine! But this isn't fair. I guess I'll see you at the lynching."

"We'll be there," Lucas said dryly.

Simone wheeled on him. "You know what? Fuck you, Lucas! And you too, Noah! I guess I don't have any choice. I have to comply, but I'm not gonna stop seeing Eric. Fuck you both for this." She slammed out of the apartment.

Noah stood and stretched. "At least we got our answer. Let's go."

135

Karma

Chapter Twenty-Five

Justine

Karma

Justine sat opposite Holly at their favorite lunch spot. They were looking through Bridal magazines for bridesmaid's dresses. Justine rarely had conflict with Holly, but today, they couldn't seem to agree on anything. Holly flipped her hair over her shoulder and smiled at her. "How are you and Lucas doing?"

Justine relaxed and smiled herself. "We're doing good. We're happy. I just wish I could see him a little more. You remember, I told you about the case he's on. But I'm seeing him tonight, so I'm happy."

"Good. Good. You must hate it when he has cases like that."

"I do, but it's what he does. He can't quit his job just because I don't like it."

"True …" Holly trailed off. She frowned again. "That's that Nine case, right?"

Justine nodded, drinking her iced tea. "Yeah. I don't like it. Simone is in it up to her eyeballs. I told you about the talk Lucas and Noah had with her. If I were her, I would have taken Noah's advice and removed myself from the situation."

Holly's face darkened. "So would I. Justine, how do you feel about Simone being around Lucas like that? Does it bother you?"

Justine looked at her warily. What the hell was Holly talking about? "Should it?"

Holly looked uncomfortable. "You know, I've gone over it in my head a thousand times. I even talked to Robert about it. He told me to stay out of it."

Justine's heart picked up its pace. "What's going on, Holly? Tell me."

Holly looked concerned. She shook her head. "I'm not talking about Lucas. I'm talking about our dear friend Simone. Justine, don't sit there and try to ignore what might be going on. You know Simone has a thing for Lucas. Don't be in denial and lose your man."

Justine opened her mouth, but shut it again. She crossed her arms on her chest. "Lucas hates Simone," she said in a small voice.

Holly looked understanding. "Did you ever wonder why? Besides, that's not your problem. Your problem is Simone doesn't hate him. Robert doesn't like her either, but do you think I'd leave her alone with him if I thought she liked him?"

Justine was still. She wasn't stupid. She knew Simone liked Lucas. She was also aware that the reason Lucas didn't like Simone was because of that fact. She didn't particularly trust Simone, but she did trust Lucas. But Holly would never broach the subject unless she had a serious reason to bring it up.

"What do you know, Holly? Do you think something is going on between them?"

Holly was quick to shake her head. "No. I never said that. But I do know that Simone did something more than just flirt with him at New Year's."

Justine blinked. "What did she do?"

Holly related the story to her in detail. Justine's mouth dropped open. "What did Lucas do?"

"He left. That's why that heifer was alone at the table when we came back from the bathroom."

Justine replayed the evening in her head. How Simone had insisted she do Patron shots with her. Probably so she wouldn't notice her antics and Simone could be a little bolder. She also thought back to how, later in the evening, Lucas wanted to leave and had been acting a bit oddly. Her mind also raced back to

Thanksgiving when Lucas had flat-out told her Simone was not her friend.

Holly was watching her carefully. "Maybe I shouldn't have said anything."

Justine sighed. "Don't feel that way, Holly. You're right to tell me Simone's up to her old tricks. I don't want a repeat of what happened in college."

"I know. That's why I spoke up."

"But I do trust Lucas. He loves me. I know he does. And I love him."

"I feel the same about Rob, Justine, but at the end of the day, they're both just men, and Simone, unfortunately, is Simone."

They parted company and returned to work. Justine had a hard time concentrating, and she was glad to get out of there. She hurried home, bathed and changed her clothes. Then she went into the kitchen and started dinner. She was still cooking when she heard Lucas come in. When he came in and found her in the kitchen, he walked up behind her, put his arms around her waist and kissed the back of her neck.

"Hey," he said affectionately.

Justine stopped what she was doing, turned around and kissed him as hard and as long as she could. He returned the kiss with just as much ardor. Justine stopped kissing him as suddenly as she'd started. She searched his eyes. He was looking back at her. He seemed to be searching her face, too.

"Is something wrong?"

"I don't like this case you're on."

He watched her calmly. "Why?"

She looked back at him, watching his eyes. "Because of Simone."

His right eyebrow went up just a tiny bit. "I don't get it. Are you afraid for her?"

Justine kept watching his eyes. "No, baby. I'm afraid for you." She watched for his reaction, studying his face intently. He didn't so much as blink.

"For me? Why?"

She went on. "Lucas, I know you don't like her. I'm not stupid. I'm not blind either. I know she wants you. So do you."

Lucas did blink then. He dropped her hands and rubbed the back of his neck. "Justine, I told you she wasn't your friend."

Justine looked intently at him. She didn't want him to move

away from her. She wanted to see his eyes. She was looking for something. Anything. "Lucas, I know what she did at that party on New Year's. Why didn't you tell me what happened?"

He shrugged. "I didn't think you wanted to know."

"Of course, I wanted to know. That's something I needed to know."

"It wouldn't have changed anything."

"What do you mean by that?"

Lucas looked down at her. She saw something in his eyes then. Anger.

"You're still her friend, right? I told you how I felt. You've seen her throw herself at me right in front of your face. You haven't done anything about it. That's what I meant, you'd rather not know."

Justine recoiled. "Why are you getting angry with me?"

Lucas looked at her and shook his head. "Never mind." He walked out of the kitchen. Justine followed him.

"Lucas, I'm still talking to you. Please don't walk away from me." He stopped and turned to face her and sighed deeply. "Lucas, do I have anything to be worried about with you working so closely around Simone?"

Lucas' jaw tightened angrily. "I can't control your friend, Justine."

Justine wanted to know his position. Her talk with Holly had really gotten to her. "You would never —"

Lucas cut her off gently. "Baby, I don't even like Simone." He picked up her left hand and kissed her ring. "I love you, Justine. Let's not have this conversation."

"I love you, too, Lucas. And I trust you."

He didn't say anything. He answered her with a kiss.

Karma

Chapter Twenty-Six

Simone

Simone sat in her office with Raphael. They were planning an outfit for the newest R&B diva to wear to a video awards show. Simone sat back in her chair and crossed her legs.

"I'm tired. Let's break for lunch. I feel like Chinese, what about you?"

Raphael grabbed his jacket. "Sounds good to me. What would you like, my dear?"

"The usual, but don't go to that place down the street. Go to the place across town."

Raphael groaned loudly and stamped his foot. "Oh, Dios mio! Come on, chica!" He started to protest, but Simone shushed him.

"Stop carrying on, Raphael. I'll treat." She handed him some money. His attitude changed in a heartbeat. Raphael was notoriously cheap. He grinned at her.

"Be back as soon as I can."

Simone waved him away. "Take your time." He left and Simone stretched extravagantly. She'd just relaxed when the buzzer to her office door rang. She pressed the button to open the door. Nine walked in, grinning his fabulous grin at her. Simone caught a glimpse of Lucas and Noah before the doors closed.

"Hey, boo," Nine said, walking upstairs to greet her and leaving Lucas and Noah downstairs.

Simone sat on her desk and crossed her legs. She smiled at Nine sexily and nodded toward the door. "Hey, Eric. I see you brought your two new best friends with you." She knew that Noah and Lucas had gotten in with Nine as his new security. Even though she didn't like it, she played along. She wasn't about to be doing no jail for no man, not even a man like Nine.

He laughed. "Say what you want, boo, but they ain't no joke. We had a little beef the other night at a club. They handled shit lovely. They may not be my best friends, but they damn sure got my back. I trust them niggas."

Simone almost laughed in his face. He didn't have a clue. "I didn't say anything bad about them. I kind of like them."

Nine put his hands on Simone's thighs and positioned himself between her legs. "Oh, you do, huh?"

Simone nodded. "And they're both really nice to look at."

Nine reached under her skirt and relieved her of her panties. He pulled her to her feet and turned her around.

Karma

"Is that so? Bend over, boo."

Simone let him have his way with her all the while she made as much noise as possible, like it was the best she'd ever had. That was for Lucas' benefit. He was still on her wish list, even though she hadn't had any problems with Nine. She knew that he and Noah had to have heard her. When Nine was done he said, "Damn, girl. That must have been all that. You did enough screamin'."

Simone licked her lips and smiled. She decided to be real with him. "It was, but I also think it did a little something for me to know someone was right outside." She winked at him. Then she stood and slipped her panties back on. Nine got himself together and looked at his watch.

"I gotta get out of here. I have a meeting." He kissed her briskly and turned to go. He reached the door, but turned back. "I almost forgot. I came here for a reason." He put his hand in his pocket and handed her a small jewelry box. Simone opened it excitedly and found herself staring at a pair of exquisite yellow diamond earrings. She clapped her hands and jiggled prettily for him.

"Thank you, Eric! They're beautiful."

He gave her another kiss. "You're beautiful," he said. He smiled at her and walked out the door.

She caught another glimpse of Lucas and Noah as Nine left. Noah looked amused, Lucas had his back to her. Simone giggled softly, and Lucas turned around. He looked slightly revolted, shook his head and turned away from her. Simone closed the door. She sat back down. There really was no use in him trying to pretend he was disgusted. She knew he wished it was him.

Soon, Raphael came back in, humming to himself and carrying their food. He put it down and hung his jacket up.

"I see Nine was here," he said priggishly.

Simone took the food out of the bag. "How do you know that?"

Raphael wrinkled his nose. "It smells like sex in here, and I saw him on the stairs with his two new bodyguards. Girl, they are so fine!"

Simone took out her chopsticks. "Which one do you think is cuter?"

Raphael looked thoughtful. "Hmm … depends on what you like, I guess. Noah's a pretty boy. Very nice. Lucas is cute, too. Well, more handsome than cute. I wouldn't kick either one of them out of my bed." Raphael had been privy to Lucas and Noah going undercover. He already knew who they were, and Simone had sworn him to secrecy, besides telling him the legal repercussions of blowing their cover.

"I know that's right," Simone said.

They laughed, talked and ate. Simone enjoyed Raphael's company. He was funny, and he always gave her refreshing advice. Not the usual don't do this, don't do that she got from Holly and Justine.

Raphael raised his soda to his lips. "So, you and Nine are getting pretty serious, huh?"

Simone laughed. "I like Eric, a lot. But picture me getting serious with someone."

Raphael smiled. "You still want to get with Lucas?"

Simone licked her lips and smiled slyly. "I'll always want to get with Lucas."

"You got it bad for him, chica."

Chapter Twenty-Seven

Lucas

Karma

Lucas and Noah left Captain Myers' office at 11 a.m. They'd just finished updating him on the progress of the investigation. Nine and his crew had brutally beaten Royce Bishop, one of his Brooklyn dealers, for taking money from their profits. Trina and Papi had walked out of Royce's apartment with three kilos of cocaine and about a hundred thousand in cash. Royce was still in the hospital. He was expected to testify against Nine's crew in exchange for leniency in his own arrest for possession and intent to sell. Nine had just added attempted murder to his long list of things they wanted him for.

Now they were en route to Nine's apartment. He and Noah were pretty much on call for him. Whenever Nine needed them, they showed up. He had a CD signing at the Mega store in Times Square at noon today. Noah settled into his seat.

"I didn't think Nine had the balls to pistol whip Royce," he said.

Lucas glanced at him. "I did."

"Really?"

"Yeah. He laughs too much. You gotta watch people like that."

"Guess you got a point." Noah looked out the window. "That boy is crazy."

"I don't know about crazy. I think he's very deliberate about everything he does. I think he thinks about it and weighs it out."

They were quiet. Evaluating the situation.

"I agree," Noah said.

Lucas looked over at his friend briefly. "I think he wants to get out."

Noah sat up. "You think so?"

Lucas nodded. "Yeah. I think he does."

"Why do you think that?"

Lucas turned the car onto Nine's street. "I don't know. Something in his eyes, maybe. His heart doesn't seem to be in it."

Noah pondered this for a moment. He scratched his chin. "Could be. Doesn't really matter, though. It's kinda late for all that. His ass is on his way down."

They collected Nine and his immediate entourage and drove to the signing. When they got there, a mob of people were waiting, and when Nine stepped out of the car, they went crazy. People were screaming his name, waving their CDs and pushing forward trying to get to him. The store had provided extra security, but Lucas and Noah fell in with Dirty Mike, Papi and Scotty to form a protective ring around him as he entered.

Once inside, Nine's agent, publicist and Simone were waiting for him.

They stood behind Nine with Dirty Mike and Papi as Nine signed CDs and chatted up his fans. Two hours later, they wrapped it up. Nine got up and put his arm around Simone, to the disappointment of his numerous female fans. The crowd was being ushered away from him by store security so that Nine could make a clean exit.

Lucas looked at the back of Nine's curly head. Nine turned, and Lucas watched his bright, easy smile as he said something to a girl clutching his CD to her chest. Nine had been very gracious and accommodating during the signing. Humble, even. Lucas' mind flashed back to watching Royce's beating. He wondered how many sides Nine had.

They all went back to Nine's place. Nine wanted some

Karma

downtime before his performance that night at a hot club in Chelsea. He disappeared upstairs with Simone. Papi and Scotty went to get the cars gassed up, and Trina was nowhere to be found. Lucas and Noah were all alone with Dirty Mike.

Noah smiled at him and threw an arm around Dirty Mike's shoulders. "What's up, playa? Why don't we go have ourselves a little chat?"

Dirty Mike looked as if that were the last thing he wanted to do, but he complied, following them outside. Noah lit a cigarette. Dirty Mike did the same.

"What's new?" Lucas asked.

Mike shrugged. "Luis the Doctor just sent us a new shipment of weight. Five kilos. It ain't cut yet, so it ain't ready for distribution. It came last night. We'll have it cut by my man Pedro and his crew down on Henry Street, then we'll put the product on the street."

Lucas and Noah shared a look.

"Five kilos? Of what, coke?" Lucas asked.

Dirty Mike shook his head and laughed. "Negative. Five kilos of heroin."

Noah whistled and flicked the ash off his Dunhill. "Damn. Y'all dealin' smack?"

Karma

Dirty Mike gave him a sardonically lopsided grin. "Why you think we got so much money comin' in? It ain't off coke and weed."

"That's a lot of dope. When are you moving it?" Lucas asked.

Dirty Mike stomped his cigarette out. "Pedro will have the drugs by 6 a.m. Monday morning."

Just under a week. They had time to set things up.

"Who's transporting?"

"Scotty and Trina usually move the product when it's pure. Pedro has his own crew. He sells some himself. Me and Papi usually move it when it's cut."

Noah tossed his cigarette in the gutter. "Anything else?"

"Yeah. Nine just made about $400,000 look legit with his magical bookkeeping."

Lucas smiled. "Is that so?"

Dirty Mike nodded. "Most definitely."

"Got proof?"

"No doubt."

Noah gave Dirty Mike a long, uncomfortable look. "Why do

you want to bring him down so bad?"

Anger glinted in Dirty Mike's eyes. "Don't be so nosy. I got my reasons."

"A'ight, bro. Don't get testy."

Lucas took his cell phone out. He looked at Noah. "I'm makin' the call."

Noah nodded.

"Cool. I'll be right here keepin' our friend company."

Lucas hit the speed dial to Captain Myers' office and relayed Dirty Mike's information. Captain Myers assured him the drugs would never make it to Henry Street.

148

Karma

Chapter Twenty-Eight

Justine

Karma

Justine had just wrapped up the five o'clock news. She looked at her coanchor. Today had been a day of big headlines. A national icon had died, and a priest had been accused of years of child molestation.

"Long day, huh?" he asked.

Justine smiled at him. "I've had longer."

Justine was filling in for the regular anchor. She stood and disconnected her microphone. She hadn't seen Lucas in four days, but they would make time for each other this evening. Lucas had promised to be there to take her to dinner at 8 p.m. Justine looked at her watch. It was a little after 5:30. If she hurried, she could pull it off. To hell with going out. She wanted a nice romantic evening in.

She snatched up her purse and briefcase, ran out of her office and hailed a cab. Her first stop was Balducci's. She picked up a gourmet dinner and dessert. Her next stop was the florist for some rose petals. Last stop, champagne.

Justine rushed home. She had 45 minutes. She put the food in the oven and jumped in the shower. A few moments later, she got out and put on her prettiest La Perla lingerie. She brushed her hair and put on a little makeup and didn't bother with a robe. Justine set the food on her finest china and tossed the rose petals. She lit every candle in her apartment. It reminded her of the evening Lucas proposed.

She just finished pouring the champagne when she heard Lucas' key in the door. She picked up the two flutes and took her time walking over. Justine felt giddy when she saw him. He was the handsomest man she'd ever seen, and she couldn't take her eyes off him.

Lucas was standing just inside the living room and had taken his coat off. He was wearing a dark gray suit, which was nice, since all she'd seen him in lately was thugged-out hip-hop gear. He was holding a bouquet of ivory roses. They smiled at each other, which melted Justine's heart. Those adoring eyes and that sweet smile. This was her man. This was her life and her future. Justine watched his eyes roam over her. She smiled sexily and handed him his champagne.

"You like it?"

Keeping his smile, he nodded and took a sip. "Oh, yeah. Lovely. These are for you, sweetheart." He gave her the roses.

Justine admired them, breathing in their heady scent. They smelled wonderful. She smiled. "They're perfect. Thank you, Lucas."

"You're welcome."

She turned and started toward the kitchen. Next, she heard Lucas' breath literally cut off as he got a look at her rhinestone-dotted thong.

"Damn," he said faintly.

Justine turned around. She couldn't help giggling. By now, Lucas had taken off his suit jacket. His tie was in his hand, and he was feverishly working on his shirt buttons as he stepped out of his shoes. The look on his face was dead serious. She laughed again and started backing up toward the bedroom. Lucas smiled as he removed his shirt and dropped his pants.

"Yeah, you better run," he said in a low, sexy voice.

Justine squealed as he chased her into the bedroom. Abruptly, she turned around and stopped him with a hand to his chest. Then she dropped to her knees and pulled his shorts down. She looked up at him. He looked pleasantly surprised. In all these months,

Karma

she'd rarely gone the oral route with him. She put her hand on his manhood. He was like a rock. When she slipped him into her mouth, he moaned shakily and put his hands in her hair.

Justine went to work on him with no mercy. She kept bringing him to the brink and then slowing down. It was torture. When he couldn't take it anymore and his knees buckled, she followed him to the floor, never letting up. Lucas sat back on his heels and gently eased her onto her side. He moved her thong aside just enough to slip in. They made love long and slow, and afterward, lay amidst the rose petals and candlelight, still on the floor, embracing each other. Justine lay on her back, looking up at Lucas, as he played with her hair.

"Thank you," he said quietly.

Justine stared back at him. "For what?"

"For doing what you did. Keeping things special. It's nice."

She snuggled into him. "Well, I'm supposed to take care of my man. I happen to love him very much."

"I can tell."

She sat up. "Ready for dinner?"

Lucas stood and helped her to her feet. He started backing her up toward the bed. "Dinner can wait," he said in her ear.

Justine was glad she'd impetuously changed their dinner plans. She couldn't get any happier than this. She was so happy. It all seemed so surreal.

151

Karma

Chapter Twenty-Nine

Simone

Simone stepped off the plane behind Nine and squinted in the merciless sun of Miami. They had flown down to attend the birthday party of the CEO of Nine's record label. It was one of the events of the year in the world of hip-hop. His CEO always put on spectacular affairs. Nine had his usual entourage with him in a stretch Navigator limousine for the ride to the hotel. His cell phone was instantly glued to his ear.

Simone settled back into her seat and put on her sunglasses. Her eyes scanned the limo. Scotty and Trina were deep in conversation, Papi and Dirty Mike were playing some game on Papi's PSP. Noah had his head back, arms folded across his chest, catching a nap.

When her eyes landed on Lucas, she was slightly taken aback to find him looking at her. When they made eye contact, Lucas broke his gaze and looked out the window. She smiled to herself. Oh, shit! What's that all about? Lucas usually took great pains to pretend she wasn't there. He hadn't been just looking at Simone. She was pretty sure he'd been checking her out on the down low.

Simone was having a hard time keeping the smile off her face. A weak moment. Bad boy, Lucas. He should never have let her see him with his guard down. It was on now. She tried in vain to catch his eye again, to no avail. He stared steadfastly out the window for the rest of the ride.

When they reached the hotel, Nine got major star treatment. He was nice enough to sign a few autographs before they were all whisked up to their floor. Nine put his hand on the small of Simone's back.

"Me and Simone are gonna hit the pool. I'm gonna need security in about 20 minutes."

"You got it, boss," Noah said.

Simone smirked subtly. It seemed to completely go over Eric's head that everything Noah said to him was tinged with sarcasm. Everyone disappeared into different rooms. Simone changed into an extremely tiny lavender bikini. She looked at Nine. He was practically drooling.

"Damn. I don't think I should let you out of here wearin' that."

154

Karma

Simone laughed, wrapping a lavender and pink sarong around her waist. She wagged a finger at him. "I dress you, Eric. You don't dress me."

He looked as if he really didn't appreciate that remark. Simone smoothed things over. She walked over to him and ran her hand over his chest. She put her mouth close to his. "Relax, Eric. Everybody's going to see me and be jealous of you. They can look all they want, but you're the only man I'm sleeping with."

He kissed her and let her go. "You fuck my head up, girl."

She kissed his throat. "I know. You've got a huge crush on me."

He laughed and moved against her. Simone moved back when he reached for her sarong. "Stop, Eric. You'll ruin my suit." She slapped at his hands, playfully.

He let her go, still laughing. "What suit?"

Simone knew he was right. The top was only called that because it managed to barely cover her nipples, and if she hadn't gotten a Brazilian wax, she would have been in trouble. She didn't care, though. She knew her body was beautiful, and she would show it off as much as she could while she was still young. Besides, she loved to shock people, and this suit was mostly for Lucas. She couldn't wait to see his reaction.

Simone and Nine hit the pool. Eric was holding her hand possessively. Simone was getting plenty of amorous leers. She loved it.

Simone looked across the pool to the bar area. Everyone was over there. Trina stood between Lucas and Noah. They joined the others at the bar, stopping to make small talk with Papi and Dirty Mike and ordering drinks. Simone sat next to Lucas. Papi and Dirty Mike tried not to ogle her. Nine frowned.

"Stop lookin' at my woman."

They grinned at each other. Papi laughed. "Man, please. Your woman is the finest woman out here. Don't look at her? You must be crazy."

Trina put a hand on her hip. "What do you mean she's the finest woman out here? What about me?"

Papi flashed her his gold fronts. "Aw, baby girl, I ain't mean it like that. You're fine, too, but lookin' at you is like lookin' at my sister. Ain't that right, Mike?"

Mike blatantly looked at Trina's ass. "Something like that," he said, sipping his drink and smiling.

Trina leaned into Noah, still playing with his hair. "Am I like your sister, too?" she asked with uncharacteristic sexiness.

Noah smiled back at her, just as sexy. "I don't have a sister."

Simone couldn't believe Noah was letting her feel all over him like that. At least she'd taken her hand off Lucas. Lucas was silent, sitting with his back turned to her. Simone put her hand on his bicep.

"Hey, Malik. How's it going?" She felt the muscle in his arm tighten up.

He turned to face her. He had the most amazing chocolate eyes. He instinctively looked her over. His eyes lingered a touch too long on her breasts. Simone smiled. Aw, shit! She had him taking the bait. He didn't smile.

"Hello, Simone." Their eyes met for a moment. Lucas shook his head and took a sip of his drink.

"Stop," he said. His voice was barely a whisper.

Simone smiled into her apple martini. Stop? He must be dreaming.

Nine gave Simone a kiss and promised he'd be back after his sound check. Simone was left with Lucas, Noah and Trina. She glanced at the back of Lucas' head. She could smell his cologne. It was turning her on, attacking her senses. She wanted to touch

155

Karma

him. She looked at him again, the way his hair curled up at the nape of his neck. Simone picked her drink up and took another sip. She decided to be ballsy.

She stood and took her sarong off, draping it over the back of her chair. She was very close to Lucas. Trina had Noah a bit preoccupied. She was coaxing him into the pool, and he was submitting. Noah took his shirt off, revealing an impressive six-pack. He slid into the water with Trina. Now Simone took her opportunity. She leaned down and whispered in Lucas' ear, "What are you thinking about, Lucas?"

Lucas remained with his back to her, eyes downcast. He turned his drink around in his hand, otherwise, no reaction. She became a bit bolder and blew lightly in that same ear. "Is it me?" she asked. She watched the hair on his forearm stand up. Gooseflesh. Good sign. Lucas raised his glass to his lips, drinking a little then returning it to the bar. He turned around to face her.

"Don't start, Simone. Leave me alone."

Simone brushed her breast against his arm. Lucas stood up and stepped away from her. Simone smiled cockily at him. "Don't be so uptight, Lucas. We both know that sooner or later this is going to happen."

Karma

Lucas laughed at her. "No, it's not. I don't want you."

She kept smiling. He was trying to convince himself, and he could barely keep his eyes off her. "You lie, Lucas. You know you do. Once we satisfy our curiosity —"

Lucas cut her off, shaking his head. "Are you out of your mind? Let it go. I'm tired of going through this with you. You've got a man. Leave me alone."

Simone pretended to pout. She turned away from him and reached for her sarong. She stuck her backside out enticingly and looked over her shoulder. Lucas stared at her for a second and walked away. Simone watched him go, deciding not to push her luck. Sooner or later, nosy Trina would stop flirting with Noah long enough to figure out what she was up to. She put her sarong back on and sat back down to finish her drink. Then she heard Trina's cell phone ring. Trina hurried out of the water to answer it. Noah got out, too, and made his way back to the bar, taking his time toweling off.

"Hey, Simone," he said, taking the seat Lucas had vacated.

Simone looked him over. "Hey, yourself. You look good wet."

Noah smiled at her. "Gee, thanks. Nice suit, by the way."

Simone returned his smile and his sarcasm. "Gee, thanks."

"Where's my boy?" he asked, lighting a smoke.

Simone looked down at herself then back up at Noah. "I obviously don't have any pockets to put him in. He must not be with me."

Noah laughed. "I don't think you've been behavin' yourself."

She shrugged. Noah gave her an admonishing look. "You gotta cool out with that, Simone. This is not a cool situation. Don't make it worse."

"How could I possibly make it worse?"

Noah sat back in his seat and exhaled. "We don't want Nine jealous. That's a separate beef that doesn't need to exist. We also don't want you obstructing justice. Remember, there's a jail sentence that goes along with that."

Simone didn't say anything. She stared into her empty glass. She wasn't trying to hear what Noah was saying. She was going to do what she wanted to do anyway.

Noah leaned toward her and spoke in a low voice. "You gotta be a good girl, Simone. We can't afford a conflict."

She turned to face him, raising an eyebrow. "Are you done?"

Noah put his cigarette out. "Yup, and I meant what I said about obstruction."

"Are you threatening me?"

Noah sighed. "Don't make me flex on you, Simone."

Simone stood up. "What's going on between you and Trina? What happened to Lissette?"

"Lissette is back home waitin' for me. Trina's just for show."

Simone looked him in the eye. "So, there's nothing wrong with a little harmless flirting, right?"

Noah looked at her disdainfully. "What you're tryin' to hit my man with ain't harmless. It's not the same, and you know it."

"It's been nice talking to you, Noah."

"Same here. Where you off to?"

"To put some clothes on."

"Good idea."

Simone went back into the hotel and took the elevator to their floor. She paused when she saw the cleaning cart in the hallway. The maid came out of Scotty's room and got clean towels from her cart. Next, she went into Noah's room, humming to herself. A lightbulb suddenly went off in Simone's head.

She had a tiny beaded purse with her, just big enough to hold her room key and some cash. She removed her room key and slipped it in the back of her sarong. Then she stood in front of 524. She knew it was Lucas' room. When the maid came out of Noah's room, Simone made a big production of having lost her key. The maid looked sympathetic but doubtful. Simone told her she had to go to the bathroom really bad. She got the same look. She produced $50 and got instant access. Simone couldn't believe it had been that easy.

She entered Lucas' room and looked around. She didn't know where he was, but he wasn't in it. Simone looked at her watch. She didn't know how long Eric's sound check was going to run, and she sure didn't want him to see her coming out of Lucas' room.

Simone was undecided on what to do next. She hadn't thought that far ahead. She stripped down to her bathing suit and waited. While she was standing in front of the mirror, primping, she heard a key slide in the lock. She smiled and licked her lips. This was it. Game over, Justine.

Karma

Lucas stepped into the room and looked totally unprepared to find her standing there. His stare turned into a frown. He opened his mouth to say something, but closed it again. He shut the door and tilted his head. Simone moved in on him.

"You don't look happy to see me."

"How did you get in here?"

Simone giggled and reached behind her. She untied her top and let it fall to the ground.

Lucas' eyes dropped to her breasts and lingered there. He took a deep breath. "Leave," he said.

Simone's grin widened as she shook her head, making her brown curls bounce. She picked up her tiny purse and plucked out a condom, then she waved it at him seductively.

"Uh-uh. Not this time. I can't do that, Lucas. Not when we both know this has got to happen. I told you that before."

He snatched the condom out of her hand. "Leave," he repeated.

Simone ran her hands over her breasts and down her body. She eased out of her bikini bottom. Lucas bit his bottom lip and finally looked away. Simone put her arms around his neck and pressed her body against his. He responded to her immediately, and he didn't push her away. When Simone looked into his eyes, she saw pure hatred there … and something else. Unadulterated lust. She brushed his lips with hers.

"I fucking hate you, Simone," he said through clenched teeth.

She touched his face. "I know. Now show me how much." She covered his mouth with hers, and they went at it with a frantic, lustful craving that had built up for way too long.

Lucas had his hands in her hair. Simone's hands dropped, and she popped the buttons off his shirt in her haste to get to his bare skin. She expertly unfastened his pants and pulled his zipper down. He sprang free, and she immediately had him in both hands, stroking him. Lucas moaned and stopped kissing her. He looked her in the face as he put his hand between her thighs. His eyes were hard and cold. The two of them stood there working each other with their hands and staring at each other until Simone started climaxing. She screamed in delight.

"Shut up," Lucas said. He pushed her backward until her butt hit the dresser. Then he lifted her up roughly into a sitting position. The condom appeared like magic. He opened it with his teeth and slipped it on.

Karma

Simone braced herself and threw her head back. This was the moment she'd been waiting for. Lucas parted her legs with no overtures that this was something that it wasn't. Their eyes met, and he hesitated for just a second. Then he closed his eyes like he was praying and went in, slow and deep.

Simone watched his face change. His lips parted, and he actually looked relieved. She smiled and twisted her hips. He groaned and opened his eyes. His face became angrier as he plunged into her, his hands on her hips, but he was breathless and overcome with undeniable pleasure. He could barely talk.

"I hate you … you … Oh, shit. Ohhh."

Simone locked her legs around his waist. They both went into a swoon, almost reaching their peak together. Simone tried to stop it from happening, but she couldn't hold it back. Her hips crashed into his, and she lost control, arching into him.

"Lucas! You bastard! Oh … my … God!"

Lucas thrust into her all the way. He put his hand over her mouth and pushed her face into the mirror.

"Shut up! Turn your sick ass over," he said in her ear. Simone had been with a lot of men. Men that other women wanted. She had never wanted to be with anybody as badly as she wanted to be with Lucas, and he was delivering. She turned over and put her forearms on the dresser. Lucas slid in from behind and masterfully obliterated any misgivings she had about seducing him. And she was far from sorry. She was ecstatic. He slowed down and started working on that most tender spot of all.

Simone bit her lip and fought back tears, she wanted to scream so bad. Her body quaked, and she exploded. She saw stars! All sorts of glorious fireworks. She'd almost recovered when her body convulsed all over again. Simone felt all her blood rush to her head, all her nerve endings were standing straight up. She was so turned on, she teetered on the brink of passing out. She started screaming. Lucas pulled her, roughly, off the dresser and down to the floor. Simone straddled him, her throat sore from screaming so hard.

They ground against each other slowly. Lucas put his hands on her hips and pushed her down until there was no room between them. Simone was in heaven. She felt her toes curl. She was so caught up she didn't realize her eyes were closed. She opened them and looked down at him. Lucas was smirking, and his eyes were still on fire.

"Bitch," he said.

"Bastard," she countered.

Lucas pushed her off him. They reversed positions. He stared at her stonily. "You happy now? You satisfied?"

Simone had no control over her body. She'd never been this breathless, this titillated, in her entire life. It was like she had an unbearable itch deep inside of her, and Lucas was scratching the hell out of it. She couldn't believe she was riding the crest to another orgasm. What kind of man was he? Simone detonated like a bomb and drenched them both. Lucas put his face close to hers and started talking in a low voice.

"Now you leave me alone, Simone. You got what you wanted. Now you know what I'm like. Stay away from me." He brought her legs up, and Simone's back arched instinctively. Lucas inhaled sharply and went crazy on her. He was coming. Hard. So was she. Lucas couldn't stifle the scream that left his lips. Neither could she. Her hips rose to meet his with each thrust. It was the most powerful orgasm she'd ever had. When it was over, Lucas collapsed onto her, and they lay there shuddering through the aftershocks.

Simone tried to kiss him, but he pushed her away and stood up. He picked her scanty clothing up from the floor and threw

Karma

them at her. Simone sat up and looked at his face. It was a unique combination of anger, sorrow, regret and resignation. He sat on the bed and put his head in his hands.

Simone got dressed in a hurry. Her body was still zinging and throbbing. It was the best sex she'd ever had, but looking at him now, she felt a stab of something in the pit of her stomach. She ran her fingers through her hair and picked her purse up. She wanted to go to him. She had to, even though she knew she was the last person he wanted to talk to. She slipped her feet into her sandals and touched his shoulder. He looked up at her, obviously offended. Simone pushed on.

"Listen, Lucas …"

"Get out," he said, quietly, roughly, shrugging her hand off him.

"But, Lucas …"

He stood up. "I said get out."

Simone looked at him. He was all she'd ever wanted. Her heart sank. He didn't belong to her. She cleared her throat. "I think I should say something to you."

His eyes blazed through her. "What? What do you want to say?"

Simone moved closer to him. He pushed her back, forcibly. Lucas looked like he wanted to hit her.

"You know what, Simone? Don't talk to me. Don't even look at me. Leave me alone. Please."

She put her hand on the doorknob. "I'm not sorry, and neither are you, not really. You and I both know it was totally worth it."

His eyes fell over her body again. She was pretty sure the spark of lust was still there.

"You're the devil, Simone. For the last time, get out." He pushed her hand off the knob, turned it and opened the door.

"Go," he said, shoving her out.

Simone stepped into the hallway, surprised to find tears stinging her eyes. Somehow, she hadn't expected to be thrown out like that. She certainly didn't expect to be called the devil. She really didn't know what she'd expected. She rarely thought that far ahead. She acted on impulse and lived in the moment.

Simone let herself into the suite she was sharing with Eric. Thankfully, he wasn't back yet. She went into the bathroom and turned the shower on. She wasn't ready to wash Lucas' scent off her, but she didn't want to smell like him when Nine got there.

Karma

She took her clothes off and stepped under the water. She thought she'd feel better than this after it happened. It had been all she'd hoped it would be, and then some. She was way more than satisfied.

Simone showered quickly and toweled off. Then she lotioned up and sprayed on some perfume. Back in the bedroom, she wrapped herself in a fluffy hotel robe and lay across the bed.

The look on his face after it was over flashed in her mind. How he called her the devil. That little statement had hurt. She closed her eyes and still felt his hands on her, him inside of her. She hugged the pillow. Fucking Justine. Queen of the fucking world.

Karma

Chapter Thirty

Lucas

Lucas woke up disoriented. He thought he was still in Miami. It took him a moment to realize he was home in his own bed, the morning sunlight starting to peek through the windows. His mind automatically went to Justine. He leaned back into his pillows and put his hands over his face. They'd gotten back to New York last night, and he hadn't called her. He hadn't forgotten. He didn't want to talk to her. He didn't want to see her. He was afraid she'd see right through him. That she'd know. He felt like the lowest form of dirt in the world for doing that to her.

Instead of pulling the covers over his head and wallowing in regret, Lucas got up, took a shower, and got dressed. He hit Noah at home and told him he'd pick him up in 20 minutes. He tried to push thoughts of the mess he'd made out of his head. Today was the day. He looked at his watch. If everything went according to plan, Scotty and Trina would be getting their asses busted right about now. Lucas had a bad feeling, and he wasn't quite sure what it was about, whether it was about what had gone on in Miami or the bust this morning. He put his jacket on and locked up. Soon, he was sitting in front of Noah's house waiting for him. Noah came out right away. He hopped in the car and slammed the door.

"Playa, playa! What's up, Luke?"

"Nothin', man." He pulled out and started driving to Nine's place. Noah fiddled with the radio, rolled down the window and lit a Dunhill. Lucas could feel Noah studying him. He glanced over.

"Holla at your boy, Lucas. What's wrong? Or do I already have an idea?"

Lucas stared straight ahead. "What idea is that, No?"

Noah pointed out the window at the diner on the corner. "Let's go have breakfast. If he needs us, he'll call. My treat."

They didn't speak again until they were seated in the restaurant.

"So, how was it?" Noah asked.

Lucas blew on his coffee. "How was what?"

Noah laughed and put extra sugar in his own coffee. "Luke, man, don't bullshit me. This is me. Noah. I know you, man. You tapped Simone while we were in Miami."

Lucas looked at him. "What makes you say that?"

Noah chuckled. "You been a bit tight, Luke. You just shut down. Maybe nobody else noticed when you two disappeared for an hour, but I did."

Lucas looked away and put his coffee down. "You checkin' me, Noah?"

Noah didn't answer him but kept his gaze steady. Lucas frowned and looked at the table.

"I seriously fucked up, Noah."

Noah remained silent. Lucas looked across the table at him. Noah was watching him patiently. The waitress came and took their orders and went away. Noah was still looking at him. Lucas hung his head.

"Okay, yeah. Yeah, I did it," he said quietly.

Noah leaned toward him. "It's not the end of the world, bro."

Lucas nodded. "Yeah, it is."

"Man, no, it's not. Look, what were you supposed to do? Simone has been throwing herself at you, damn near since you met her. Shit, I saw her in that bikini, Luke. Hell, I wanted to knock her ass off. The way I see it, yeah, you fucked up bad, but when you really get right down to it, Luke, it wasn't your fault. You was hoodwinked, bamboozled ..."

Lucas smiled a little. "Led astray."

Noah laughed. "Shit, Luke, you ain't land in that ass. That ass landed on you!"

They laughed together and gave each other dap. Lucas sat back and put his arms across the back of the booth. "That's what I'm supposed to say?"

Noah shook his head. "Believe me, dawg, you ain't sayin' nada. I been this route with Nadine. To this day, she ain't got me to admit to anything. We got divorced because of 'circumstantial evidence.'"

They laughed again. Lucas felt a little lighter. He loved Noah like a brother, and he knew, even if he couldn't make everything right, Noah could make him laugh. Seconds later, the smile evaporated from Lucas' face.

"I didn't mean for that shit to happen, Noah."

"I know it."

"I feel really bad."

"I know."

The waitress brought their food. When she left, Lucas sighed. "If Justine finds out …"

"Justine is not gonna find out. You ain't gonna tell her. I ain't gonna tell her. Simone ain't gonna tell her either. Nobody else knows. How's she gonna find out?"

Lucas raised an eyebrow. "What makes you so sure Simone won't tell her? She's devious, No."

"I don't think she will, but let's hope it's not on her agenda."

Lucas stared out the window. Deep in his heart, he knew he'd blown it. All he could do was sit and wait for the bomb to drop. Noah leaned toward him again.

"Lucas Cain, tell me I don't see you goin' out like this. You know the game, playa. You know what you gotta do. Get your game together and pimp 'em both. If Justine does find out, you can't be like, 'Oh, darling, sweetie, I'm sorry. Please forgive me.' You gotta be like, 'Look, baby, I don't know what you're talkin' about. That bitch is crazy.'"

Lucas looked at him. Noah kept talking.

"I'm serious, Luke. And if Simone steps to you, you gotta tell her, 'Bitch, fall back,' and shut her ass down completely and totally. Come on, man, what happened? Bein' in love take all the bastard out of you? I know it's messed up, but sometimes that's how it's gotta be. You hear me talkin' to you?"

Lucas finished his coffee. "Yeah, I hear you."

Karma

Noah sat back. "Good. Then act like this shit never happened."

Lucas nodded slowly. Noah was right in a way, and it was pretty much his only option. Noah smiled at him suddenly.

Oh, God, he knew what was coming. Lucas laughed and shook his head.

"You know I gotta ask, Luke. I wouldn't be me if I didn't. How was it? Don't be shy."

"Noah, your ass is outta control."

"Yeah, okay. Maybe a little. But, Luke, please don't front on your boy."

They stared at each other.

"I know it was good, Luke. Simone looks like it woulda been real good."

Lucas nodded. The corner of his mouth went up. "Oh, yeah. It was good. It was like, you know when you were a kid and you always get denied a piece of candy? Then when you finally get that candy, it's like the best candy in the fucking world? You wanna eat the whole bag, right? Noah, it was some damn good candy. Some of the best candy I ever had."

Karma

Noah grinned and let out a low whistle. "Goddamn! Candy ass."

They started laughing, and Noah's cell phone rang. He looked at Lucas and flipped it open.

"Yeah? What? Calm down, man. We already on the way." He hung up and grinned at Lucas.

"Showtime," he said and paid the bill.

They hurried outside and rushed over to Nine's place. Lucas' cell phone rang while they were on the way. He looked at the number. It was Captain Myers. Lucas put the phone on speaker and clipped it to the visor. Myers was brief and direct.

"This was a big one, fellas. Very big and very messy. We rolled on Scott and Katrina Dillard at 5:45 a.m. We seized eight kilos. Five heroin, three cocaine. We also seized two Uzis, and a .45-caliber handgun. When we made the bust, the Dillard kids and their flunky in the backseat decided they wanted to go down like Bonnie and Clyde. They fired on our officers, who naturally, fired back."

Lucas kept driving. "Anybody hurt?" he asked.

Myers paused and went on. "We have one officer currently fighting for his life. It doesn't look good. He was shot in the head.

Katrina Dillard was DOA at 6:15 a.m., shot just under her left eye. Scott Dillard, shot once in the right shoulder, was placed under arrest at the hospital. Unidentified pal was also DOA. Shot through his aorta."

"Damn!" Noah said. He lit a cigarette.

"What else?" Lucas asked.

"Pedro Salazar's apartment on Henry Street was raided. We confiscated 10 kilos of heroin, a large amount of ecstasy, various drug-cooking and cutting paraphernalia, a shitload of automatic weaponry — and get this — almost half a million dollars."

Noah whistled.

"It was a great bust, fellas. Nine's ass is next. Katrina's out of the way. Scott looks like he's a cop killer, and King Rio, I hear from the Feds, is going to have a lot of problems being paroled. This crew is going down. It's just a matter of time."

"Anything else?" Lucas asked again.

"Yeah. I want you guys to be real careful. The shit's gonna hit the fan. Anything you find out, I need to know ASAP. Check in as soon as you can."

They ended the call, and Noah flicked his cigarette out the window. "No wonder Nine was flippin' on the phone. Damn."

Lucas glanced at him. "What's the matter, No? You feel bad about Trina?"

Noah shrugged and sighed. "Not really. She was cool, but she was fucked up, too. You can't live your life like that. I feel a little sorry for her. Maybe if she had another way to go, you know?"

Lucas glanced at him again. "You hit it, didn't you?"

Noah smiled and looked unremorseful. "Of course, I did."

"What about Lissette?"

"We cool, but I ain't never made no promises. Shit, Luke, I know how I am. I ain't no playa tryin' to change. I tried that, and it don't work for me. When I die, they're gonna bury me with my pants around my goddamn ankles."

Lucas laughed and shook his head. It was funny, but he also knew Noah was dead serious.

They pulled up in front of Nine's and before they got out, Noah discreetly checked his weapon. Lucas did the same. They shared a look. It was on now. From now on, they didn't know what they were walking into. Their covers could very well be blown, and they could be totally in the dark about it.

"I got you, bro," Noah said.

"I got you back."
They gave each other dap and walked in the front door.

Karma

Chapter Thirty-One

Simone

Simone could not believe everything that was happening. Trina was dead! Scotty was in the hospital, and Nine had been on the phone all morning. She had no idea things were going to end up like this. Should she have listened to Noah and Lucas when they told her to get out?

Nine set an empty coffee cup down in front of her. She picked it up. "You want a refill?" she asked with concern. Everyone stared at Nine. His silence made her edgy.

Nine got up and paced back and forth. "Well, they killed Trina. And there's nothin' we can do about it either. Be different if it was another crew, but we can't play that with 5-0."

"Damn straight," Noah said.

Nine gave him a weak smile.

"We gotta lot of stuff to do. Trina needs funeral arrangements, and we gotta do something to try and bail Scotty out …"

Papi shook his head. "Man, we ain't gonna be able to do nothing for Scotty except pray."

Nine frowned. Simone knew he wanted to help his brother.

"He's the only one left that they can pin that shot cop on, Nine. If he dies, you can kiss Scotty good-bye." That came from Lucas.

"I know," Nine said.

Papi slammed his fist on the table and stood up. "Yo, why you ain't mad?"

Nine stopped pacing. The look he gave Papi frightened Simone. "What did you just say to me? Papi, you think I ain't mad? I just lost my sister, my brother's in the joint, I had to shut down operations, and on top of that, I just lost a whole lotta money. With the police all over my ass like this, I know the Feds are involved. I'm shut down, Papi! Yeah, I'm mad as hell, but what am I supposed to do about it? You can't fight the law like you'd fight some punk-ass drug dealers that's tryin' to creep up on you. There's only three ways this shit can end. Death, jail, or I could try to disappear." Nine sat down looking exhausted and pissed at the same time.

Simone sat down next to him. Even with Lucas and Noah undercover, she never really thought about Nine's involvement with the drug trade. He was always smiling when he was with her. She couldn't believe she was sitting here watching his empire crumble.

The whole room became very still when Nine pulled his Heckler and Koch 9 mm pistols out of his waistband. He began to laugh.

Taking a bottle of Belvedere from the freezer, Nine placed one gun on the counter and took a big swig. He smiled, but not the sweet smile Simone liked. This one wasn't warm. It was mean.

"Light us up a tree, Papi," Nine said. Papi pulled one, already rolled, out of his cigarettes. He lit it up and passed it to Nine. Walking back over to the counter, Nine picked up his gun and started smoking the joint. Simone stiffened when he approached her with his guns out. He smiled at her. "Don't worry, baby. I ain't tryin' to hurt you." He kissed her. "I was gonna marry you."

Simone was stunned. Before she could reply, Nine kissed her again. He turned abruptly to Dirty Mike and Papi.

"Which one of your punk asses snitched on me?"

Papi's mouth dropped open. "Eric, what you talkin' about, man?" he asked.

Nine continued to smoke the joint. "Nobody but us knew about that delivery. One of y'all let the cops know about it. I wanna

170

Karma

know which one of you is the snitch." Nine was not yelling, he was screaming threats. His demeanor made the hairs on the back of Simone's neck stand straight up.

Papi looked at Dirty Mike a long time. Mike was watching Nine's gun hand. Papi jumped up suddenly and pulled his pistol out. Lucas and Noah were on their feet in a heartbeat.

"Chill, Papi. Fall back. I got his Judas ass." Nine stepped to Dirty Mike and put the gun against his temple.

Noah advanced on him "Whoa! Nine, put the gun down. Don't shoot."

"You wanna die too, Tommy? I'll tell you what. We can all die today." Nine turned back to Dirty Mike and cocked his gun. Simone wished she were anywhere but here. She would never have thought Nine capable of all this.

"I've known you my whole life, Mike. I can't believe you did this shit. Look at this mess you made. What is this about? Is this about Desiree?"

Mike looked straight at Nine. "My sister was your brother's woman. He beat her ass and got her addicted to heroin. She fuckin' died from that shit. You think I was gonna let that go? She was blood."

171

Karma

"Man, that was my brother. That was Rio, not me."

Mike looked back coldly. "Guilty by association."

Nine jerked back like he'd been slapped. Even then, Simone still felt for him. "Mike, Trina is dead because of you."

Mike nodded. "And Desiree is dead because of Rio. And thanks to me, when — and if — he ever gets outta the joint, he ain't got nothin' to come home to."

That was it. Nine laughed wildly. "Say good-bye, Mikey."

Simone screamed. As Nine pulled the trigger, Noah came up on his right, grabbed his gun hand, and brought him down, but he was a second too late. The side of Mike's head blew out, spraying blood and brains everywhere. Papi brought his gun up to aim at Noah, but Lucas moved so fast he was just a blur. Lucas stepped between Papi and Noah as Papi started shooting. Lucas crouched and shot Papi twice in the chest. He went down like a ton of bricks. Simone was still screaming in the background.

Noah tried to get Nine to drop his gun. Nine reached for the gun inside Noah's jacket, but Noah put a knee in Nine's diaphragm and cut off his air. Then Noah connected a solid punch to Nine's face, but not enough for a knockout.

Lucas was coming up on Nine, gun aimed at his head. Nine let his own gun go and pulled Noah's gun free. Quickly, he smashed Noah's nose and tried to squeeze a shot off at Lucas. It still had the safety on.

Noah knocked the gun away, and it skittered across the floor. Nine went for his own gun. It was a foot away, but Noah was right on top of him. Nine reached. So did Noah. Simone held her breath. She didn't know who she wanted to get there first. Nine's hand wrapped around the handle. He laughed as he brought the gun up.

"Beat you to the punch, Tommy."

Noah grabbed his hand. They were locked in a desperate struggle for the gun. Noah was winning, with leverage on his side. Nine gritted his teeth and slammed his forehead into the bridge of Noah's already-injured nose. Noah let loose a string of curses, but he didn't let go of the gun. Lucas appeared from nowhere and put his foot on Nine's neck. Nine stared into the barrel of Lucas' gun.

"Let the gun go," Lucas said in a low, deadly voice. Simone was more frightened of Lucas at that moment than she had ever been of anyone in her entire life.

Nine continued to struggle. Lucas cocked his gun and applied pressure to Nine's throat. That was it. He couldn't breathe. Simone could feel the tears behind her eyes as she caught her breath.

"Do it now, or I will kill you! I ain't playin'."

Nine was defeated. He let the gun slip out of his hand. Noah wrestled him onto his stomach and pulled his hands back. Nine was genuinely shocked when Noah pulled a pair of plastic cuffs out.

As Nine turned, Simone looked at his face. With a mean, crazy smile plastered to his face, Nine was staring at Dirty Mike's slumped-over body.

172

Karma

Chapter Thirty-Two

Karma

Lucas

Lucas hung up his cell phone and turned to Noah. "They should be picking him up in a minute. The Feds are on their way. They want to check the place."

Noah nodded. He had Nine facedown on the floor with his foot planted, possibly unnecessarily, firmly in the small of his back. Noah lit a cigarette and winced. His face was starting to swell. It was probably going to turn eight different colors. He looked at Lucas.

"Thanks, bro."

"Anytime."

Lucas looked around the room and took in the scene. Mike's blood and gore were everywhere. Papi was lying in a spreading pool of blood. Lucas, fortunately, had to shoot only a few people in the course of his career, but he'd never killed anybody before. He knelt and felt for a pulse. He wasn't surprised when he didn't get one. Papi aka Hector de La Cruz was dead.

"You okay?" Noah asked.

Lucas nodded and went to the other side of the center island. Simone was on her knees with her head down, hugging herself. She was shaking like a leaf. For the first time since he'd met her, he felt sorry for her. He got on one knee and put his arm around her.

"Simone? Come on, get up."

She let him help her to her feet. When she saw Mike, she freaked out and started screaming. He didn't blame her. It definitely wasn't a good look for him.

"Get her outta here, Luke," Noah said.

Lucas folded her into his arms and led her out of the room. Simone had blood on her face and blouse. She'd been standing right behind Mike when Nine blew his brains out.

Lucas took her down the hall to the bathroom. She was still hysterical. When Lucas tried to let go of her, she clung to him, locking her arms around his neck.

"Lucas! Oh, my God. Please, get me out of here."

174

Karma

Lucas looked down at her. She didn't appear to be faking it. He rubbed her back, tentatively.

"It's all right. You've got to calm down. We've got the situation under control. We won't let anything happen to you. Just calm down."

After a minute or two, Simone simmered down. It was the weirdest thing, but Lucas became very aware of her. Maybe it was all the extra adrenaline, but he felt himself becoming aroused standing there, holding her in his arms, her soft, full breasts pressed against his chest, her body trembling against his. He took a step back, releasing her. A tiny frown formed on his face.

"You okay, now?"

She nodded and gave him a weak smile. "I guess."

He handed her a towel. "You need to wash your face. I'll wait outside."

Simone touched his arm. "No, don't go. Please. I'll just wash my face, Lucas. No funny business. I promise. Just don't leave me alone."

Lucas nodded and leaned against the wall. Simone looked in the mirror. She shuddered with revulsion at the sight of Mike's blood on her. A small choking sound escaped her throat. Lucas thought she was going to throw up, but she didn't. She wet her face and soaped up with one of the fancy French soaps in the soap dish. Lucas tried in vain not to look at her ass as she bent to rinse off. His mind returned to Miami. Yeah, it had been good, but maybe it was because it had been wrong to do it. Forbidden fruit. He looked at the floor. He'd just killed a man, and all he wanted to do was sink himself into Simone as far as he could go. Just then, Justine's lovely face flashed in front of his eyes like a beacon. Lucas quietly moved into the hallway.

Sirens started screaming, and Lucas went into the kitchen with Noah. They hauled Nine to his feet and took him into the living room. Simone was perched on the edge of a sofa. She looked at Lucas.

"You left me alone, Lucas," she said softly. She had a far-away look on her face.

Nine stopped walking. His eyes turned a totally different shade of green when he looked at Simone. "Lucas? Simone, please tell me you don't know these motherfuckers."

Noah pushed Nine down into a chair. "Yeah, man, we go way back. Just like bucket seats. Mind your business. Simone, mind your mouth."

Nine shook his head. "You were my woman. How could you not tell me? Did you have anything to do with this?"

Lucas looked at Nine. "You don't ask the questions. Simone, don't talk to him."

The police and the Feds arrived by then. Nine was taken into custody. The coroner removed the bodies, and Lucas, Noah and Simone took a trip to the hospital for trauma. Lucas didn't feel like he needed it. He wasn't hurt, but it was protocol. The doctor looked him over, seemed concerned that he wasn't more upset, and gave him two prescriptions: Valium and Ambien. Just in case.

He went outside and called Justine. He got her voicemail. He missed her. He hadn't seen her since the day she'd surprised him with the rose petals and the pretty underwear. He tried again. Still got her voicemail. Lucas slipped his phone back into his pocket and rubbed his goatee, which he was growing back, slowly. He sighed deeply. Where was she? Probably covering this story. If that was the case, he wouldn't be seeing her anytime soon. He looked at his feet, suddenly hit with such a wave of loneliness it almost took his breath away.

"Cain? You all right?" Captain Myers put a hand on his shoulder.

175

Karma

Lucas didn't speak for a moment. He was on the last crest of the wave. Felt like he was choking. He swallowed hard and shook it off.

"I'm good."

Captain Myers looked doubtful. "You sure?"

Lucas nodded, but didn't look up. "Yeah, I'm all right."

Myers patted him on the back. "Great job you and Ramsey did. With the information we collected with your help, Nine is history. Prepare for your promotion."

Lucas nodded again. "What happened with the cop that was shot earlier? He make it?"

Myers dropped his head. "Passed on."

Lucas grunted softly. Too bad. "How's Noah?" he asked.

Myers chuckled. "That bastard broke his nose. Ramsey's extremely pissed off."

Lucas gave him a small smile. "Guess I better find my old friend."

"Do that, Cain. Go have a drink. I don't want to see you two for the next two days. If I need you, I'll call."

"Thanks."

Karma

Lucas went back into the hospital. He found Noah talking with Simone. Noah tried to smile but ended up grimacing. His face was swollen from Nine busting his nose with the gun, then slamming his forehead into it. Lucas grinned at him. They showed each other love with dap and the one-shoulder hug.

"Damn, No. You look busted, man."

Noah laughed. "Yeah, I know I look a hot mess, but I'll heal, and soon, I'll be back to my gorgeous self. Prettier than you, Luke."

Lucas laughed, too. "Fuck you, Noah. Never happen. This black don't crack, but obviously light skin do."

They shared a laugh.

"Fuck you back," Noah joked.

They went outside, Simone trailing behind, like she didn't quite know what to do with herself. Probably still shell-shocked. Noah lit a Dunhill.

"You get in touch with Justine?"

"Nah. Can't find her. Left her a message."

Noah shrugged. "Well, then, let's go get liquored up."

"I'm with that."

Noah turned and regarded Simone. "You wanna come? You

had a pretty bad day, too."

Simone bit her bottom lip and looked at Lucas. "Is it okay with you?" she asked.

Lucas shrugged. It really didn't matter to him one way or the other. At that point, he just wanted to put the day behind him. They got into Lucas' car and drove to a bar named Raffles in the East Village, at Simone's suggestion. It was a nice neighborhood bar with a small dining room, a jukebox and pool tables in the back.

"Why here?" Noah asked.

Simone smiled. "So, if I get a little too tipsy, I can stagger my ass home without bothering you guys. I live a couple blocks away."

Noah laughed. "Smart move. You got a sofa? I might have to stagger my ass with you."

They sat down and settled in at the bar. Simone sat between them. Noah took his cigarettes out and offered one to Lucas. Lucas took it and lit it, inhaling deeply. Simone let a small smile creep over her face.

"I didn't know you smoked."

He blew the smoke out slowly. "I used to. Now it's just once in a while."

Karma

Noah waved for the bartender. He came right over. A cool white guy with long blonde hair and ripped blue jeans. His pearly white smile faltered when he looked at Noah.

"Damn, dude, what happened to you?"

Noah smirked. "Got hit in the face with a gun."

The bartender's smile disappeared altogether.

Simone giggled. "Relax, Kevin. He's a cop."

His smile returned with relieved laughter. "Shit! I thought I was gonna have to call for one."

Simone shook her head. "No need. You've got two right here. These are my friends, Noah and Lucas. This is Kevin, one of my favorite people."

Noah and Lucas shared a look. Lucas wondered if they'd slept together.

"And you're one of mine, Simone."

Yeah, they had. He didn't care. He was suddenly very thirsty. Lucas looked at Noah again. Noah cleared his throat.

"Enough of the goo-goo eyes, Kev. Time to get us drunk."

Kevin grinned. "No problem. What are you drinkin'?"

"Glenlivet."

Simone shook her head. "Not tonight, fellas. Let's drink tequila and Coronas."

Lucas put his cigarette out. "Sounds like a plan," he said.

Noah eyed them both warily. "Oh, it's like that? All right, I'm down. I guess y'all will know when to pour my ass outta here."

Kevin grinned. "Cool. Patron or Cuervo?"

"Patron, darling." Simone batted her eyelashes at him.

Lucas shook his head. Almost back to her old self. At least she wasn't flirting with him. Kevin winked at her and poured three shots, giving them each an ice-cold Corona. He set out some limes and a shaker of salt.

"Uh, you can leave the bottle," Noah said.

Lucas reached for his wallet, but Noah waved him off and paid the man. "You ain't payin' for nothin' tonight, Luke. You saved my life. Papi was gonna shoot me, sure as shit."

"You know I've always got your back, Noah," Lucas replied. He threw back his shot and drank half his beer. Simone poured him another one. Noah held his shot up. Simone held hers up, too.

Karma

"Don't think I don't love ya, man. My kid thanks you." He and Simone threw back their shots.

Lucas knocked off his second one and drank the rest of his beer. He smiled. "Fuck you, Noah."

They laughed. Simone poured another round as Kevin brought three more beers. Simone turned to Lucas. "You were great. Like a superhero or something."

Noah laughed. "Nah, more like Shaft."

They all laughed. They talked and drank and laughed some more. Lucas found he didn't really mind Simone's company as long as she behaved herself. After about two hours, he tried Justine again. Still got her voicemail. He left another message. When he hung up, Noah wasn't there.

"Where's Noah?" he asked Simone.

She drank some of her beer. "He went to the bathroom. What's wrong? You couldn't get Justine?"

Lucas glanced at her. "Nope." He absently picked up his shot glass. It was empty. He put it back down. Simone picked up the bottle and poured three fresh shots. Kevin returned.

"You guys okay over here?"

Lucas nodded. His tongue was starting to feel a little thick.

Simone laughed. "Just great. Three more Coronas, please." She slurred the word "please," and giggled. Lucas raised an eyebrow and lit one of Noah's cigarettes.

"You drunk, Simone?" he asked, blowing smoke out the side of his mouth.

She nodded. "A little. You?"

"A little."

Noah came back to the bar. He was talking on his cell phone in low tones, one finger stuck in his other ear. He swayed almost imperceptibly before he sat down. Lucas looked at the bottle of tequila. It was almost done. He knew he was drunker than he thought he was. Noah hung up. He was smiling.

"Lissette's pickin' me up. I'm gettin' laid. You want a ride, Lucas?"

Lucas put his cigarette out. "Why would I need a ride?"

"'Cause your ass is drunk, that's why."

"No, I'm not."

Noah laughed. "Yeah, you are. I know you are, 'cause I am."

Lucas stood up. The room spun in slow motion. He sat back down.

179

Karma

Noah snorted. "Told you so. Want a ride?"

"Nah, I'll just take the subway up to Justine's."

"You sure?"

"Positive."

"Suit yourself."

Simone stood up and stretched. Her blouse rode up alluringly, showing off her navel. Lucas looked at Noah. He was looking at her like he liked what he saw. Simone smiled at him. Noah looked unashamedly at her ass.

"Damn, Simone. You're kinda fine, ain't you?"

She laughed. "You're drunk, Noah. Stop looking at me like that."

"Shit, I can't."

They did a bit of back-and-forth and finished the bottle. Simone was sitting with her back partially toward Lucas. She was leaning against him, casually. He could smell her hair. It smelled nice. After awhile, Lissette walked in and made a big deal over Noah and his face. They settled the tab and walked out into the night air. Noah tried one last time to give Lucas a ride. He refused. Noah made him promise not to drive, and he did. Then Noah and Lissette drove off, and Simone smiled at Lucas.

"Walk you to the subway?"

Lucas looked at her. She didn't seem too steady. Hell, he wasn't that steady himself. He looked at his watch. It was still early. Just after eight. He could still get to Justine's at a decent hour in case she had to work tomorrow.

"I'll walk you home."

Simone looked flattered. "You're worried about me? Lucas, I didn't know you cared."

He smiled. "Don't be a smart-ass. Which way?"

Simone grinned and pointed east. She took a step and stumbled. Lucas reflexively caught her by the arm. She tucked her arm through his.

"Maybe I should hold on. We can hold each other up."

Lucas made no comment, but he let her hold on to him.

Simone leaned on him, putting her head on his shoulder and pressing her breast into his arm. He remembered that breast. Soft, round and perfect. Skin like velvet. He put his hands in his pockets. Simone shifted and held on to his bicep. She gave his arm a squeeze. "Nice arms. You work out?"

He knew she meant it as a joke, but he frowned down at her. He also knew he was in a weird mood. Had been all day.

"Don't start, Simone."

She laughed and held his arm tighter. "Don't start none, won't be none!" she sang out. They kept walking.

"Are you upset about Papi?" she asked, cheer still in her voice.

"I guess so." He didn't feel like talking about it. She kept going.

"Don't be. He was a piece of shit."

Lucas smiled. "What does that make Nine?"

Simone snuggled against him. "I used to think he was just misguided. Forced into something he didn't want to do. Then this morning, he just blew Mike's brains out like that … yuck!" She shuddered against him. A jolt of electricity went up his spine. Shit! He had to get away from her before all that tequila helped him make another bad decision.

She stopped walking. "This is me."

Lucas politely disengaged her from his arm.

Simone looked up at him, light brown eyes sparkling. "You were great today."

"Just did my job."

A slow smile slid across her lips. "Well, thanks."

"You're welcome. Good night, Simone." He turned to walk away, but Simone held his arm. Lucas looked down at her. Her eyes were suddenly brimming with tears.

"Don't go, Lucas. I think we both need someone tonight."

He moved away from her.

"I can't help —"

Simone moved quickly. She cut him off by sticking her tongue in his mouth. Her mouth was soft and hot. He kissed her back. Simone put her arms around his neck, molding her body to his. She started to move against him right there in the street. The friction was shockingly wonderful. He pulled her to him, placing his hand on the small of her back. Then he became aware, and startled, that they were grinding against each other in public. Simone broke the kiss and took him by the hand.

"Come inside," she said softly.

Obediently, Lucas followed her into the building.

Karma

181

Chapter Thirty-Three

Justine

Justine and Holly sat in Holly's car outside Simone's building. They stopped by to make sure she was okay in the wake of what had happened. Justine had been busy all day covering the story.

"Maybe I should have gone home first. I know Lucas is probably looking for me."

Holly shook her head. "He's probably tied up at the precinct. Hell, we don't even know if Simone is here."

Justine rummaged through her purse again. "I can't believe I lost my cell phone. Today of all days. I know he called me."

Holly handed Justine her cell phone. "Here, use mine. Call him."

Justine flipped her phone open and was about to make the call when Holly got her attention.

"Oh, shit," she said in a quiet, stunned voice.

Justine looked up. She followed Holly's gaze. Across the street, Lucas and Simone were standing in front of her building, talking. Simone was all leaned up on him. Justine blinked. Lucas said something to her and turned to walk away. Simone put her hand on him. She said something, and he stepped back. He said something to her. The next thing Justine knew, Simone kissed him. Lucas put his arms around her, and they were all over each other. All the air left her lungs. She couldn't breathe.

"Oh, my God. Oh, shit. Oh, no," Holly said.

Simone took Lucas by the hand and led him inside. Holly looked at Justine. Justine felt sick. She opened her mouth to say something; nothing came out. She closed her mouth. She felt the tears start to fall. Lucas! Oh, Jesus, Lucas! She felt like she was going to die. Holly put her hand on top of hers.

"Justine?"

Justine snatched her hand away. A scream was at the back of her throat. "I want to go home," she said, in a small tight voice.

Holly was still looking at her. "Don't you think —"

Justine cut her off. "Please take me home."

Holly started the car. "I think —"

Justine hit the dashboard with her fist. Holly jumped. "Just get me the fuck away from him!" she screamed at Holly.

Lucas. Lucas betrayed her with Simone. Simone. Again Simone. She felt like she was losing her mind. Justine put her hands in her hair and curled into a ball. Her breath hitched, and she started to scream, then sobbed. Distantly, she felt the car moving. Felt Holly's hand pat her. Heard her trying to calm her down and drive at the same time. All Justine could see was Lucas kissing Simone. Them grinding against each other. Knew by now they were screwing each other's brains out. She screamed like someone stabbed her in the heart. Screamed his name.

"Lucas! Why? How could he do this?"

Holly was driving fast, trying to get her home. "That fucking Simone. That's how," Holly said more to herself than to Justine.

Justine was so hurt, she sank to the floor of the car. Holly put her free hand on her shoulder.

"Get up, girl. Don't let him do that to you. Don't let that bastard get the best of you. Fuck him. Whorish bastard."

Justine stopped screaming. She grew eerily quiet. Silent tears ran down her cheeks. She couldn't believe what her own eyes had just witnessed. She felt as if she'd been hallucinating. She thought he was better than that. Didn't think he'd ever do this to her in a million years. He'd done it, though. Threw everything they had to the winds just to stick it to Simone. She hated her. Right now, she hated him, too.

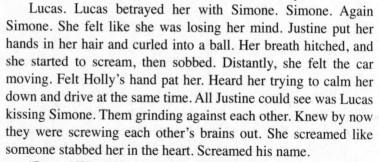

184

Karma

Justine closed her eyes and moaned. That statement was foreign to her. More than foreign, it was just plain wrong. How could she hate Lucas? She loved him. She moaned again. She wished she'd never seen him. She felt Holly park the car. Holly got out and came around to her side. She opened the door and put her hand on Justine's shoulder.

"Come on, baby. Let me help you."

Holly took Justine up to her apartment. She helped her to the sofa and went to the bar. Holly took out the Belvedere and poured two stiff drinks straight up. She ordered a pizza and kicked her shoes off. Then she sat down next to Justine and handed her the vodka. Justine drank half of it.

Holly was looking at her. "I'm sorry, girl."

Justine felt the warmth of the vodka spread through her. "I thought he loved me."

Holly frowned. "I think he does. It's that whore, Simone."

Justine swallowed the rest of her drink. "He should have been stronger. I thought he was."

Holly sighed. "He's only a man, Justine."

Justine got up and poured another drink. Then she picked up her phone and called downstairs. She asked the doorman if he'd mind running next door to get her a pack of cigarettes. He asked what brand. She said it didn't matter. She returned to her seat and looked at her ring.

Karma

"We were supposed to get married, Holly."

Holly sipped her drink. "Are you calling the wedding off?"

"I don't know."

Holly looked away. "You love him, but can you forgive him? I mean, can you act like this never happened? 'Cause, sweetie, that's what it's gonna take for you to go on with your wedding plans."

Justine didn't speak for a long time. She looked at her engagement ring again. She wanted to be with him. She needed him. Could she forgive him? Trust was out the window. If she couldn't trust him, what did they have? Nothing. An image of him kissing Simone popped back into her head. How could he do this to her? She drank the vodka.

Holly was watching her with guarded eyes. Justine jumped when the doorbell rang. She answered it and accepted the smokes from the doorman. She gave him a big tip. Justine felt Holly's eyes on her as she took one out and lit it. She was instantly dizzy. Dizzy and feeling the effects of the alcohol. She sat back down, smoked her cigarette and drank her drink. After a while, she looked at Holly.

"I don't think I can call it off."

"Why? You pregnant?"

Justine dismissed her with a flip of her hand. Another sip. Another puff. "No, Holly. I'm not. I … I can't imagine my life without him in it. I don't want to. I love him, Holly. I've loved him from the moment I saw him. Lucas does it for me. He's my be-all and end-all. Anybody after him would be like switching from champagne to grape soda."

Holly chewed on her bottom lip. "Damn, girl, you got it bad."

"I thought he had it bad, too."

A frown creased Holly's forehead. She put her arm across the back of the sofa and leaned toward Justine.

"We've been friends a long time, Justine. I love you like a sister. I want to talk to you. Open and honest. Is that all right with you? Can you handle it?"

Karma

Justine stared at her. She wasn't in the mood, but she knew Holly wouldn't leave her alone until she'd said her piece. Part of her knew what she was going to say. The other part knew she was right. She studied her shoes.

"Go ahead. But know in advance, no matter what you say, Lucas' ass is guilty — busted — wrong —"

Holly put her hand up. "Stop. Lucas is all those things, I agree, but let me play devil's advocate."

Justine put her cigarette out and lit up another one.

"Justine, why didn't you fight for him?"

Justine drained her glass, stood up and started pacing slowly. There was a little swerve in her step. She smoked her cigarette nervously. "What are you talking about?" she mumbled.

Holly's eyes followed her. "You know what I'm talking about. You've known practically since you started seeing Lucas that Simone wanted your man. I told you, he told you, hell, Simone showed you. Why didn't you do something about it?"

Justine poured another drink. She took a long swallow and grimaced. Holly was frowning.

"You're going to be pissy drunk in about two minutes. Slow down. And what's with the smokes? You haven't smoked since college."

Justine smirked. "You started it, and by the way, I did try and do something about it. I had words with Simone on more than one occasion."

The frown stayed on Holly's face. "When some heifer is sniffing around your man, you do more than 'have words' with her. You have to let her know you ain't fooling around."

Justine put the cigarette out, lit another one. Holly wrinkled her nose.

"You tryin' to kill yourself?"

Justine drank some more. It tasted horrible, but she still felt the pain. She'd stop when she was numb.

"Maybe."

"What about tonight? Why didn't you stop him tonight? You weren't supposed to run. You were supposed to let him know you saw his ass. You were supposed to jump out of the car and start fucking both of their cheating asses up. Why didn't you do that?"

Justine didn't answer her. Seeing them like that had shocked her. If she'd had something sharp at that moment, she would have stabbed her own eyes out. She'd felt like she was awake in a nightmare. The hurt had been overwhelming. Like someone had poured molten lava down her throat. The last thing she'd wanted was confrontation. She was in such a state of disbelief she just wanted to get away, erase what she'd seen. Not her Lucas. Never that, as he would say. She sat down and put her face in her hands. The tears came back.

Karma

"You don't understand. He was supposed to not let it happen. I trusted him. I thought he was stronger than he is. He was supposed to be a man and put her in her place." She was wiping away tears.

Holly looked at her. "He looked like he was being a man to me. He also looked like he was about to put her in her place." She took a long sip of her own drink.

Justine froze. She and Holly stared at each other.

"That was messed up, Holly."

Holly shrugged. "This is a messed-up situation."

Justine continued to stare at her. Sipped and puffed. "You're saying this is my fault?" Justine was starting to slur her words.

Holly looked at her, not unkindly. "What I'm saying is I think you could've taken a stronger stand to keep your man from straying. Especially tonight. You may not have been able to stop anything else, but you could've stopped tonight from happening.

I would have."

"So you do think it's my fault?"

Holly nodded. "In a way, yeah, I do. I'm sorry. I'm just being honest."

Justine put her cigarette out. The doorbell rang. Holly got up and paid for the pizza.

"You need to eat something," she said.

Justine stretched out on the sofa. The room was spinning, and she didn't feel well.

"You want me to stay?" Holly asked.

Justine put her hands over her eyes. "No. I just want to sleep."

Holly picked up her purse. "I'll call you tomorrow."

"Thanks, Holly."

Holly slipped out quietly. Justine rode that drunk seasick feeling into a fitful sleep.

188

Karma

Chapter Thirty-Four

Lucas

"Damn!" Lucas woke up with a start and sat straight up. Unable to get his bearings in the dark room, he reached out blindly. His hand crept over silky cloth until it found the soft but firm flesh of Simone's round bottom. She stirred slightly under his touch and turned over. Lucas eased slowly out of the bed and felt his way to the bathroom. He flicked on the light and winced. The glare was brutal in contrast to the darkness he'd just left. An old saying sing-songed through his head.

Whatever happens in the dark always comes to the light.

Lucas sighed. "Please, Lord, not today. Not ever." He turned on the cold water and splashed away any sleepiness that lingered. Clumsily, he grabbed a towel and wiped his face without looking in the mirror. Then he went in search of his clothes. They were draped over the back of a chair in the bedroom. Still trying not to make too much noise, he dressed quickly and felt around in his pockets for his car keys. They weren't there. He tried to locate them without turning on the light. His fingers danced lightly over the top of the cherrywood dresser. Nothing. Lucas swiftly moved to the nightstand and did his finger dance. He just found them when the light popped on.

"Lucas?" Simone sat up in bed with a slight frown on her face, the red satin sheets pulled up modestly to her breasts.

Lucas straightened up automatically and didn't bat an eye. "Simone," he answered flatly. He wasn't going to pretend that he wasn't trying to escape.

Simone's frown deepened, and she sat a little straighter. "Lucas Cain, I know you're not trying to slip out of here in the middle of the night. Tell me I'm wrong."

Lucas laughed a little, almost as if he didn't mean to do it out loud. "Why do you have to say my whole name? Lucas Cain ..." He trailed off and picked his keys up. "This isn't a movie. It is what it is. Keep the drama to a minimum." Lucas realized he was going into bastard mode. He didn't care.

Simone got up and covered the distance between them in three steps. She glared at him and stuck an accusatory finger in his face. Lucas looked at it mildly and shook his head with a small smile that felt strange on his face.

Karma

"No, you didn't just say that to me. You were going to walk out of here and leave me asleep. How could you do that after last night? Why would you do that?"

Lucas shrugged. "Because I didn't want to go through this. This isn't necessary, Simone."

Simone stepped back and raised an eyebrow. "What isn't necessary? To treat me with a little respect? Lucas, you just slept with me. How do you expect me to feel?"

Lucas repeated his shrug and looked at his watch. "Just let it be what it was."

"Oh, I see. So, we're not friends or anything, right? We don't talk. We just fuck, right?"

Lucas shook his head and laughed softly. He was tired of this, and he didn't want to be bothered. "Okay," he said with indifference.

"Okay? We're not even friends, Lucas?"

He started to walk away but turned back. He looked her over slowly. A quizzical look crossed his face. "Me and you? Friends? Simone, I thought you and Justine were friends."

Simone jerked her head back like he'd hit her. They stared at each other for a long hard moment. Simone broke eye contact first. She looked away. Without looking up, she asked her question.

"When will I see you again?"

This time Lucas actually laughed out loud. "In your dreams. Don't do this, Simone. It was what it was. It's not an affair. Keep it light."

Simone looked as if she wanted to press the issue but thought better of it. "All right, Lucas."

Lucas gave her a disdainful little smile. "All right then."

Simone walked him to the door looking like she wanted a kiss but wasn't really expecting one. Good thing. She didn't get it.

Karma

Chapter Thirty-Five

193

Karma

Justine

Justine woke up when she heard her front door open. She sat up slowly and ran her fingers through her hair. Sunlight was streaming in through the windows. Had she slept that long? She looked at her watch. It was 9:30. She was dying of thirst. She got up and went into the kitchen without looking at Lucas. Picking up a bottle of water, she opened it and took two long swallows. Lucas followed her into the kitchen. He was standing in the doorway, looking at her with those beautiful eyes of his. So damned handsome. Her heart ached just looking at him.

"Been drinking?" he asked.

"Yup." She put the cap back on her water. Felt the weight of it in her hand. Their eyes met. Lucas was showing her his poker face. Waiting for her to say something. That image of him and Simone grinding against each other reared its ugly head again. She loved him. She hated him. Justine threw the water bottle at him as hard as she could. It hit him in the chest with a satisfying smack. He flinched from the impact, picked the bottle up, and put it on the counter. Then he slowly ran his hand over the back of his neck and looked at her. Justine felt a slow heat in her temples. Her hands turned into fists, and she rolled up on him. "Don't you want to know why I did that, Lucas?"

He didn't answer. He looked down at her. The sadness in his eyes was depthless.

"I'm talking to you, Lucas!" She meant to say it loud, but it came out a scream. She raised her hands and shoved him backward in frustration.

"Justine —"

Justine's hands became fists again. She rained a barrage of punches on him, hitting him with all the strength she had. She wanted to hurt him as much as he'd hurt her. Lucas' hands went up defensively, but he made no attempt to strike her back. Her fists kept flying. Lucas grabbed her wrists, and she twisted her body, trying to break free. She wrenched her right hand loose and slapped him hard across the face.

"Stop," he said. He turned her around easily and pinned her arms down, locking his across her body. She fought against him, and he pulled her closer, disabling her from moving. She started screaming, tears streaming down her face.

Karma

"Let me go! Don't touch me! Let me go, you bastard! Dirty, lying, cheating bastard! Let me go!"

Lucas let her go like she was on fire. She whirled around to face him. His face expressed pain, remorse and sorrow. He dropped his head.

"I'm sorry," he said simply.

Justine looked at him like he was crazy. "Excuse me, but did you say you were sorry? How could you do this to us? We were supposed to get married. I was supposed to have your babies. You threw everything away to lay down with slutty-ass Simone. What's the matter? I'm not enough woman for you?"

Lucas rubbed his face where she'd slapped him. He looked at her. "Justine, I'm sorry, baby. I fucked up. I am so sorry. I didn't mean for it to happen, but it did. I never wanted to hurt you. You're the love of my life. You're more than enough woman for me. Please don't —"

He reached out to touch her, but Justine recoiled. Snatched herself away from his grasp. He looked hurt and fell back.

"I told you not to touch me. Dammit, don't touch me! How dare you? You want to touch me with those same hands you had all over Simone?"

"Justine —"

She put her hands over her ears. "Shut up! Shut up, Lucas! There's nothing you can say to make this better. I never thought in a million years you'd destroy us like this. I thought so much of you. Loved you so much. Trusted you completely. I feel like you reached into my chest and pulled my heart out with your bare hands."

Lucas sat down and put his head in his hands. Justine saw him suffering. Good! She turned up the heat.

"I thought you were different, Lucas. You came into my life like a knight in shining armor. Made everyone I'd ever dated look like dog shit. You swept me off my feet. My Prince Charming. You were all I could have hoped for. Best of all, you were just as in love with me as I was with you. I guess I was wrong. Either that, or you're one hell of an actor."

Lucas leaned back in his chair. The pain in his eyes was enormous. "I do love you, Justine. I love you more than anybody. I always loved you. I always will." He stood up and went to her. Justine backed away. He kept coming, a look of determination in his eye. He backed her into a wall, placing one hand on either side of her so she couldn't get away. Lucas put his face close to hers. Justine's hands curled into fists again. Lucas noticed.

Karma

"You want to hit me? Go ahead. I deserve it, and I won't hit you back. You hate me? Fine. Right now, I hate me, too. I'm sorry, Justine. I am not a perfect man. I was wrong. I betrayed our relationship with a woman I don't even like. I'll spend the rest of my life making it up to you."

Justine looked down at her engagement ring. She started to take it off. She heard Lucas' breath catch in his throat. He took her hand before she could get it all the way off. He pushed it back on. "No, baby, no. Don't take your ring off. We're stronger than this. Please. Don't take it off. Don't leave me. I need you."

That moved her. That, and the panic in his face. She'd never seen him look like that. Lucas was scared. Scared she didn't love him anymore. Scared he'd lost her. The tears started again.

"Looks like you didn't need me last night."

"I tried to call you all day after everything was over. Paged you constantly. You didn't call me back."

Justine folded her arms across her chest. "I lost my cell phone. Was it good?"

Lucas tilted his head and frowned. "What?"

Justine shifted her weight to one leg. "I asked you if it was good."

Lucas took a step back. His hand went over his goatee. Nervous gesture. He took a deep breath and let it out. "What kind of question is that?"

Justine tapped her foot impatiently. "A valid one. I want the answer. It must have been a really great piece of ass to make you throw our relationship away. Tell me, is she better than me?" Her voice was starting to rise.

He looked at her a moment longer and walked away. Justine became enraged. He was going to stay and take this dose of medicine. She followed him into the living room.

"Don't you walk away from me, Lucas!" She grabbed his arm, and he turned around. "What did you find in her that you didn't have right here? Lucas, I gave you all of me. Were you tired of me? Bored? I did everything I could to make you love me. I tried to keep you happy. Why couldn't you stay in love with me?"

196

Karma

Lucas looked like he wanted to touch her, but he kept his hands to himself. "I am in love with you, Justine, and I'm staying in love. Simone can't hold a candle to you. She doesn't mean anything to me. It was a long, bad day, and it just happened. We were drunk."

Justine almost laughed. "You're kidding me, right? Don't give me the drunken excuse. You should be able to control yourself. You probably wanted her for a long time."

Lucas narrowed his eyes. "What?"

Justine stepped right into his face. "You heard what I said."

Lucas looked at her coolly, his jaw tightened. "I know you're upset, so I'm gonna let that go," he said quietly.

Justine put her hands on her hips. "Please, don't tell me you have an attitude. Don't have the audacity to be angry, Lucas. You have no right to be."

Lucas sat on the arm of the sofa. "You just accused me of wanting Simone for a long time. You should flip that around, Justine. Open your eyes. Simone has been throwing herself at me since we've been together. She flirted with me right in front of you. I told you about her. I told you she wasn't your friend."

"So you finally slept with her."

He looked at the floor. "I'm not making excuses. I'm pretty sure you know what happened to Nine."

Justine nodded. "I was covering the story."

Lucas stood and rubbed the nape of his neck. "Then you know Nine blew Mike's brains out. Simone got splashed. It freaked her out. Noah and Nine fought over the gun. Nine bashed Noah in the face and broke his nose. Papi was going to shoot Noah. I shot Papi."

Justine put her hand over her mouth. She knew Papi was dead. Killing somebody was a good enough reason to get drunk, but he wasn't off the hook. "I didn't know."

"I tried to call you."

"I lost my cell phone."

"You said that."

They looked at each other.

"You can't justify what you did."

"I'm not trying to." Lucas picked up his jacket and slipped it on. Justine's eyes widened. She stepped in front of him to block his way.

"Where are you going?"

"I think it's better if I leave. I know you don't feel like looking at me right now."

Justine sighed. That was the problem. She could look at him forever. "Where are you going?" she asked again.

Karma

Lucas looked as if it finally registered. He shook his head. "Do you keep asking me that because you think I'm going to Simone? Sweetheart, please, don't get it twisted. I'm not having an affair with her. I don't want to leave you for her. I —"

Justine held her hand up, stopping him midsentence. "Yeah, Lucas, I know. No feelings. You just fucked her."

He looked away, then moved closer. "I'm going home. I think you need some space." He reached out to touch her. When she didn't move away, he lifted her left hand and kissed her palm. Her ring glittered prettily, and in spite of herself, Justine felt that same electricity she'd always felt for Lucas. She looked at him and wiped the tears off her cheeks. She saw some serious pain in his face. Yes, he was paying, but his debt was huge.

"I love you, Justine," he whispered.

She didn't return the sentiment, just kept looking at him. Lucas walked to the door. Justine moved past him and opened it. Lucas stepped over the threshold.

"I'll call you," he said. It came out sounding more like a question.

She refused to meet his eyes again. He was wearing down

her defenses. She looked at the floor instead. "No, Lucas. I'll call you." She closed the door. Not quite a slam.

She heard him walk away. She looked out the peephole at him. He got halfway to the elevator and did an about-face. He stood there indecisively for a moment, as if he wasn't sure how to proceed, then he turned around and instead of taking the elevator, he took the stairs.

Justine went into the bathroom and turned the water on in the tub. She called her job and requested the next three days off, then she went into the kitchen. She picked up the bottle of water that she'd hit him with and took a highball glass off the shelf. Back to the living room for the Belvedere. Back to the bathroom for the tub. She took her clothes off, got in, and poured the vodka. Two swallows and a sip of water. Pain, rage, revenge and love were running a race in her heart. Justine whimpered and put her arms across her chest like she was dead. She slid down until only her head was above the water and waited to see which one would win.

Karma

Chapter Thirty-Six

Simone

Karma

Simone leaned against the counter and nibbled at her thumbnail. She wondered, briefly, if Holly was going to come threatening to kick her ass again. Holly really needed to mind her own business.

Simone tried to imagine the look on Justine's face when she'd seen them. A tiny smirk appeared on her lips. It had been good, too. He was great. Even when he was a little drunk. She felt a pang of guilt, then shook it off. Justine would land on her feet again. With Justine's history, she'd probably still marry Lucas, and he'd never cheat on her again. They'd stay married forever and have five kids, a dog and a gigantic house in Westchester County or out on Long Island. She'd live in a perfect world, just as she'd always done. Little bitch.

Simone sighed. She realized she had most likely burned her bridges. She knew she wouldn't be forgiven for the same thing twice. She shrugged. She was outgrowing Holly and Justine anyway. Simone knew they tried hard to be her friends, that they'd done their damndest to try to love her. She felt bad that she couldn't reciprocate. It had been a long time since she'd loved anyone but Simone.

She would miss them, though. She'd miss Nine, too. He loved her. She had feelings for him, but they weren't what he needed for her to feel. Only one person had managed to crack the ice over her frozen heart, and he didn't even know it. He didn't want her. Not like that. He never would, especially now.

She had felt something for Lucas. Still did. Simone finished her tea. She took her cup back inside and rinsed it out. Maybe she'd go to L.A. and see what was happening out there. There was nothing left for her here. Maybe she could convince Raphael to go with her. He was indispensable to her. He was also the only person around that was still her friend. Simone put her jacket on and picked up her bag. She felt that small stab of guilt return. She thought about the last thing Lucas said to her, then she laughed.

"No … Fuck you, Lucas." She felt the guilt slip away as she walked out of her apartment.

Karma

Chapter Thirty-Seven

Justine

Karma

Justine sat at her desk tapping her steepled fingers together. It had taken her two days to decide her course of action. She still hadn't called Lucas, and he hadn't called her. She loved him, but he had to pay for what he'd done. Simone, she was going to handle in her own time, in her own way. She smiled to herself. Everyone thought she was soft and helpless. When the dust cleared, she was going to prove that she could be just as mean and fucked up as everybody else.

Justine had taken her engagement ring off that morning and put it in her jewelry box. She looked at her naked finger. Revenge wasn't particularly sitting well with her, but people make you like you are sometimes. The knock she was waiting for came at her office door.

"Come in."

Darius walked in and took his usual seat on the edge of her desk. His eyes were serious and full of concern.

"You all right, Justine?"

She smiled at him and stood up. She'd dressed carefully for

this. A nicely tailored Donna Karan blouse over a pair of skintight jeans. Conservative from the top up. Trashy from the bottom down. Jeans so tight she could barely sit in them. She smiled. Lucas had loved these jeans, but whenever she'd worn them out, he never strayed too far from her side. He always told her she had the nicest ass he'd ever seen. These jeans were proof. Darius' eyes followed her appreciatively.

"Why do you ask?" she said.

Darius raised his eyes. "I don't know. You seem a little distracted."

Justine nodded. She had, but that was intentional. She was trying to get his attention. She had. She stuck her hands in her back pockets and arched her back. Darius' eyes were following her every move.

"Maybe a little," she said.

Darius stood and moved toward her. He smiled. "You know, I give great massages. You look a little stressed out."

"Just a bit." She sat back down, and Darius went to work on her shoulders. Justine moaned luxuriously and gave in to the massage. It was nice, but Lucas gave better ones. She closed her eyes and pretended it was him.

"You like that?" Darius asked.

Justine smiled. "It's wonderful. Thank you."

She heard the smile in his voice. "My pleasure."

Justine sighed and laughed a little. "Oh, no. It's definitely mine."

Darius put his face next to hers. "You flirtin' with me, Justine?"

She looked at him from the corner of her eye. "Depends. You flirting with me?" she countered.

Darius straightened back up. He stopped the massage. "Where's your ring?"

Justine leaned back in her chair until her head rested comfortably against him. "Took it off."

He moved away from her. "Why?"

She turned around and told him the truth. "Because I didn't want it on anymore."

Darius returned to his seat on the edge of her desk. "You're not with him anymore?"

Justine stood up and his eyes went back to her behind.

"We had a falling out."

"Is that so? What about?"

Justine put a hand on her hip. "I'm hungry," she said, changing the subject.

Darius stood back up. "So am I. You wanna get something?"

Justine picked up her bag. "I wouldn't mind that at all. You ready?"

"You know it." Darius held the door open for her, and they were on their way.

They went to Coldwater's, a seafood place in the East Fifties. The conversation stayed light until they were halfway through their entrees.

"What happened?" Darius asked, putting his fork down.

"I don't know. It just fell apart."

Darius looked at her a long while. "Yeah, okay. What made it fall apart?"

Justine sat back in her seat and remained truthful. "Too many people in our relationship."

He took a sip of wine. "How so?"

Justine cleared her throat and toyed with her napkin. "Well, one person."

Darius narrowed his eyes. "He cheat on you?"

She nodded.

He touched her hand. "Sorry." Darius looked sincere.

Justine shook her head. "Don't be."

"Is there anything I can do?"

She smiled at him. As a matter of fact there was. "Just be there for me."

He leaned forward. "I'm always here, whenever you need me. For anything. You know that."

"I appreciate that, and I'll hold you to it."

Darius drank the last of his wine. "You better."

He paid the check, and they headed out of the restaurant. It was nippy out, so Darius pulled the collar of her coat up around her neck.

"Tucking me in?" Justine asked with a smile.

He smiled back. "If you need tucking in, I'm your man."

Darius looked as if he wanted to kiss her, but she wasn't quite ready for that and shied away. Instead he touched her arm.

"You want me to see you home?"

She shook her head, still smiling. "No, I'm good."

He moved closer to her. "Hail you a cab?"

203

Karma

She laughed. "Be serious."

Darius rolled his eyes. "Oh, yeah. I forgot they don't stop for black men. Excuse me."

They laughed a little, and he moved in for that kiss again. Justine put her hand on his chest. She had a moment of déjà vu. She remembered standing in front of a restaurant with Lucas and placing her hand on his chest. It was a different circumstance, though. She had wanted to touch Lucas. Been dying to. Had to. She was trying to hold Darius at bay.

"Whoa. It's a bit too soon for that."

He looked sheepish. "I'm sorry. I couldn't help myself."

She laughed at him and hailed her cab. Darius held the door open for her.

"Good night, Darius."

"Good night, Justine."

She gave the driver her address, and he sped off. Justine sat back for the ride. She wasn't smiling now. Darius deserved a little payback, too, for omitting the fact that he was married. She felt very little guilt for involving him in her plan. She took her cell phone out and checked her messages. No Lucas. He was still playing the waiting game. How respectful. It was a pity he wasn't when he'd spent his night with Simone. Justine returned her phone to her purse. She sighed. The old saying was true. Payback was a bitch.

Karma

Chapter Thirty-Eight

Lucas

Karma

Lucas sat in the closed courtroom next to Noah, bearing witness to Nine's indictment. Numerous counts of sale and trafficking, money laundering, racketeering, assault and murder. The cherry on top of his disastrous sundae was assault and attempted murder of a police officer. Noah had actually smiled when they read that one.

Lucas looked at Nine, who still couldn't manage to keep the smile off his face. It was there, but very small. He didn't look any the worse for wear, even though, right now, he should have felt the weight of the world on his shoulders. Nine shifted in his seat, and their eyes met. Then the smile fell off his face, and he looked at Lucas as if he'd gladly kill him if he weren't shackled. Lucas smiled at him. Noah followed his lead and smiled, too. He even gave him a discreet little wave. You could almost see the steam come out of Nine's ears.

"Asshole," Noah said under his breath.

They sat through the rest of the indictment and left the building with everyone else when it was over. Outside was a media circus.

This story was huge because Nine was huge. He was at the top of his game in the hip-hop world, and the fall was going to be long and hard. It was one of the biggest stories going. There were so many camera crews you would have thought they were here for the Grammy's or something.

Noah donned a pair of sunglasses to partially hide his bruised face. He turned to Lucas. "Ready for my close-up. How do I look?"

"How do you think?"

Noah made a face. "Later for you, man. I still look good."

Lucas was about to come back at him when he saw Justine. She was standing to the left of the steps in one of the better spots with her back to him. Noah cleared his throat.

"I see her," Lucas confirmed.

"You all right?"

"I don't know."

Noah lightly touched his shoulder. "If you ain't, you will be."

Karma

Lucas kept his eyes on Justine. He didn't answer Noah. He didn't tell him he wasn't too sure about that. He resumed his descent down the steps. Noah followed him. It had been two weeks. Not a word from her. His head told him to move on. His heart told him that moving on was out of the question. He wasn't going anywhere until she made him go. He mentally checked himself, glad he had dressed carefully. Tasteful black pinstripe, black overcoat. He passed a hand over his face, also happy that his beard had almost returned to its former glory. He knew he was okay. He and Noah came to a stop at the foot of the steps.

"You want me to hang around?" Noah asked.

Lucas looked over at Darius holding his camera up.

"Might be a good idea." He was pissed at the sight of Darius. Darius seemed so into his job, he hadn't even noticed him yet. Just as well. Lucas shut him out of his mind and focused on Justine. Justine was totally gorgeous, simply dressed in a chocolate skirt and cream-colored top with a light winter jacket. Her hair was being gently tousled by the light breeze. Lovely. Lucas put his hands in his pockets and waited for her to wrap up. When she did, she gave Darius a big smile and made an OK sign with her left hand. Lucas felt a stab of pain in his heart when he noticed she wasn't wearing her ring. He looked sideways at Darius. He felt a malice for him so strong he could taste it. Noah looked at his boy.

"I got him, Luke. Handle your business."

Lucas turned his attention back to Justine. She was looking at him. They stared at each other. He could tell she still loved him from that first look, but things were still all wrong. They needed to stop the bullshit and fix this. He walked up to her, never breaking his gaze.

"Hey," he said.

Justine tried not to smile. She sucked her cheeks in a little and pursed her lips. She told on herself, though. She was blushing furiously.

"Hey," she replied.

Darius appeared at Lucas' side. "You all right, Justine?" He looked at Lucas.

Lucas' hand curled into a fist. He was contemplating swinging when Noah threw his arm around Darius' shoulders.

"What's up, bro? Let me holla at you a minute." Before he could protest, Noah had him walking in the opposite direction. Justine watched them walk away and turned back to Lucas.

"Noah is crazy," she announced, looking slightly amused.

"He is. You took your ring off."

She looked at her naked hand. "Yeah, I did."

Karma

"What does that mean?"

"It means I took my ring off."

Lucas looked down at her. She looked back up at him. He touched her arm. She didn't pull away. "Justine, we need to talk."

She nodded. "I agree. I've been meaning to call you, but you slipped my mind."

Lucas blinked. "I slipped your mind?"

Justine looked indifferent. "It happens. I slipped yours."

Ouch. That hurt, but he'd take it. He deserved it.

"Have dinner with me?" he asked.

"Okay, Lucas."

He was surprised she gave in so quickly. It must have shown on his face.

"Don't look so shocked. We have to decide where this is going."

"You're right."

"But not tonight. I'm busy."

Lucas smiled at her ruefully. "All right. When?"

"Friday. Is that okay with you?" She was torturing him. Friday was three days away.

"Perfect."

She surprised him again by reaching out and touching his face. "Your beard looks nice."

He covered her hand with his. They locked eyes again. He knew she loved him. Hell, she hadn't gone anywhere, he had. He was sorry, too. Real sorry.

"Justine —"

She shook her head. Her eyes filled with sudden tears. "Uh-uh. Don't. Not now. Talk to me Friday."

He nodded. "Okay."

She slipped her hand out of his and dabbed at her eyes. "You should go now, Lucas."

He took a step back. "Okay."

A tiny smile played at the corners of her mouth. "Let's go to Gideon's."

"Whatever you want."

"I'll meet you there. Eight o'clock."

"It's a date. Why Gideon's?"

Justine smiled at him. "That's where we met. See you Friday." She walked away toward the news van, leaving Lucas undecided on the way he felt about that.

Chapter Thirty-Nine

Simone

Simone was waiting for the ax to fall. She hadn't heard from anyone in more than two weeks. She didn't dare call Holly or Justine. Not straight-out. She'd rather call Lucas and have him curse her out. She didn't quite dare do that either.

She looked across the room at Raphael. He was on the phone with their jeweler, making arrangements to get a watch on loan for a client to do a photo shoot. He ran a hand through his short platinum blonde hair and smiled at her. She tried to smile back, but it wouldn't come. After a few minutes, Raphael thanked the jeweler and hung up. He came over and sat next to her.

"What's wrong, chica? You look a little sadder every day."

Simone hadn't told him anything about what happened. She wasn't sure she wanted to now. She remained silent. Raphael looked worried about her.

"Is it Nine?"

She shook her head. She sat back in her seat and folded her hands over her stomach. "I'm thinking about moving."

Raphael's perfectly arched eyebrows went up. "Really?

Where to?"

Simone watched his face for a reaction. "Los Angeles."

He made a face. "Why would you do that?"

She shrugged. "There's nothing left for me here. Why not start fresh somewhere else?"

Raphael looked shocked. "What do you mean, nothing's keeping you here? What about your business? Your apartment? Your friends? Simone, what about me?"

Simone stood up. "I think I can be the same stylist on the West Coast that I am on the East Coast. I can sublet my apartment. I don't have any friends anymore, and I was going to give you the option of coming with me."

Raphael stood also. "You want me to come with you? Are you serious?"

"I'm very serious. I think it's time to go."

Raphael studied her face like he was trying to read her mind. "Simone, what's going on? You haven't been yourself in weeks. I thought it was all this business with Nine, but it's more than that, isn't it?"

Simone sighed deeply and stuck her hands in her back pockets. "A lot of stuff has happened."

Raphael looped his arm through hers and gently led her to the window. It was their favorite place to talk. They sat down facing each other. Simone sighed again.

"I never told you what happened in Miami, did I?"

Raphael shook his head.

"I slept with Lucas."

Raphael's mouth dropped open. "No, you didn't! You guys having an affair? Is that what's wrong?"

Simone almost laughed. "Are you kidding? Lucas doesn't like me enough to have an affair with me. He probably doesn't like me at all. He just lusts me."

Raphael looked thoughtful. "What if he did like you? Maybe it's not all lust. You think you could take him from Justine?"

Simone sucked her teeth and waved her hand. "Raphael, please. Let's not play 'let's pretend.' I'm a big girl. I know for a fact I'll never be Lucas' favorite person. I also know for a fact, he'd never leave Lil' Miss Perfect for me. I think he'd rather eat rat poison."

"Dios mio. Ain't that a little harsh?"

"Lucas is a little harsh. At least with me."

An evil smile lit up Raphael's face. "I wonder what Queen Justine would do if she found out?"

"That's the problem. She did."

"So? What did she do?"

Simone looked out the window. "Absolutely nothing. No screaming, no tears, no offers to beat my ass. Nothing. I haven't heard from her or Holly since she found out."

"That's why you want to leave town?"

"To be honest? This total silence and lack of action is spooky. I don't like it."

Raphael's brow furrowed with concern. "You think they're plotting on you, chica?"

Simone shrugged. "I don't know. Holly, maybe. I wouldn't expect that from Justine."

Raphael shook his head. "I don't know, Simone. She and Lucas are supposed to get married. She might be getting her ninja suit out for your ass."

"Nah, not Justine. Too ladylike and dainty. That would be totally out of character for her." Simone seriously doubted Justine would have the heart to step to her. She didn't think she had it in her. More than likely, she had just decided that Simone didn't exist in her perfect world anymore. Holly, she figured, had done what she promised and washed her hands of her. She looked at Raphael. He still wore that look of concern.

"I'm telling you, chica, don't sleep on Justine. That's some serious shit you did. You should watch your back."

Simone yawned. "Yeah, okay."

"I'm serious."

Simone nodded but blew him off. She was having a mighty hard time imagining Justine in ninja mode.

211

Karma

Chapter Forty

Justine

Justine got out of the cab in front of Gideon's intentionally late. She was supposed to have met Lucas half an hour ago, but she wanted to keep him waiting. She'd taken the extra time to make sure he'd break his neck when he saw her. A black Marc Jacobs dress, tight in all the right places, three inches above the knee, and a heavenly show of cleavage. His favorite perfume. Her hair loose and flowing the way he liked it. Justine went inside and checked her coat. She had on the diamond bracelet Lucas had given her. She looked down at it, remembering when he'd given it to her. She felt butterflies in her stomach, and her heart started beating faster. She was dying to see him.

She tried to calm those feelings down as her eyes scanned the room for him. Finally, she spotted him at the bar, his back to her. There was a shapely caramel-colored sister in a tight red dress and a long blonde weave standing next to him, obviously trying her best to chat him up. Justine felt a tingle of jealousy. Lucas was still her man. He would remain her man until she said he wasn't. She watched them for a moment. She could see his face in the mirror behind the bar. He looked at his watch, sipped his drink, and said something to blonde without turning his head. She laughed like he'd told the world's funniest joke and touched his bicep. He looked down at her hand, stepped away and said something else. The blonde hyena laughed again.

Justine looked back into the mirror. Lucas was looking right at her. She felt that familiar jolt of electricity. Damn, Lucas! Standing there, all fine, in that navy blue pinstripe and a heifer he wasn't even interested in hanging all over him. He was staring at Justine in the mirror. He gave her a small smile. Against her will, she smiled back. Damn, Lucas!

Justine made her way over to the bar and stepped between Lucas and blonde. Lucas looked down at her with the same small smile. So damn handsome. Justine felt a tap on her shoulder. She turned to face Goldilocks.

"Excuse me, but we were talking. You need to back up."

Justine put her hand on her hip. No, this chick didn't just talk to her like that. She narrowed her eyes. "You need to back up. That's my fiancé."

The woman threw her hands up and backed away. "All right, all right. My bad." She gave Lucas one last look and walked.

Justine watched her slink away, then turned to Lucas. "She had some nerve. I need to back up?" She looked at Lucas. He was still smiling at her.

"What are you smiling at?" she asked, a touch of heat in her voice.

"You checked her."

"Damn right, I did."

Lucas moved into her personal space. Justine was immediately overwhelmed. She could smell his cologne, feel the warmth from his body. She wanted him to touch her. She didn't realize she'd missed him this much. She found herself standing there staring back at him, lips parted, heart pounding and blushing like crazy.

"You okay?" Lucas asked. He had a tiny spark of satisfaction in his eyes. He knew what he was doing to her. Casting his spell, working his magic.

Damn, Lucas! Justine gripped the edge of the bar and tried to snap out of it. "Aren't you going to order me a drink?"

"Of course. What would you like?"

"An apple martini."

He leaned away from her and ordered her drink, leaned back,

and set those eyes on her again. Justine looked at her hands to keep from making eye contact. She still felt him watching her. The bartender set her martini down. When she picked it up, her hand was shaking, so she put it back down. Her blushing intensified.

"Let's sit down," she said without looking at him.

"All right. You want me to carry your drink?" There was a hint of a smile in his voice.

She turned away from the bar and went to the sitting area. They sat down opposite each other, and Justine finally took a sip of her drink. She closed her eyes, then opened them.

"Much better," she said. She looked across the table at him. That spark of satisfaction was still there. He was perfectly aware of his effect on her.

"Weak in the knees?" he asked good-naturedly.

Justine looked him in the eye. "Don't get too smug, Lucas. I'm still very angry with you. You are far from being off the hook."

He looked at her hand. "Still not wearing your ring?"

She reached into her purse, took her ring out and put it on the table between them. Lucas looked at it and then back at her. Good. She had wiped the smile off his face. She felt his confidence falter and hers grow. Justine leaned back in her chair and crossed her legs. She took a sip of her drink and put it down.

"I've got a very special mission for you, Lucas."

He sat back and took a sip of his own drink. He didn't look happy. "What's that?" he asked unenthusiastically.

"Convince me to put it back on."

Lucas rubbed his beard and stared at the ring. He didn't say anything.

"Come on, Lucas. I'm waiting."

He sat up straight. "Justine, I don't want to play games with you. I don't know if I can convince you to put your ring back on. I can only do what I can to try and fix this."

She sipped her drink. "I'm listening."

He looked at the table, eyes so downcast they almost looked closed. A lush fringe of black lashes, so masculine in their beauty against the smooth chocolate of his skin. Justine recrossed her legs. In that moment, she wanted him so bad it was a dull ache. She wanted to hate him, but this was Lucas. Her Lucas. She thought if she couldn't have him, she'd stop breathing. He looked up at her. Justine fought hard to keep from jumping across the table to put her lips on his.

"I guess the first thing I can do is own it. I do own it, Justine. I realize what a terrible, treacherous, thing I did. I realize how much I hurt you. I understand that you'd be justified if you told me you never wanted to see me again. What I did was inexcusable, unconscionable and probably unforgivable. I can't tell you why I did it. It wasn't anything I found lacking in you. I should have had more self-control." He paused when the waitress asked them if they were okay. He nodded and thanked her. She left with a smile. Lucas picked the ring up and looked at it thoughtfully. When he put it back down, he laughed without mirth. He returned his eyes to the table.

"I remember when we first met, I didn't want to admit I was, but I was afraid of you."

Justine drank the last of her martini and raised an eyebrow. "You were? Mr. Mack Daddy, playa, playa?"

Lucas frowned at her. "Don't say that. That might have been true, and I'll admit it, before I met you. But even given what I've done, it hasn't been true since I met you."

It was Justine's turn to laugh mirthlessly. "Lucas, shut up. I can't even believe you twisted your mouth to say that."

A dark look fleetingly shadowed his face letting her know he didn't appreciate being disrespected. He looked as if he thought about coming back at her, but changed his mind.

Karma

"When I said I was afraid of you, what I really meant was I was afraid of failing you. I was right to be. I did fail you."

Justine studied his face. She'd never seen him look so sad, or so handsome. He looked away and finished his drink. In stark contrast to the emotion she'd just felt, the lure of her attraction for him was starting to make her angry. Angry at him for pulling her to him, like some kind of testosterone-filled magnet, and angry at herself for wanting him so badly. She wanted to deflate him, to humble him and make him weak. She wanted to hurt him.

"You're right. You did fail me."

A flash of hurt passed over his face, but he didn't look back at her. Justine signaled the waitress and ordered two more. Lucas surprised her when he reached into his breast pocket and took out a pack of Dunhills and lit one. He inhaled and blew the smoke out slowly.

"When did you start smoking?" she asked.

He still didn't look at her when he answered. "I used to smoke years ago, when I was a Marine. Guess I just picked it back up. I thought maybe I'd told you that."

Justine reached over and plucked one out of the pack. "Wasn't me. Maybe you told Simone. May I have a light, please?"

Lucas gave her another inky look and lit her cigarette. "When did you start smoking?" he made the mistake of asking.

Justine sat back and blew smoke through a tight smile. "I used to smoke in college. Guess I just picked it back up after you fucked Simone."

Lucas' jaw tightened, and he looked at the floor. The waitress brought their drinks. They both picked them up and drank deeply. The waitress had heard the tail end of what Justine said as she removed their empties. She looked at Lucas with disdain. He smirked at her and blew smoke in her face. Then she looked at Justine.

"You want me to keep 'em coming?"

Justine smiled. They shared a "wronged sister-girl" sympathy look.

"That might be a good idea."

The waitress glanced at Lucas. "If you have a problem, give me a holler."

Karma

Lucas laughed a bit dangerously. "You want a tip or not?" He blew smoke at her again.

She frowned and walked away. Justine heard her say something about a trifling-ass nigger under her breath.

Justine wanted him contrite; she knew she couldn't handle Lucas in fuck-you mode. She touched his hand.

Lucas removed his hand to pick up his drink. Took a sip, put it down. He lit a cigarette again and resumed talking.

"The second thing I can do is apologize." He looked at her. "Justine, you have no idea how sorry I am. I am so sorry. I truly regret what I did. If I could take it back, I would. If I could erase it, I would. I wish to God it never happened. I'm sorry I hurt you. I'm sorry I failed you. I'm sorry I wasn't the man you needed me to be."

Justine sat back and regarded him. He did look as if he were sincere. She reached for his cigarette and took it from him. When she put it to her lips, she swore she could taste him. They stared at each other as she smoked the rest of it. When she put it out she was honest with him. "I believe you. I think you really are sorry. I think you really regret it. I think if you had it to do over, you wouldn't."

"I wouldn't," he agreed.

Justine looked at the ring, then into his eyes. "I've got to ask you, Lucas, was it worth it?"

"Not at all. No question," he answered without hesitation.

"What's the third thing?"

He was quiet for a moment, as if mulling over exactly how to say what he wanted to say. Finally he looked at her with those big brown eyes. "The third thing is that I should beg your forgiveness. Justine, don't cross me out of your life. You saw how things have been between us. It was like a fairy tale. I know I really messed things up, but please, baby, forgive me. Let's try to move on. Let's go back to us. What we have is special. We can't turn our backs on it." He paused again as the waitress did her thing. She gave Lucas a stink look and removed their empty glasses.

"Anything else?" the waitress said to Justine in a kind voice.

Justine smiled at her. "No." Then she looked at Lucas. "Take me home, Lucas."

He frowned. "So, this is over?"

Justine stood up. She smoothed her dress as Lucas watched her. "Take me home, Lucas," she repeated. She picked her drink up and drained it. He looked faintly amused and drained his, too.

"Let's go," he said. He stood and paid the tab, leaving the waitress a $20 tip in spite of herself, or maybe because that was his normal way of doing things. Justine picked her ring up and gave it to him. He looked at her like he didn't know what to do next. He didn't say anything, he just put it in his shirt pocket. They collected their coats, and Lucas drove her home. They didn't say much. There wasn't much to say.

He parked the car and turned to her. "Do you want me to come up?"

"That would be nice." She got out of the car, and Lucas followed her. They stood side by side in the elevator, not speaking. Lucas walked her to her door.

Reaching for her keys, Justine turned around and faced him. "Want a nightcap?"

He looked at her oddly. "When did you start drinking so much?"

Justine smiled at him sweetly. "Since you fu —"

He cut her off. "Okay. Never mind."

She opened her door and stepped inside. She was tipsy but she was holding up well. She looked at Lucas. "Are you coming in?"

He leaned his sexy ass against the door frame and looked down at her. "You sure you want me to?"

Yes, she was tipsy, and maybe she should just go to bed, but she wasn't ready for him to leave. She missed him. She wanted him. "Positive," she said, moving aside to let him in.

They took their coats off and resumed their staring contest. Justine moved closer to him. Lucas watched her patiently. He was waiting for her next move. She reached into his shirt pocket and removed her ring. She put it in his hand, then ran hers down the lapels of his suit.

"What have you been doing without me?"

"Suffering."

She looked at him coolly. "Good."

Justine reached up to undress him. She stepped back and looked at him standing there in his undershirt and his trousers. Yeah, he was fine. But it wasn't just that. She loved him, and she longed to feel his hands on her body. Finally, she pushed that bitch Simone to the back of her mind. She took her shoes off and turned her back to him.

"Unzip me," she ordered.

Lucas complied. She turned back around to face him and took her dress off. It, too, was added to the clothing pile. They watched each other without speaking. Justine took a deep breath and let it out. Lucas was the love of her life. No matter what happened later, she was putting his infidelity on the back burner. Tonight, they belonged to each other. She held out her left hand, palm down.

"You can put my ring back on." He slid the ring onto her finger and looked at it. When Justine tried to put her hand down, he wouldn't let her go. She pushed her hair behind her ear with her free hand. "What?" she asked.

He pulled her to him until their faces were almost touching. Justine's heart sped up. He was looking at her very seriously. Lucas kissed the finger with the ring without breaking his gaze.

"If you wanted to hurt me back, you did when you took my ring off."

Justine kissed his neck. He was delicious. "I did?" She moved up to his ear, making little circular motions with her tongue. He moaned.

"You did." He put his hands in her hair and turned her face to his. "I'd appreciate it if you didn't do it again."

She straightened up. Lucas' hands moved from her hair to her hips, grazing her sides. Justine shuddered involuntarily. It felt like he had tiny electric charges in his fingertips. She reached behind her and unhooked her bra and tossed it over her shoulder. "You want me to keep it on?"

Lucas was looking at her breasts when he answered her. "Please keep it on." He licked his lips.

"You know what I want, Lucas?"

"What, baby?"

Her breasts were distracting him. He looked like he wanted to put his mouth on her. His hands started to drift up her sides, but she pushed them back down to her hips and put a finger under his chin, lifting his head so she could see his face.

"I want you to make love to me like you never want me to take it off. Like you want me to forgive you. Make me feel like you love me. Show me, Lucas."

Lucas pulled her to him, and Justine put her arms around his neck.

"Is that all? Justine, that's easy, because it's true." He looked at her through those long eyelashes with those big, beautiful, dark chocolate eyes.

Justine kissed his forehead. "I love you, Lucas."

Karma

He put his lips to hers, held them there, then took them away. Justine chased him with her own lips. They kissed softly at first. Leisurely little pecks and lingering closed-mouth kisses. Lucas hands discovered her breasts, cupped them briefly, then made slow circles over her nipples with his thumbs. Justine gasped, and he slipped his tongue in her mouth. That was it. She melted. She was in this moment with him. For this moment, she was his. She'd never been able to resist his kisses.

He was taking his time with her, being slow and deliberate. He wasn't really probing. It was more like he was tasting her. She took as much of this slow torture as she could stand. She went for his spot. Justine broke the kiss and took his bottom lip into her mouth and ran her tongue over it. She gently raked her teeth over his lip and sucked with a light, even pressure. Some small sound escaped him. Lucas stood up with her, and Justine crossed her legs behind his back. Then Lucas walked into the bedroom with her and laid her down. Justine looked at him. He wanted her to. Standing there strong, and handsome and confident. Pleasing her was not a problem. She knew he could, with little effort. He gave her a smile. She knew then that it was on. She was going to get him in top form, and that was dangerous.

Lucas approached the bed and dropped to his knees. He smiled at her again as he removed her panties. When he put his mouth on her, Justine got a bad case of the shakes. She cried out and grabbed fistfuls of the sheets. Lucas was intent on not rushing through this. He stayed there like he had all the time in the world. When Justine's body shook with her first orgasm, he went in nice and slow and deep. Justine wrapped her legs around him, and he went deeper. He alternated that slow, sexy grind with a nice little jackhammer. Justine opened her eyes. Lucas was watching her. His little smile was gone. He kissed her and slowed up again.

"I love you, Justine."

Before she could say anything, her back arched, and she started to work her hips faster. Lucas kept up with her. She felt like she couldn't catch her breath. Her toes curled. She opened her mouth and screamed his name. When she looked at his face, the little smile had returned. Lucas shifted a bit and had her entire body trembling and bucking furiously. She looked up at him and felt a flash of raw anger as the thought of Simone enjoying her man sailed through her mind. Fortunately, the thought didn't stay there long. She was rocked by another orgasm. He took her there one more time, shouting her name. This time he joined her. He kissed her long and hard. She kissed him back with the same passion. Yes, he loved her, and she loved him. She didn't want to leave him. He took his weight off her and lay next to her. She turned to face him.

221

Karma

"Are you staying?"

"You want me to?"

"Yes."

"Okay."

They didn't speak for a long while. They just lay there watching each other. The thought of Lucas' hands all over Simone and him being so intimate with her was almost too much to bear. Justine was caught in a maelstrom of emotion. She and Lucas were supposed to live happily ever after. Damn both of them for doing this. She didn't want Lucas out of her life. She wanted him. She was in love with him. But she didn't know if she was capable of forgiveness. She might have had an easier time forgiving him for cheating if it had been someone else, but he'd cheated with Simone. Simone, of all people. She sat up and wiped a tear off her cheek. Lucas sat up with her. He didn't try to touch her.

"I don't know how to fix this, Justine."

"Maybe you can't."

"I can try."

Justine sighed and got out of bed. "This is going to take some time."

Lucas walked over to her. "I'm sorry."

She crossed her arms over her chest. "I believe you. Don't say it anymore."

"All right."

"I'm angry with you, Lucas. I know I'm repeating myself, but I'm really fucking angry with you!"

He looked at the floor. "I know it."

"This is hard."

He nodded.

"I close my eyes, and all I can see is you and Simone. You doing all those sweet and wonderful things you do to me, to her. And her enjoying it. Screaming my man's name. Maybe you were screaming hers. Her sucking the joy out of my life like some kind of fucked-up, jealous, sex-crazed vampire! I hate that bitch!"

Lucas looked extremely uncomfortable. Justine kept going. "Did you know this is the second time that whore has done this shit to me? She slept with my boyfriend in college."

Lucas continued to avoid her gaze. "I didn't know that. Maybe it's got more to do with her wanting to hurt you than actually wanting me."

Justine shook her head. "It was both. Lucas, how could you sleep with her? Why did you do this to us?" They stared at each other. Justine felt like she was going crazy, being pulled two ways at once. "I love you, Lucas."

He looked caught off guard, like that was the last thing he expected to hear. "I love you, too."

She moved closer. "I know I shouldn't, but I love you, I can't—"

He took her into his arms. "Then don't. We'll try. We'll work on it." He kissed her, and she was gone again, back to that "just the two of us" world of love and delight he always took her to. They made love again in the shower and later back in the bedroom. They fell asleep holding each other, neither one wanting to let the other go.

Lucas left her, reluctantly, the next morning to go to work. They kissed and promised they would work this out. When he was gone, Justine went back to her bedroom and took the ring off again. She put it in her jewelry box and shut the lid. She stood there wondering how hate and love could live in her heart at the same time.

Karma

Chapter Forty-One

Simone

Simone was pissed. She didn't want any part of this. She didn't have time for this! She stared at the subpoena on her desk. Forget this. She wasn't testifying against Eric. She got up and put her coat on. Angrily, she snatched the subpoena up and stuck it in her bag, locked her office up and went downstairs to hail a cab.

It took her no time to get to Midtown South. She glanced at her watch. It was almost five o'clock, but she didn't think cops kept regular hours. She hoped she'd find Captain Myers in his office. She went inside and upstairs. The frosted glass in his door was dark. Dammit! She knocked anyway. No answer.

"Look what the cat dragged in," someone said from behind her.

She turned around and saw Noah standing there. He wasn't smiling. He was regarding her very coolly. Simone chose to ignore that.

"Hi, Noah. Would you happen to know where your captain is?"

Noah, Simone noticed, was back to his old handsome self.

His face had healed nicely, and he looked quite Adonis-like in his deep gray suit. He narrowed his equally deep gray eyes.

"What brings you here?" he asked protectively.

Simone sucked her teeth. "Noah, please. I'm not looking for Lucas. That is, unless he can help me with this subpoena." She held it up, and Noah barely looked at it.

He smiled a little. "Yeah? I really can't imagine Lucas helpin' you with anything."

Simone drew back. "Excuse me?"

He looked at her hard and cold. His gray eyes glittered like ice. "I didn't stutter. What's the subpoena for? They want you to testify against your boyfriend?"

Simone frowned. "He's not my boyfriend anymore, Noah."

Noah's smile became steely. He feigned surprise. "Oh, really? Then why not testify? Do something nice for once."

Simone stepped back. "I know you're probably pissed at me, Noah, but I could use some help."

Noah put his hands in his pockets and laughed at her. "I wouldn't help you across the street, Simone."

Karma

Simone was genuinely startled. She hadn't expected this from Noah. He took a step toward her. "What's the matter? You thought I was the nice one? I got a newsflash for you. Lucas is the nice one. Why did you call me after that shit went down? You think I'd have a nice long chat with you after you tripped my boy up like that?"

Simone retreated. She'd never had a reason to feel afraid of Noah before, but at the moment, he was downright menacing with that steely little smile and heavy-hitting attitude. "I was just trying to find out what's going on. Nobody's talking to me."

Noah looked at her like she was stupid. "No shit? Nobody's talkin' to you? Gee whiz, I wonder why?"

Simone folded her arms across her chest. "I don't understand why everyone is so angry at me. Lucas was there, too."

Noah's eyes flashed. "You don't think he's payin' for this? You're talkin' to me like I haven't been here watchin' you do your dirt. Every chance you got, you hemmed him up. Takin' your clothes off and shit. Did you want him that bad, or do you hate Justine that much? What do you got? You ain't got Lucas. What was the point?"

She shrugged and smiled at Noah's righteous anger. "Maybe I just wanted to fuck him."

The smile fell off Noah's face. His right hand shot out of his pocket so quickly she didn't have a chance to get out of the way. His hand circled her arm like a vise. Noah was gripping her arm so hard, he cut her circulation off and it hurt like hell. When she cried out, he pulled her to him and spoke into her ear.

"Shut up. Listen to me, Simone —"

Simone tried to pull away from him. He pulled her back.

"You're hurting me! Stop it!"

Noah returned his mouth to her ear. "I said, shut up. This little cat and mouse shit with Lucas is over. You hear me? It's a wrap. Stay away from him. Don't even talk to him. Do you understand?"

Simone looked at him defiantly. "Let go of me."

Noah tucked his lips in and applied more pressure on her arm. Simone realized what he was doing. He was applying direct pressure to a nerve.

"Do you understand?" he repeated.

"Yes, all right, yes." This time when she went to snatch her arm away, he let her go. She couldn't believe Noah had flexed on her like that. He actually put his hands on her! She rubbed her arm. It still hurt like hell, and it was also going to leave a mark.

Karma

"I never thought you'd put your hands on a woman, Noah." She looked at his face. Dark and stormy. His anger was coming off him in waves.

"What woman? You don't qualify. You ain't a woman to me. You live your life like this? You're lucky somebody hasn't killed your ass for the shit you do. You keep it up, somebody's going to."

Her subpoena had fallen to the floor during Noah's brutal little nerve trick. Simone bent down and picked it up. Noah put his hands back in his pockets.

"As for that subpoena, there's nothing you can really do about it. See your ass in court."

Simone was still rubbing her arm. "Abusive prick."

Those gray eyes glittered again. "Fuck you, Simone. Now leave the building before I have you escorted out, bitch." He turned his back on her and walked away.

Tears burned the back of her eyes. She'd really done it this time. All her bridges were burned. After the trial was over, she was out of here. She looked at Noah's retreating back and glared at him.

Chapter Forty-Two

Karma

Justine

Justine was ready to put the next part of her plan into action. She put her coat on and went in search of Darius. She knocked on his office door and poked her head in. He wasn't there. She checked the cafeteria and lingered near the men's room. No Darius. Damn! This was throwing everything off. She left the building and looked around. Finally, she spotted him at a hot-dog cart. Justine smiled brightly and walked up behind him.

"I found you! I've been looking for you all over the place."

He turned to face her with a smile. "Well, you did find me. What's up?"

"I was wondering if you were busy tonight."

Darius looked pleasantly confused. "You tryin' to date me, Justine?"

She laughed. "It's Friday night. I don't want to be alone."

"Oh, so you do want to date me."

"Call it what you want. Do you feel like hanging out with me?"

He laughed. "Do you think I would pass up a chance to spend

time with you?"

Justine smiled. "I was hoping you'd say that."

Darius looked surprised when she took his arm. "So, where are we going?"

"No place special. Just dinner and a movie."

"Okay, I'll follow your lead."

Justine winked at him. "I was hoping you'd say that, too."

After dinner and a movie, they walked out into the brisk night air. Darius stopped her and put his arms around her. He kissed her. Justine tried not to stiffen up as she felt his body press into hers. She pushed him away, breathlessly. She didn't want to kiss him anymore, but she played it off. She smiled.

"Whoa! Did you miss me?"

He laughed low and sexy. "Think I didn't?"

Justine eased herself out of his embrace. Away from the evidence of his arousal. He looked down at her.

"Where are we going with this? What do you want from me, Justine? I already got hurt by you once."

Justine smirked. "You hurt me, too, you know."

He looked sheepish. "Yeah, okay. You got that one."

"Just be there for me, Darius."

He gave her a peck on the lips. "I will be. However you want me. Even if I think you're using me."

Damn! "Using you?"

"Yeah, I kinda got the feeling you're tryin' to get even with that asshole."

Justine couldn't keep the frown from forming on her face. It was instinctive. Darius gave her an astute look.

"What's wrong? You don't want me callin' him an asshole? Well, he is." Darius dug in with both heels. "Pompous bastard. Flexin' on people like he's the man. Like he can kick somebody's ass. He should have been takin' care of his woman."

"Whatever, Darius. I'm not trying to get back at him. You know that's not my MO." She was a poor liar.

He smiled at her knowingly. "Nah, I guess that's not how you get down. So, what is it that you want?"

Justine sighed. "I just got used to not being alone. I feel very alone right now."

He laughed. "So … you want me to be filler?"

She stopped walking and touched his face. "Darius, I don't know what I want."

They stared at each other, and Darius covered her hand with his. "Baby, for you, I can be filler," he said. Darius leaned in and kissed her again. He seemed to have found his groove. This kiss was much better, but he still couldn't top Lucas. They stepped apart with a bit of urging from Justine.

She leaned back against him. "All right then." They started walking again, and she was wondering what Lucas was doing now.

231

Karma

Chapter Forty-Three

Lucas

Lucas was driving back up the Long Island Expressway with Justine at his side. She called him three days ago to invite him to Thanksgiving with her parents. He looked over at her. She was staring out the window, eyes weighed down with exhaustion.

"You okay?" he asked.

Justine yawned and sat up. "Yes. It was just a long day. Thank you for coming with me."

Lucas cut off another car and set off a procession of car horns. He was pissed at her. "Thank you for coming with me? What kind of shit is that, Justine?"

She studied him for a moment, then looked out the window. "I didn't tell them you cheated on me. Just that we were having problems, okay?"

Lucas changed lanes again. "Are you punishing me?"

To his amazement, Justine smiled and answered with a decent amount of glee in her voice. "Yes. Are you mad?" A hint of smugness was in her voice.

Lucas sped up. "Baby, I love you."

Justine settled into her seat. "Do you?"

He glanced at her again. "You want me to spend the rest of my life apologizing to you, I will. You know I will." He looked at her.

He wondered how long it was going to take for her to forgive him. It had been more than a month. He wasn't trying to rush her, but this was wearing him out. Not to mention the fact that he really wasn't used to taking shit off women. He'd take it though, because he loved her and he was wrong.

Justine didn't speak to him again until he parked the car. She unbuckled her seat belt. "Are you coming up?"

"Do you want me to?" This was becoming a routine conversation.

She smiled at him. "Don't be silly. Of course, I want you to."

Lucas followed her out of the car and into the building. When they got into the elevator, Justine grabbed his lapels and kissed him passionately. Lucas moaned and enjoyed the unexpected kiss. This was where he wanted to be. He'd never felt this way about anyone but her. She tasted so good to him. So sweet. She smelled so good, and her body felt so right. He loved her. He'd do anything for her. The elevator doors popped open, and they stepped out. Justine let them into the apartment. Quickly, they shrugged out of their coats. As he took off his suit jacket, Justine removed his tie and draped it over her own neck. She bit her bottom lip and looked up at him with sorrowful eyes.

"I hate you for what you did to us."

Lucas dropped his head. Here we go again. He felt like she'd hit him.

"All right." Hate was a pretty strong word. Lucas knew she didn't hate him. She was mad and hurt, but if she hated him, he wouldn't be standing here.

Justine started taking her clothes off. She didn't stop until she was standing before him naked. She was beautiful, lovely, but she looked so sad. He had put that look in her eyes.

"Lucas, Lucas, I feel like every time we're here like this, it's like watching the same scene over and over again in a sad movie. Don't you feel it?"

He nodded silently.

"You have to understand how I feel. Lucas, I love you. I'm supposed to not want you anymore. Not want you to touch me anymore. I can't do it. I need you, Lucas. I don't want to go

234

Karma

through this every time we make love, but I truly am having a hard time forgiving you, and at the same time, Lucas, I just can't let you go. I don't want to."

She led him into the bedroom and helped him out of his clothes. When he touched her, she started crying soundless tears. "Oh, Justine, I am so sorry." He would have done anything to turn back the hands of time. It hadn't been worth it. To see her like this broke his heart. He wanted to tell her not to cry. That he was sorry. Instead he made love to her. Sweet and slow the way she liked it. When she thought they were done, he started all over again. Made love to her. Showed her how he felt. He wanted her to be his wife. To have his babies. Lucas was far from a crying man, but his face was wet, and he knew why. Justine started to shiver in his arms. He let himself go with her. "I love you. I need you. Don't leave me. You're mine, Justine. Please, sweetheart."

Justine was grasping him when it was over. They clung to each other.

The next morning, Lucas took a shower and got dressed for work. Justine was sitting on the bed, watching him. As he finished with his tie, the phone rang. He wondered who could be calling her that early. Justine walked out of the room, giggling into the phone. Something about it hit a nerve with Lucas, but he let it go. Maybe it was Holly. He went into the kitchen. Justine was putting on the kettle.

235

Karma

"Who was that?" he asked.

She turned her back to him and reached for her apple cinnamon tea. Lucas felt sudden heat for her and was tempted to rip the tea out of her hand and make her look at him. A bad feeling settled, malignantly, into the pit of his stomach.

"Holly," Justine replied. She never looked up from her tea making. Just kept going about her business.

Lucas narrowed his eyes. Yeah, okay. Holly. Sure, it was Holly. "What are you doing today?"

Still transfixed in tea preparation, Justine remained with her back to him. "Not much. A little Christmas shopping with Holly. She loves to shop on Black Friday." She turned around and seemed startled by the look on his face. "What?" she asked.

The phone rang again. Justine blushed, probably without realizing it. She picked up the phone and informed the caller that she'd call right back. Lucas looked at her.

"Is everything all right?" he asked. His voice was calm, but his skin was crawling.

Justine smiled at him. "Perfect," she said. She hugged him. "You okay?" She hugged him a little tighter.

Lucas continued to stare at her. Somewhere down the road, she must have forgotten he read people for a living. It was his job to discern whether or not things were right or wrong. This had "wrong" written all over it. He hugged her back.

"I'm good."

Justine smiled up at him. "I'm glad you stayed." She put her head on his chest.

Lucas gently pushed her away from him. "You sure?"

Justine frowned. "Why are you acting funny all of a sudden?"

Lucas' eyebrows shot up. "Me? I thought you were acting pretty strange yourself."

She looked at him harshly. Fire lit her eyes. "What are you saying, Lucas? Are you saying you don't trust me? I know that can't be what you're saying. 'Cause if you're trying to act like you don't trust me, you've got a lot of nerve, Lucas Cain. After you fucked over me the way you did, you're gonna try and act like that? I don't think so."

Karma

Lucas blinked. Who the hell was this? He was getting tired of her flipping on him. Fuck this. He loved her, but he was done with her treating him like a punk. It was time to flex on her. He moved so close to her, so quickly, she put her hand up in shock. Lucas grabbed her hand and pulled her even closer. The wind went right out of her sails. A trace of fear crossed her eyes.

"I love you, Justine, and I'm trying to make it right. I'm tired of this shit, though. I've had enough of you flippin' on me and talkin' to me like I'm soft. If you don't want me anymore, be woman enough to let me know, but stop what you're doing. I will not be disrespected." He pushed her away from him as gently as he could. He wasn't trying to hurt her. He just wanted to get his point across.

They stared at each other. Lucas was angry, and Justine looked as if she hadn't expected that from him. Lucas walked out of the kitchen and stopped in the living room to put his coat on. Justine was right behind him. He opened the door to leave, and she grabbed his arm. Lucas looked down at her. The tears were back.

"Lucas, wait. Don't leave like this. I'm sorry."

He snatched his arm away and stepped back. "Stop playin'

with me, Justine. I mean it."

She looked afraid. "I know you do."

"If we're gonna work on this, then let's do that, but this has got to stop. It's tearin' me up."

"Okay."

"I'll call you." He stepped over the threshold and closed the door behind him before she could say anything. Then he sighed. That bad feeling was still there.

Karma

Chapter Forty-Four

Karma

Justine

Justine had been sitting at her desk doing a little Christmas shopping on the Internet when Holly stuck her head in her office. Justine was surprised but delighted to see her.

"Hey, girl, what brings you here?"

Holly sat down across from her. She didn't look happy. "Guess who I just heard from?"

Justine frowned. "Simone?" The name felt nasty on her tongue. Like she wanted to scrape it off.

Holly frowned, too. "Yeah. It was strange to me because we've had almost two months' worth of silence, then suddenly, there's her ring tone going off on my cell phone."

Justine leaned back in her chair. Holly was watching her intently.

"What did she want?"

"Said she was moving to L.A. after the trial."

"Is that so?"

"So she said. Something else was real strange."

"What's that?"

"She says she's been getting strange phone calls. Threatening calls. She says it sounds like one of those voice disguiser gizmos."

Justine laughed. "Holly, are you serious?"

Holly didn't laugh. "She says if it's one or both of us, she wants it to stop."

"You're kidding, right?"

Holly looked at her pointedly. "Did you call her?"

Justine stood up. "Come on, Holly. That's not me. Why would I do that?"

Holly sat there looking so concerned. Justine knew where she was going with this.

"I don't know why you're doing a number of things you've been doing since this thing with Lucas. Smoking, drinking, being secretive …" Holly walked over to her. "Honey, I know you love Lucas, but don't let this turn you into someone you're not."

Justine frowned. Mind your own business, Holly. "You think I called her?"

"I think something in you snapped when this happened. I think you need to talk to somebody and work through this thing."

"You think I called her?"

Holly looked sad. "Yeah, honey, I think you did."

Justine moved away from her. "If she thinks I called her then why didn't she just step to me? Stupid bitch."

Holly shrugged. "Maybe she didn't want a confrontation."

Justine laughed again. "Holly, she guaranteed a confrontation when she slept with Lucas."

Holly gave her a troubled look. "Justine, I think you need a little therapy. Don't look at me like that. Therapy is not a bad thing."

"I'm not crazy, Holly. I'm just hurt."

"I know. I hate to drop this on you and run, but I've got a short lunch today."

"Yeah, Holly." Justine wanted her old friend to leave.

Holly hugged her. She hugged her back.

"I love you, girl. Everything will be okay."

Sure, Holly. Justine nodded. "Okay."

"I'll call you before the week is out."

"Okay." Justine watched Holly leave and returned to her seat.

Therapy? Justine had her own brand of therapy for

everyone involved.

241

Karma

Chapter Forty-Five

Karma

Simone

Simone was in her office with Raphael going over her fitting schedule for the week when the doorbell to her office chimed. They both looked at each other. They weren't expecting anyone. Simone sighed and pushed away from her desk. She just hoped it wasn't Justine. Raphael was looking at her expectantly. He knew her business. He was her new best friend.

"You want me to get that, chica, or you wanna act like we ain't here?"

The bell chimed again. Fuck it. Simone had never in her life been afraid of Justine, and even though things were a little freaky, she wasn't about to start now. She got up and went over to the sewing table and picked up her sharpest pair of scissors.

"You know what? If it's her, let the little bitch in. If she steps to me, I'm gonna let her have it."

Raphael paled a bit when she picked up the scissors, but he went to the door and opened it with his hand on his hip and his fiercest face. Simone was surprised to discover she was scared. She was even more surprised that Justine had her this shaken.

Raphael threw the door open and clapped his hands.

"It's cool, Simone. It's the cavalry!" he yelled to her.

Lucas stepped through the door with Noah right behind him. Simone felt her heart rip in her chest at the sight of Lucas. After everything, she still wanted him badly. Noah looked at her with his icy-grey eyes. He took in the scissors and Simone's tight grip on them.

"What are those for?" he asked, taking an intimidating step toward her. She didn't like Noah anymore. He was a cold bastard. Simone moved away from him.

"They're for your ass if you came here to hurt me."

Lucas stepped between them.

"Nobody's gonna hurt anybody. I need to talk to you. Now put the scissors down."

Simone looked into his eyes. He didn't look happy, but he didn't look like he came here to kill her. She reluctantly put them down. Noah turned to Raphael.

"We'd like to speak to her privately," he said.

Raphael puffed his chest out. "I think I should stay. I sense some hostility up in here."

Noah advanced on him. "You gonna sense somethin' else, 'up in here' if you don't get your little strange ass out."

Raphael flinched, then snapped his fingers in Noah's face. "Oh no, you didn't say that to me —"

Lucas put his hand on Raphael's arm. Noah was smiling at him sinisterly, cracking his knuckles.

"Raphael, we don't have time for this. We're just going to talk to her and leave, okay? Calm down."

Lucas smoothed Raphael's ruffled feathers. Raphael was momentarily placated.

"Okay, papi. Twenty minutes."

Lucas nodded. "That's fine."

Raphael got his coat and headed for the door.

"Raphael?" Lucas called to him.

"Yes?"

Lucas' eyes darkened. "Don't call me papi."

Raphael's hand went to his mouth. "I forgot. Sorry."

Lucas eyed him until he shut the door. Once he was gone, he turned to Simone. "I talked to Holly. She says you've been getting some prank calls. Justine's been calling you?" he asked.

Damn, he was right to the point. Simone decided to play with him. "Not even a 'how have you been?' Lucas?"

"I don't care how you've been. This isn't a social call."

She gave him a seductive look. "Did you miss me?"

Lucas looked at her like she was soaked in something nasty. His hands went up like he was going to grab her, but he dropped them just as quickly. "Don't make me hurt you," he said. It was barely audible.

Simone walked away from him to put a little space between them. So much for a bit of harmless flirting. She glanced at him. He looked like he wanted to yank her head off her shoulders with his bare hands. Simone started to pout. So much animosity. This wasn't all on her. Lucas moved away from her, too.

"Like I said, I hear you think Justine's been calling you."

Simone folded her arms across her chest defensively. "Holly has a big mouth, but yeah, I know it's Justine. She even called me from your cell. I'm not lying. I'm not imagining things. And she either spray-painted my doors, or she had someone else do it. I had to report that for insurance purposes, but I didn't say I knew who did it. If she does anything else, I'm getting a restraining order. End of story."

Lucas sat on the edge of her desk. "Have you seen her? I mean, standing around, maybe thinking you didn't see her?"

Simone shook her head. "No. She's not hanging around in a Halloween mask or anything."

Karma

"No lurking?" Noah asked.

Simone narrowed her eyes at him. "I refuse to talk to you, asshole."

Noah reclaimed his sinister grin. Lucas put his hand up.

"Then talk to me. Any lurking?"

"No, Lucas, no."

"You feel like you got anybody following you?"

Simone felt unnerved by that. It didn't have to be Justine straight-out. It probably wouldn't be. Justine had a certain public celebrity status, and she wouldn't want her name involved. She could just as easily pay someone to do something to her. She said as much to Lucas. He shook his head.

"I don't think it's that bad. She's probably trying to scare you. Did she do anything else? Anything weird happen? Anything not seem right?"

Simone shook her head. Lucas stood up.

"Before you go getting a restraining order, do me a favor and let me talk to her. I'm sure she'll stop if I make her aware that I know what she's doing."

Simone rubbed her palms on her jeans. "This is totally out of character for her. I wonder what would make her snap like that."

Noah laughed sarcastically. "Some ho tryin' to ruin her life would be my guess."

"Nobody asked you, asshole."

Noah kept that evil look on his face. "Is that my new name? Don't fuck with me. I got somethin' for your ass. That's a promise."

Once again, Lucas stepped between them. "That's enough. If anything else happens, I want you to get in touch with me. Call me right away."

How sweet. He's trying to protect me. She reached out and touched his arm. He knocked it away roughly.

"Don't touch me. Don't ever put your hands on me."

"I was just going to thank you."

"No need. Let me know what's goin' on." He and Noah walked out, but not before Noah gave her one last nasty look.

246

Karma

Simone shivered. Everyone had gotten so cold. Her mind went back to Miami. Lucas sure hadn't been cold then. He'd been on fire. She sighed. He must really hate her. Today he'd deliberately kept her name out of his mouth as if it had a bad taste. She smiled to herself. To hell with all of them. Soon she'd be in L.A. starting over.

She settled down in her chair and her smile became smug. It did give her a great deal of satisfaction that Justine was flaking off the wall like chipped paint. Little Miss Perfect wasn't so perfect after all. As a matter of fact, she was starting to look like Little Miss Crazy.

Chapter Forty-Six

Justine

Justine stepped into the shower and turned the water on. She stood under the spray and started to lather up. She was seeing Darius tonight, and she wanted this to be it. She was going to let him have what he wanted so she could get what she wanted.

Her mind drifted. She thought about the phone calls she'd had Lucy make to Simone. It hadn't been hard to get Lucy to do it. Lucy had met Lucas and Simone. She didn't like a bone in Simone's ass. When Justine told Lucy what happened, she'd been so angry, she helped Justine devise a plan of retribution. At least for Simone. Lucy made the calls herself. Except for one. Justine had called one night on Lucas' cell, but she hadn't left a message. She regretted that one. Lucy's boyfriend was a drug dealer. Not big time, but not small time. He'd gotten someone who owed him money to spray-paint Simone's doors.

Justine got out of the shower and dried off. She put on her best perfume, then took her hair down and curled it. When she was finished combing it, she realized she was wearing it the way Lucas liked it. She also realized she was wearing his favorite perfume. Oh well, some habits were hard to break. Besides, she really didn't want to. After all, Lucas was still her man until she said he wasn't. It was becoming a mantra.

Justine put on her makeup and walked naked into the bedroom. When she turned on the lights, she almost had a heart attack. Lucas was sitting there in the dark, at the foot of the bed. His elbows were resting on his knees, hands clasped, head down. He was staring at the floor.

"Lucas? What are you doing sitting here in the dark?"

He stood up and looked at her. His eyes were infinitely sad. He spoke softly. "You look lovely. That's how I always think of you. Lovely."

Justine went to him, a little ball of fear forming in her stomach. "Lucas, what's wrong? Are you okay?"

His eyes took her in, moved over her body. He lifted his hand and traced the outline of her body with his finger. Justine trembled. He smiled at her, but it was a sad smile.

"You look like you're on your way out."

Justine shifted on her feet. "I am. Yeah, I am."

He moved closer to her. "Really? Where are you going?"

"Nowhere special."

248

Karma

"Nowhere special? You look special." He put his hand in her hair and ran his fingers through it. Justine moved away from him so he wouldn't mess it up.

"No, just to dinner with a few of my colleagues."

Lucas took his coat off and pulled his sweater over his head. He was naked from the waist up. He rolled up on her until her back was against the wall. He looked down at her.

"Don't go. Stay here with me."

Justine had never been able to resist Lucas. He took her hand and put it over his heart. She sucked in her breath and bit her lip. She was going to cry, the gesture was so sweet. She loved Lucas with all she had, but this was something she had to do. The die was already cast.

Lucas moved her hand to his face. His beard was soft. He moved against her, and her knees got weak.

"Where's your ring?" he asked.

Justine was quick to answer. "I took it off to shower." He reached for the light switch and turned the light off. They stood in the dark not speaking, Justine's hand against his face. He kissed her forehead tenderly.

"I love you," he said in that same soft voice.

"I love you, too," she answered. And it was the truth. She loved him dearly.

"I'm here for you, sweetheart. I'm not going anywhere."

Justine slipped her hand away from his face. That ball of fear grew bigger. "Lucas, what's wrong?" She tilted her head so she could smell his breath. This was strange, and she wanted to know if he'd been drinking. His breath was fresh.

"This is my fault," he said.

Justine put her head on his chest. His heart was pounding. "What are you talking about?"

Lucas put his arms around her. That skin on skin contact, their two bodies meeting, was a sweet sensation. It had her distracted.

"Don't get yourself into trouble because of me."

Justine moved away and hit the lights. Damn, Holly! She's like a broken refrigerator. She can't keep anything. "What do you mean by that?"

He stared at her. Stared through her. "Baby, I know what's going on. Why would you do that? Why?"

Justine frowned. "Do what?"

Lucas looked at her like he was weighing her innocence. He leaned back. "Have you been harassing her?"

Oh, no. He knows. He wasn't supposed to find out about that. "What? Harassing who?"

Lucas approached her like he was scolding a bad child. "I think you know who I'm talking about. I know, Justine, okay?"

She walked away from him, opened her lingerie chest, pulled out some pretty underwear and started to get dressed. First, she slipped into her panties and put her arms through her bra straps, fastened the back and moved to her closet. Lucas stood there watching her, his arms across his chest.

"You need to stop, Justine. It's no good."

She reached into the closet, took out a sexy black dress and put it on the bed. Lucas looked from the dress to her.

"You wearin' that to dinner?"

Justine gave him a rueful smile. "What do you care? You're in here accusing me of harassing your fucking girlfriend." It fell out of her mouth before she could stop it. She regretted it the moment it was out there. Lucas had never put his hands on her in anger, and he really didn't now, but he reached out and grabbed her. Justine let out a gasp of surprise as he shook her like a rag

Karma

doll. Shook her so hard her teeth rattled.

"Don't you say that to me! I don't have a girlfriend! I have you. You're going to be my wife! What are you doing? I beg you every day, Justine. I'm begging you now. I know you don't want to let this go. I know you've got some kind of vendetta going on. Don't do this. Forget it, baby. Let's just try to salvage what we've got. Please."

Justine pulled away from him and picked her dress up. She took it off the hanger, but Lucas snatched it out of her hand. Justine was tired of this. She grabbed her dress and attempted to pull it out of his grasp. When she heard fabric ripping, she was really pissed. When she jerked it out of his hand, he let go at the same time. Justine tumbled to the floor with her ruined dress in her lap. She looked up at him. He was angry. She didn't think she'd ever seen him that angry before. Something in his face had changed.

"I don't know where you're going, but you won't be wearing that," he said.

Justine got up and calmly threw her dress in the trash basket. Then she turned to Lucas. "I don't believe you put your hands on me," she said for lack of anything better to say. She realized things were happening a lot faster than she'd planned.

Lucas deflated. "Justine, I didn't. Not like you're tryin' to say I did. I would never hit you, and you know it."

She smirked. "Maybe not, but you're not above shaking the shit out of me, are you?" She rolled her eyes at him and went back to her closet. She pulled out a red dress equally as sexy as the black one. Lucas ripped that one off the hanger himself and threw it on top of the first one.

"If you're dining with your colleagues, wear a fuckin' suit," he said through his teeth.

Justine stared at him incredulously. "Lucas, what's the matter with you? You come in here accusing me of things, shaking me and throwing my clothes in the garbage. What's the matter with you? Are you crazy? We've never been like this."

Lucas went to her. "I'm not crazy. I'm not drunk. I'm definitely not stupid. Stop what you're doing, Justine."

"What am I doing, Lucas? You came in here with an agenda. Tell me. What am I doing? You don't know anything! You only know what somebody else accused me of. I can't believe you're not on my side."

Just like he'd done the night he'd met her, he stepped all into her personal space. "Sweetheart, I'm always on your side."

Justine sucked her teeth and went back to her closet. Lucas stepped in front of her. "Where are you going?" he asked.

She tried to push him aside. He wouldn't budge. When she tried to move around him, he blocked her path. Justine was infuriated. Before she could check herself, she reached out and slapped him. Lucas' head went back, most likely in surprise, rather than due to any real pain. Lucas was messing up her plans. She needed him to leave. She slapped him again, harder this time. Now Lucas grabbed both her wrists. He pushed her back until the back of her knees hit the bed. Down she went. Lucas fell on top of her, pushing the wind out of her. She put her hand under his chin and tried to push him off her.

Meanwhile, her legs had a mind of their own. They opened and let him in, locking behind his back. She hastily unbuckled his belt and pushed his pants down with his underwear. His breath was harsh in her ear. She maneuvered herself and forced her panties aside. Then she put her hand on him and led him into her. He was like a rock. They both sucked in air at the contact. Her back arched.

251

Karma

"Oh, Lucas! Oh, God! Don't you leave me!" The words flowed out of her mouth with no script. She wanted this man more than she wanted anything else. He sucked her bottom lip into his mouth, and Justine began her inevitable quaking. She fell into her first orgasm, and a picture of him and Simone flashed through her mind. Fucking bitch! Justine cruelly raked her fingernails up Lucas' back, knowing she was hurting him.

Lucas made a sound in the back of his throat and kept going, twisting and turning with her. He ended up with her bottom in his palms, slamming into her like tomorrow wasn't coming. He cried out first. Justine put her hands in his hair and pushed them both up and off the bed until it looked like a feat of magic. Like they were floating on her shoulder blades. They fell back onto the bed, breathing hard and not speaking.

Justine looked over at Lucas. He was on his back, staring at the ceiling. He looked like he had the weight of the world on his shoulders. She touched him, and he sat up. She was taken aback. Lucas had never before acted like he didn't want her to touch him.

"Lucas?" she said his name hesitantly. He put his face in his hands and sat there on the side of the bed. Justine got to her knees and crawled over to him. She gingerly put her hand on his shoulder. He didn't knock it off. That was a good thing. "Honey?" He didn't respond, instead he stood up and got dressed. Justine stayed on her knees, watching him. He didn't say a word, even as he put his coat on. She climbed off the bed and followed him to the front door. This time she stepped in front of him.

"Wait a minute," she said.

Lucas wouldn't look at her. "Wait for what?"

Justine put her arms around his waist. He didn't return the gesture, but he didn't push her away.

"You look so sad, Lucas."

He finally looked at her. "Do I?"

For the second time that day, he seemed to be looking through her. Like he was trying to see what she was thinking. He leaned down and looked into her eyes. "Where did you go, Justine?"

She dropped her arms. The question startled her. "What do you mean?"

"I feel like you're a different person. How can we get back to us if you're not here?"

Justine felt sadness wash over her. He was right, of course. "I'm here," she said in a small voice.

Lucas touched her hair again. "No, you're not, but that's okay. I'm in this for the long haul. I just need to leave right now."

"Why? Where are you going?"

"Home. I need to think. So do you." He opened the door. "I'll be back tomorrow. Is that okay?"

"Sure."

He kissed her and left. Justine closed the door behind him and went into the bathroom. She had to take another shower and redo her hair and makeup, but she wasn't going to put this off any longer. It was time for the moment of truth.

Karma

Chapter Forty-Seven

Lucas

Lucas couldn't stay away any longer. He spent the night alone in his Brownstone and drove straight to Justine's first thing in the morning. He parked out front and entered her building, bouncing his keys in his hand. He felt a little better. They'd talk this out. They'd start over if they had to. He loved her, and he was marrying her, come hell or high water.

He got off the elevator and walked to her apartment. As usual, he stuck his key in the lock and went in. He'd taken his jacket off and was about to lay it over the back of the sofa when alarms went off in his head as his brain started registering what he was actually seeing. He closed his eyes real slow and opened them again, just as slowly. He wasn't hallucinating. All this shit was still here. Two glasses on the coffee table. He walked deeper into the room to survey the entire scene. His eyes fell on Justine's dress thrown haphazardly across the arm of the chair. Male clothing in a heap near an end table. Something shiny caught his eye. He kicked it with his foot. The breath left his body, and he felt like someone was actually squeezing his heart when he saw it was an empty condom wrapper.

Lucas closed his eyes. His heart was beating so fast, he thought it would jump right out of his chest. He felt a scream building in the back of his throat. Justine. Justine. Justine. Oh, baby, why? Hadn't he done enough to destroy this relationship by himself? Anguish rose up in him strong and deep. Lucas shut down. He dropped his head and folded his arms across his chest. It was the posture he assumed when he was a boy and he was trying hard not to cry. He stayed that way for a long while.

Then he heard a noise from the kitchen. Lucas tilted his head in that direction and opened his eyes. His arms fell to his sides. Justine said something, and he heard male laughter. The rage came back. It bubbled up in Lucas so fast, for a moment, he couldn't see. His eyes grew cold, and his heart rate slowed.

He silently went to the closed kitchen door. His fury was palpable and white hot. He felt as if he were breathing fire, like a dragon. He put his hand on the door and swung it open. Justine was in a short, frilly little robe with her back to him. Darius was wearing his boxers, facing him. The sudden movement of the door made him look up. Darius looked directly into Lucas' burning stare.

"Oh, shit," he said, quietly. Justine's head popped up from what she was doing. She looked at Darius, then over her shoulder at Lucas. If her eyes could've gotten any bigger, they would have fallen right out of her head. She jumped so hard, she knocked the bowl she'd been mixing pancakes in right off the counter. It shattered and batter splashed everywhere.

"Lucas!" she half-screamed.

Lucas moved just inside the kitchen and let the door shut behind him. Darius started backing up. Lucas looked at him with murderous intent as his hands balled into fists.

"Where you gonna go, man? There's only two ways outta here. Through me or out the fuckin' window. It's your choice. Either way, your ass better start prayin'."

Darius stopped moving, realizing he was backing himself into a corner. Lucas rolled his head and cracked his neck, smiling malevolently. He shook himself out and got ready to move. Justine just stood in the middle, looking terrified, both hands over her mouth. Darius was trapped. His eyes darted around the room searching for a weapon. Lucas shook his head.

"Don't do it. You pick something up, I'm gonna make you

eat it."

Justine looked back at Darius, then to Lucas. She started pleading with him. "Lucas, please, don't do this. Just let him leave. Just let —"

Lucas didn't even look at her. "Don't talk to me, Justine."

He gave Darius the "come on" gesture with his fingers. "Let's go, motherfucker, you been here long enough." He walked around Justine, just to get him moving.

Like the idiot he was, Darius didn't let the chance go by.

Lucas smirked. Did he really think he could just skip by him and leave? Lucas was fast, and he knew it. He let Darius get almost to the door, then he was on him. He grabbed him in a headlock and threw him to the floor. Lucas dropped down on his diaphragm with his knee. Justine screamed. Lucas hit Darius in the mouth as hard as he could. Blood sprayed as his lip split. Lucas knocked the skin off his knuckles, but it was worth it to feel a couple of Darius' teeth break. Lucas didn't give him a chance to recover. His nose was next. Lucas smiled grimly when he punched him and felt the cartilage give way. More blood. Lucas put his hand in Darius' hair and pulled him off his back before he started choking. Finally, he left him alone and let him struggle to his feet.

Karma

But in his anger, he underestimated him. Even though he was hurt, Darius rushed him. Lucas was taller, but they probably weighed about the same. Darius tackled Lucas so hard that he knocked him off his feet. Lucas heard Justine scream his name and saw an explosion of stars as the back of his head slammed into the hard kitchen floor and bounced back up. Darius growled and punched him in the face. Lucas turned to avoid major damage, but he was too late to stop him from opening a cut above his left eyebrow. Blood ran into his eye, and he winced and knocked Darius off him.

They both scrambled to their feet, ran at each other and just started fighting. Street fighting, old-school style. Justine was screaming for them to stop. They pounded each other furiously, each one refusing to lose. Lucas let all his rage out on Darius and fought him hard and close, not letting him get too far away from him like he did earlier. He bided his time and finally knocked his ass out with a hard blow to his jaw. Darius went down like a ton of bricks, a surprised look on his face. Lucas nodded and stood over him.

"That's right. I caught your ass out there." He wiped his face.

His hand came away bloody. He glanced at Justine, who'd fallen silent and retreated to a corner, then she went into the living room. Lucas followed her, picked up Darius' clothes and returned to the kitchen. Darius was just coming to. He threw his clothes at him.

"Get out. If I come back and you're still here, that's your ass."

Lucas went into the bathroom and shut the door. Locked it, but not before he stopped by the living room and retrieved his jacket. He didn't want his gun out there like that. He clipped the holster back on his belt and looked in the mirror. He had a deep cut above his left eye, a scrape across his right cheek, his bottom lip was beginning to swell and his ribs hurt like hell. He looked at his hands. They were a mess. All scraped up, and his right thumb was jammed. He washed his face gingerly and tried to stop the flow of blood over his eye. It took a while, but it finally slowed down.

Lucas put his coat on and went back into the living room. Justine was sitting on the edge of the sofa, staring into space.

"Your lover gone?" he asked.

Justine looked at him. She looked pretty pissed off herself. "He's not my lover, Lucas. And, yes, he's gone." She stood up and walked over to him. Lucas felt that white hot anger start to rise again. Justine curled her hands into fists and talked through her teeth. "What the hell is wrong with you? Are you crazy? Why did you do that?"

Lucas surprised himself by actually laughing. "What did you expect? Did you think I was gonna shake his fuckin' hand and congratulate him?"

She put her finger in his face. "Don't you curse at me, Lucas."

He knocked her hand away. "Fuck you, Justine. Don't come at me like that after what you just did."

Her eyebrows went up. "Fuck me? How dare you talk to me like that! What did I do, Lucas? What's the matter? You bent out of shape because I stepped out of this relationship and slept with someone else? Huh? How does it feel? Are you hurt? Angry? Do you feel betrayed? Do you want to hit me? How does it feel to know somebody else had his hands all over your woman? Tell me, Lucas. Tell me exactly what you're feeling right now."

Lucas looked at her. As much as he loved her, it was taking a tremendous amount of willpower not to snatch her up and strangle her until she stopped breathing. He shook his head. "Tit for tat,

Justine? Two wrongs don't make a right."

"Maybe not, but it makes us even."

The anger was dissipating, mixing in with another long unfelt emotion. Hurt. All his life, Lucas had made it his business not to get too close to a woman. He didn't need a psychiatrist to tell him where it came from. His mother — the one thing in his life he could never get over. He let Justine in. She was right for him. He knew she was. He ruined it. Everything that had transpired from the moment he met Simone was his fault. Justine had been with another man. She left him, too. His love. Grief and sorrow washed over him like a monsoon. He started shaking, and his breath hitched in his throat. Justine's look of anger turned to worry in a heartbeat.

"Lucas?" She laid a hand on his arm, and he lost it. He grabbed her and held her as tightly as he could. Justine was caught off guard, but her arms went around him.

"I'm sorry," he said in a harsh sob. The tears came. He couldn't quite believe he was standing here crying, more than crying, bawling. He hadn't cried like this since the day his mother left. Justine put her fingers in his hair and held him.

257

Karma

"Me, too," she said, crying with him just as hard.

They sank to their knees, Lucas wetting her hair with his tears. "My fault. It's all my fault. I ruined us. I killed everything. I'm sorry."

Justine clung to him, held him as tightly as she could, sobbing softly in his ear.

"I made you not love me anymore. That's the only way you could do that. If you didn't love me any more."

Justine looked stricken. "No, Lucas, no." She kissed his lips and put her cheek to his.

"Then why? To get me back? You got me back, Justine. You paid me back."

They stayed on the floor together for a long time, crying and holding each other. Lucas was the first to disentangle himself. He had to get out of there. He needed some air. He didn't understand this thing between him and Justine anymore. He felt he should be angrier than he actually was. He was more hurt than he was anything else. He stood up, slowly, wincing at his aching ribs. Justine also got to her feet. Lucas wiped his face with his hand. They looked at each other.

"What have we done?" he asked her.

"I don't know."

He looked down at her. "I wish to God you hadn't done that."

She nodded. "I wish you hadn't slept with Simone." It wasn't a dig. She was just saying how she felt.

"I understand."

"Do you want your ring back?"

Lucas leaned back and let out a deep breath. He put his hands behind his head. He hadn't even thought about it. "Wow. You just hit me with that. I can't deal with it. No way can I deal with that right now."

She nodded again and looked at the floor. That question had sent his mind reeling again.

"Do you want me to take it back?"

"No, Lucas."

Anger started creeping back in. "Then why did you —" He cut himself off. He was getting aggravated. "Never mind. This is going in circles. I can't talk to you right now."

258

Karma

He looked at Justine. She looked sorry, and she looked ashamed. She should, but she was still his love. Or was she? He didn't know anything anymore. His emotions were ping-ponging off the walls. The air felt heavy. He realized he was about to start hyperventilating.

Justine was looking up at him, her hands clasped between her breasts like she was praying. She didn't speak. Her eyes were great saucers of worry. "Lucas ..." she said.

He closed his eyes. His temples were starting to throb. "I gotta get outta here. I have to go." He reached for the doorknob.

"Lucas —" Justine started.

He turned on her in exasperation. "Justine, please. Stop saying my name. Just stop right now. I'm exhausted. Please, just let me go. I'll call you. I promise, but you've got to let me get out of here right now. I can't breathe."

Justine moved aside. "I'm sorry."

Lucas laughed a wild and bitter little laugh that was missing all its humor. "Yeah, me, too. You're sorry. I'm sorry. We're all just so fucking sorry. I gotta go."

He left quickly and rang for the elevator. Anger, guilt and sadness weighed him down. He felt like he was awake in a nightmare, and he finally felt like everything wasn't going to be okay.

Chapter Forty-Eight

Justine

Justine walked out of her office and locked the door. She was on her way to the newsroom to sit in for the news at noon, and she was running late.

"Justine."

She whipped around at the sound of Darius' voice. She hadn't seen him in a week. Not since the day Lucas had found them together.

"Darius."

He was still a bit of a mess. He had a bandage across his nose and a few bruises, but he'd gotten his teeth fixed.

"How have you been? You all right?"

She nodded and shifted her folders to her other arm. "Are you okay?" she asked, not out of genuine concern, but because it was polite. She was done with Darius. He'd served his purpose.

"Do I look like I'm okay? Where have you been, Justine? You could have called."

Yes, maybe she could have, but she didn't want to. She didn't answer him.

"You used me. I knew it, but I went along with it, so that's my bad. How are you feeling about yourself right about now, Justine?"

She looked at her watch. "I'm late," she said, avoiding his eyes.

"Do you believe in karma?" Darius ventured.

Justine stared at the floor. "Not really," was her answer.

"Well, I do. You got me back for what I did. You got him back for what he did. You're next, Justine. Karma's gonna come back around and bite you on that pretty little ass of yours. You better get ready." He turned and walked away.

Justine smiled. She had one more thing to do. Everybody else better get ready. She walked to the newsroom and sat in for the twelve o'clock. When the broadcast was over, the producer told her she was needed on the road to cover Nine's trial.

Karma

Chapter Forty-Nine

261

Karma

Lucas

Lucas, never a great celebrator of holidays, was determined to make this Christmas a good one. There'd been so much sadness, pain and anger in the last few months. He was tired of it. He made up his mind. He wanted his woman, and if she'd have him, he was willing to do whatever it took to keep her. He was sick of playing games and being in emotional turmoil. He was putting everything behind him, and he was marrying Justine in February. He wrapped his hand around the small, robin's egg blue Tiffany box in his pocket. He smiled to himself. He was in the best mood he'd been in, in months. It was Christmas Eve, and he was going to see his baby.

He used his key and let himself into her apartment. Instantly, he shook off a tremor of recall. The last time he'd used his key, Darius had been here. Lucas forced that picture out of his mind and looked around for her. A quick search of the house left him with only the bedroom to look in. He found her there, curled up under a big white comforter. She slept peacefully, her mouth slightly open. Lucas smiled. Probably drooling on the pillow. He often teased her about that.

Lucas took the box out of his pocket and put it on the nightstand. Then he took off his clothes and climbed into bed with her. He brushed her face with his fingertips, and she stirred. He leaned down and kissed her until she was awake. Her arms went around him automatically. Lucas made love to her slow and easy for a long time. He didn't stop until she was satisfied. When it was over, they lay there together, spent and happy. His heart felt much lighter. He sat up and took the Tiffany box from the nightstand. Justine looked from the box back to him. He took her hand and placed the box in it.

"Merry Christmas," he said.

Justine opened the box slowly and gasped at the ring inside. A small circle of diamonds. She looked at him as he slipped the ring onto the ring finger of her left hand.

"Is this my wedding band?"

Lucas laughed and shook his head. "No, baby. This is a promise ring. It's thin, so you can wear it with your other rings. On the same hand. With this ring, I'm promising you that I belong to you and only you. You are the only woman in my life. I don't want anyone else. Please, sweetheart, forgive me for what I did."

Karma

Justine looked at the ring on her finger and back at him. "I love you, Lucas. Forgive me for what I did."

Lucas gave her a sad smile. "I made you do that." He got up and went to the jewelry box and got her engagement ring. He slipped it on her finger. "I love you, Justine. I can't live without you. Every breath I take is for you. If you leave me, I'll die. Marry me, please."

Justine accepted the ring. She smiled at him. "I take it you've forgiven me."

Lucas nodded. "I have. I made my peace with it."

She kissed him. "I forgive you, too. Let's get married."

"I'm all yours," he said and proceeded to make love to her again. They stayed in bed all day until it was time to go to Holly's for Christmas Eve dinner.

Chapter Fifty

Justine

Justine sat in the back of the courtroom and watched as first Noah, then Lucas, gave testimony on Eric Dillard. It had been a long day, and she was ready to wrap it up. She looked to her right, at the back of Simone's head. Justine fingered her engagement ring. Simone had almost cost her everything. She wanted to pay her back so she could move on. She wanted to have some closure with her. Simone seemed to sense her looking at her. She glanced over her shoulder, and their eyes met. Justine gave her a tight smile. Simone looked away quickly. Simone was afraid of her! It was laughable. She hadn't been afraid when she was after Lucas.

Justine returned her attention to Lucas' testimony and made some notes. When the prosecutor was done with Lucas, they had a recess. Everyone stood and started to file out of the courtroom. Justine stood and lingered a moment, staring at Simone, who remained seated. She wanted to go over and stick a thorn in her side, but she decided against it. She stepped into the hallway and waited for Lucas and Noah. Noah came out first.

"Hey, Justine. You waitin' on us or layin' in the cut for

Simone?" he asked with a smile.

Justine laughed. "I was waiting for you guys. Where's Lucas?"

"Talking to Captain Myers. He'll be right out."

Simone chose that time to come out. She was hurrying so fast, she almost walked right into Noah. She realized her mistake and jerked away from him. Throwing her head back quickly, she kept walking without speaking to either of them. They turned in unison and watched her go.

Noah smiled wickedly. "I don't believe she likes us anymore, Justine."

Justine smirked. "Good, then the feeling's mutual."

Noah looked down at her. "You been behavin' yourself?"

Justine kept her smile, but frowned a little. She was never admitting to anything. Better to let them think what they wanted. "Of course. Haven't you?"

Noah grinned. "Sorry. Don't know how."

They shared a smile as Lucas came out with the captain. Captain Myers took one look at Noah and Justine and frowned.

Karma

"Ramsey, what are you doing? This is a trial. No interviews." He looked at Justine sternly, as if she should know better. She couldn't suppress her smile.

"Captain Myers, I assure you, I wasn't asking for an interview." She looked at Lucas.

"This is my fiancé," Lucas said, moving closer to her.

Myers' mouth fell open. "You're kiddin' me, right, Cain? You're engaged to Justine Greer?"

Lucas smiled and nodded. "Yeah, I am."

Myers chuckled and shook his head. "Some guys have all the luck. You know, it's a wonder you guys pulled this thing off."

"Ah, but we did," Noah said.

Myers nodded. "Yes, you did. That clown's going away for a long time. Good work," he said and walked away.

Justine eased between Lucas and Noah and took them both by the arm. "You guys were good today. Like your captain says, you're going to send him away for a long time. I'm very proud of you both." She led them out of the courtroom.

Simone was standing on the courthouse stairs ending a call on her cell phone. She looked deeply troubled as she put the phone back in her bag. She turned around and saw the three of them standing there, so she walked over.

"I don't know how you just managed that shit. Maybe you're paying someone to do your dirty work for you. I warned you though, if you don't leave me alone, I'm getting a restraining order against your little ass," she said to Justine.

Justine was truly at a loss. She had told Lucy to put a stop to that business when Lucas found out. As a matter of fact, Lucy was on vacation in St. Marten with her drug-dealing boyfriend at the moment.

"What are you talking about?" she asked Simone.

Simone stuck her finger in Justine's face. "Don't pretend you didn't just make one of your prank phone calls, Justine. Calling me a bitch and talking about how you're gonna kill me," she said loudly.

Lucas stepped in front of Justine. "Whoa. Wait a minute. Lower your voice. Justine didn't call you. She was right here and take your hand out of her face."

Simone looked at Lucas and dropped her hand. She looked momentarily confused. "So, if she was with you, then who's calling me? Who was that?"

Noah looked amused. "Seems like you've got yourself a problem. Maybe you should talk to the police."

Simone looked at him like she wanted to hit him.

Noah inched toward her. "Go ahead. I dare you," he said with a cold smile.

Justine maneuvered around Lucas to face Simone. "It wasn't me. Maybe your boyfriend doesn't want you testifying against him. Have you ever thought of that?"

Simone's eyes widened, and her hand flew to her mouth. "Oh! I never thought of that. Oh, my God. What am I supposed to do?"

Justine shrugged and smiled at the panicked look on her face. Was she really asking her for advice? She must have forgotten they were no longer friends. "I really don't know what to tell you, Simone. Noah says you should talk to the police."

Simone's beautiful face twisted in frustration. "I am talking to the fucking police. There's two detectives standing right here that are involved with this goddamned case! Neither one of them is doing one damn thing to help me. You're all standing there laughing at me, like you think this shit is funny! Somebody just threatened to kill me, for God's sake!" She was yelling at Justine, but she was looking at Lucas. Justine looked up at him, too. Lucas was watching Simone with cold eyes. He took his wallet out and withdrew a business card. He held it out in Simone's general direction.

"This is Captain Myers' number. If you don't see him when you go back in, give him a call as soon as possible. He'll be able to help you with protection."

Simone took the card from him. "Thank you, Lucas."

He nodded at her and put his arm around Justine. Simone took her time and noted the gesture. She eyed them both and walked away. Justine folded her arms across her chest and regarded Lucas and Noah.

"Well, who looks crazy now?"

They all turned and watched Simone disappear into the courthouse.

Karma

Chapter Fifty-One

Simone

Simone took the Number Six train up to 110th Street with Raphael. They were making a special trip to see his cousin, Manny. She wasn't crazy about the neighborhood, but she glanced over at Raphael with his short, platinum hair, peg-leg jeans, engineer boots, short leather motorcycle jacket, and black lacquered nails. He walked as if he didn't have a care in the world and spoke to several people. His demeanor put her at ease. She tried to relax. She was getting tired of always looking over her shoulder. Simone was getting paranoid with a capitol P, seeing people following her, screening her calls. Ever since that day at the courthouse when Justine said maybe Nine was responsible, Simone had been terrified.

Maybe Justine's harassment had been simply that. Harassment. She'd been trying to get her back for sleeping with Lucas. Eric was a different story. She remembered how he reacted when he found out she knew Lucas and Noah. He looked like he wanted to kill her. Simone believed he could, too. All too vividly, she recalled that day she watched him almost gleefully blow Dirty

Mike's brains out. She remembered how it felt to get splashed with all that bloody gore. It hadn't even fazed Eric. If he could kill someone he grew up with like that, she knew he had no problems getting rid of her.

She followed Raphael into a seedy-looking building. Raphael rang for the elevator.

"You sure you want to do this, chica?" he asked her, his eyes filled with concern.

Simone looked worried. "Don't you think I should?" she countered.

He put an arm around her and kissed her cheek. "I do, Simone. I don't think you have much choice."

The elevator arrived, and they stepped inside. They rode up to the eighth floor. Raphael rang Manny's doorbell, and he answered it right away.

"Raphael! How's it going?"

Simone swallowed a giggle as Raphael exchanged dap and a one-shouldered hug with his cousin. Hell, she'd never seen him act so manly!

"Good to see you, Manny. This is my friend, Simone."

Karma

Manny was a good-looking guy with longish hair and a buff body adorned with a myriad of tattoos which were plain to see because he was sans shirt. He gave Simone the once-over and smiled at her with teeth so perfect, they had to be veneers.

"Ah, Simone. Come in. Sit down."

They entered the apartment and followed Manny into the beautifully decorated dining room. The place was so nicely tricked out Simone wondered why he didn't relocate to a nicer building.

"Have a seat. Can I get you anything?"

Simone shook her head, and Raphael requested a soda. Manny said he'd be right back.

"Your cousin's cute," she said.

Raphael smiled. "Runs in the family."

"This apartment is to die for. Why does he live here?"

Raphael looked at her and rolled his eyes. "Don't be a snob, Simone. It's not bad up here. Besides, this is where he's most comfortable." He looked at her knowingly.

"Oh. This is where he does his business?"

"Bingo."

Manny returned with Raphael's soda and a gray metal briefcase. He sat next to Simone and popped it open. There were four handguns inside, each in its own cozy compartment.

"I didn't bring out the big boys. One of these should be enough for you to protect yourself. As a matter of fact, I think this one would be perfect for you." He picked up a nicely made .32 and handed it to her. Simone tested the weight of the gun. It wasn't too heavy, but she put it down quickly. She wasn't a big gun fan; she just needed to protect herself.

"What makes it perfect for me?" she asked.

Manny picked the gun up again and aimed at a vase on the highboy. "Well, it's fairly lightweight, a heavy enough caliber to take someone out, and you're a big enough girl to handle the little kick it's got."

Raphael leaned forward. "This is the one you like?" he asked Manny.

Manny nodded.

"Good. She'll take it."

Simone turned to him, slightly annoyed. "Raphael, what about the other ones? I mean, I should at least look at them."

Raphael shook his head. "Simone, we're not comparison shopping for a pair of jeans. This is a gun. We don't know guns. Manny does. If he says this is the one for you, I'm inclined to believe him. Mission over. Case closed. Buy the gun."

They stared at each other for a moment. Simone reached into her purse and took out her wallet. She managed to smile at Manny.

"So ... how much?"

269

Karma

Chapter Fifty-Two

271

Karma

Lucas

Lucas and Noah left the precinct together and stepped outside into the flurry of snow that had been falling for the better part of the day. They both donned wool caps and pulled their collars up. They shared a look. It was New Year's Eve. Last year, they'd gotten lucky and had the time off. This year, they weren't so lucky. They had Times Square detail. Noah pulled his gloves on and shook his head.

"I ain't really feelin' this shit, Luke. We ain't had to watch the ball drop up close in years."

Lucas pulled his gloves on, too. "We wouldn't have had to do it now if Myers wasn't on vacation. This shit is sour grapes for the bust."

Noah nodded. "Yeah, that prick, Silvestri. Why do they always let him take over for Myers? I can't stand his prejudiced ass."

Lucas looked at Noah. "Well, he can't stand our black asses either. You know, it's killin' him that we got promoted."

Noah scowled. "He shouldn't even be able to do this shit to us. He's runnin' that 'we needed the benefit of their experience' shit. Fuck that. People know the deal. Ain't no fool tryin' to be out there tonight doin' the shit we lock people up for. Not tonight. This is some bullshit."

"I agree."

Noah was still scowling. "Let's go. I wanna get this shit over with."

Lucas looked at his watch. "It's only seven. You can't rush the clock, No."

Noah stayed scowling as they got into their unmarked car. "Shit, I can try."

They drove to 45th Street and parked the car. Both of them were reluctant to get out. Noah lit a cigarette.

"What were you planning on doing after this shit detail? Meetin' up with Justine?"

Lucas nodded. "Something like that. Nothin's written in stone. What about you?"

Noah blew smoke out the window. "No plans. Lissette is out of town, and Nadine's got little Noah."

Lucas laughed. "Why didn't you say something? When we finish this, we'll go get a drink. I can't let you ring in the New Year alone, No."

Noah grinned at him. "Gee whiz, you're such a good friend."

They laughed.

"Shut up. Let's go."

They walked over to Times Square and disappeared into the mass of people. The teeming crowd was relatively well behaved to be so dense. They didn't issue any tickets, just shut down a few revelers with open containers. Time went by pretty fast, and before they knew it, the ball was dropping. The crowd grew more excited as they counted in the New Year. Lucas thought he'd go deaf when the crowd screamed "Happy New Year" collectively. He winced and turned to Noah, who had his fingers stuck in his ears.

Lucas laughed at him. "Happy New Year, No!" he yelled.

Noah blinked at him comically. "What?"

Lucas threw an arm around his neck. "I said, 'Happy New Year!'"

Noah patted him on the back. "Right back at you, bro. Now, let's go get that drink. I swear to God, I just went deaf."

Karma

Chapter Fifty-Three

Simone

Simone sat in her dark living room amidst all the boxes that she'd packed up. She was ready to get out of here. She couldn't wait for this stupid trial to be over. She also couldn't stop shaking. She was tired of constantly looking over her shoulder. She smiled wryly. She had thought Justine was losing it, but she wasn't. Now Simone felt she was drifting further and further away from her own sanity.

Moments ago, she could have sworn someone had followed her into her building, but it had only been some weirdness with the shadows and the lights. She was tired of living in constant fear. Simone stood up and wiped her palms on her jeans. She shrugged to herself and went into the kitchen to get the bottle of champagne she'd stuck in the refrigerator earlier. She thought of calling Raphael to join her, but she wanted him to have and enjoy this last New Year in New York. She wanted him to have some fun, not be stuck in the house babysitting her frightened ass.

Simone popped the cork and turned on the television. Dick Clark's "Rockin' Eve" was just starting. She poured herself a flute of champagne to calm her nerves and take the edge off. By the time the ball dropped, she was halfway through the bottle.

274

Karma

Chapter Fifty-Four

Lucas

Lucas didn't get annoyed with Noah often, but he was working his nerves a bit right now. Noah wanted to stay at the bar and keep drinking; Lucas wanted to go home to Justine. He leaned on the bar and watched Noah get his mack on. He was currently flirting with a tall, dark-skinned sister with goddess braids down her back. He smiled a little, his irritation easing up a bit. Noah had always been the way he was, and he wasn't changing for anybody. He'd tell you as much himself.

"Is that smile for me, or are you just reflecting on how damned handsome you are?" The line was so smooth and delivered with so much aplomb, it caught him off guard. He raised an eyebrow and turned to see who it came from. A petite, mocha-colored honey with movie star good looks wearing a shockingly tight dress that was just about the same color she was stood next to him. He almost did a double take to make sure she wasn't naked. She smiled at him sexily and moved in real close. The lady smelled like flowers.

"Where'd you learn a line like that?" he asked, taking a sip of his drink.

She looked him over with obvious pleasure. "Who said it was a line? Just stating facts. You are quite handsome. I'm sure you know it."

Lucas laughed. Another beautiful, ballsy woman. He'd had enough of that, but he didn't see a reason to insult her, even though he wanted her to go away.

"So ... what are you doing here all alone on New Year's?" she asked, setting down her Cosmopolitan.

Lucas didn't want her to get too comfortable, so he was honest with her. "I'm not alone. I stopped in with my partner to get a drink after work."

"Partner? Please, tell me you're not gay."

Lucas laughed and shook his head. "No. I'm a cop."

Her eyes brightened. "Really? I bet you look real sexy in your uniform."

"I don't usually wear one. I'm a detective."

She moved even closer until her left breast was touching his arm. Lucas straightened up and looked at her.

"Even better. My name is Celine, by the way." She offered her hand to him.

Karma

Lucas looked at it and picked his drink up. Celine's name was so close to Simone's that it made him shudder. She ignored the rebuke and kept talking.

"So do you have a name or what? You can't possibly be as shy as you're pretending to be."

Lucas laughed again and raised himself up to his full height. Time to put an end to this shit. "That's the first time I ever heard that one. I'm not shy. I'm engaged."

Celine laughed wickedly. "Hell, I'm married. So what?"

Lucas frowned and moved away from her. He looked at her seriously and put his glass down. "Nice to meet you, Celine. Good night and Happy New Year."

She looked disappointed. "Are you dismissing me?"

"Uh-huh," he replied.

She shrugged her heavenly shoulders. "Your loss. Happy New Year." She picked up her drink and slowly walked away.

Lucas watched her go with no regret. She was beautiful, but he already knew she wasn't worth it. Simone had taught him a tough lesson, but he'd learned well. Nobody was worth losing Justine. He looked over at Noah, who looked to be whispering sweet nothings into the tall girl's ear. She was smiling seductively, and Lucas knew his boy well enough to know he probably wouldn't be sleeping alone this night. He finished his drink and put his coat on. Time to go. He walked over and tapped Noah on the shoulder.

"Yo, man, I'm out."

Noah peeled himself away and surprised him. "All right. Give me a couple of seconds."

Lucas fell back and gave Noah his space. He watched them exchange numbers.

Noah put his coat on and joined Lucas at the door. Noah laughed at the look on his face. "What's up, dawg? Why you look so shocked? Thought I was hittin' that tonight, didn't you?"

"Damn sure did, No. What happened?"

They stepped out into the snow and started walking toward Lucas' car. Noah lit a Dunhill and looked pensive.

"Nothin'. That's just it. Nothin' happened. I was just havin' fun, but I didn't really feel like doing anything, you know?"

Lucas smiled and nodded. "Yeah, I do. That didn't have anything to do with Lissette, did it?"

Noah frowned at him. "Come on with that shit, Luke. I got punked once. I ain't goin' out like that again."

Lucas laughed and shook his head. "Noah, you know as well as I do that it didn't go down like that."

Noah inhaled and smirked. "Yeah, you right. Had a nice little wife, a great kid, nice house … I threw it all away 'cause I couldn't keep my pants up. Probably 'cause I was hangin' out with your ass, Luke."

Lucas turned and looked at him, not without affection. "Nah, don't blame me for your shit. Your ass was like that when I met you."

Noah laughed. "True, true."

They reached the car and got in. They were quiet for a moment. Lucas took his cell phone out and called Justine. Her phone rang until the machine picked up. He frowned and tried her cell. Same thing. Went to voicemail. His heart sped up as he snapped his phone shut. His mind went instantly to Darius, but his instinct didn't. His instinct told him there was something seriously wrong. That dark feeling of dread, the feeling that something bad was going to happen — the feeling he'd been having for months suddenly dropped down on him huge and dark. Overwhelming.

Noah was looking at him. He flicked his cigarette out the

277

Karma

window and watched him as he replaced his phone. "Something wrong?" he asked.

"Can't find Justine."

Noah's frown mirrored his own. "Think something's wrong?"

Lucas put on his turn signal to pull out. "I know it is."

Noah sat back in his seat. "It's probably nothing." His eyes, however, betrayed the calm in his voice. They shared a look, and Noah spoke before Lucas could. "I think we should go."

Lucas peeled away from the curb a lot faster than he should have.

Karma

Chapter Fifty-Five

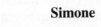

Simone

Simone was brooding. She was leaning against the French doors that opened to her terrace, surveying the contents of her life packed up into boxes. It wasn't fair. She didn't really want to leave New York. Her life was here. And who was she running from? Justine? Life was funny, but that had to be the biggest joke of all. Her actually being afraid of Justine. Hell, she'd steamrolled all over Justine since she'd known her. Simone looked down at her right hand and realized she was still holding the champagne bottle. She smiled to herself and took a swig, thinking back to when she first met Justine.

She met Holly and Justine at the same time, at the same campus function. Justine had been okay at first, but as Simone grew to know her, she found that all she wanted to do was knock the shine off Justine's perfect world. Everything about Justine radiated perfectionism and overachievment. She was a doted on only child and had a handsome and equally overachieving boyfriend. Justine was pretty, vivacious, at the top of her class, and worst of all, almost cloyingly sweet and deserving.

After all Simone had been through, she found Justine particularly hard to swallow. She could identify with Holly more. Holly was from the projects and hadn't had such an easy time getting to where she was either. But Justine … prom queen, valedictorian … There'd been times, a lot of times, when Justine hadn't done anything. Simone had just wanted to punch a hole in her balloon and wipe the smile off her face.

Then they'd gotten older, found jobs in their professions, and all was well. There were times, though, when Simone felt like retching when she saw Justine's sweet little face on TV. They went places, and people asked for her autograph like she was the goddamn Queen of England. Simone hated it. People fawning over her. Then came the icing on the cake. Lucas.

Simone didn't want her to have him. Justine got everything she wanted. Why him, too? It just wasn't fair! Lucas was one fuck of a catch. And he was fine as hell. No, it wasn't fair. Fuck her and her happily-ever-after. In a way, she deserved her share of pain.

Simone smiled again. She knew that what she'd done with Michael in college didn't even touch the devastation Justine had gone through when she'd slept with Lucas. Simone grinned. That sure had wiped the smile off her face and stopped her from skipping. Poor Queen Justine. It had changed her into a different person. A heartbroken person. A real person, with real problems, for once, not just a black Barbie living in a happy bubble.

Karma

Simone took another swig from the bottle, that evil smirk still playing at the corners of her mouth. She'd knocked Mr. Cain down a few pegs, too. Pre-Justine, she knew she could have had him fairly quickly. Post-Justine, that shit had been almost impossible. Never in her life had Simone thrown herself at any man the way she'd done with Lucas Cain. But it had been worth it to see his resolve disintegrate. It was almost funny. It was definitely worth it. Period.

She sat on the sofa and made herself comfortable. Yet another sip from the bottle. Fuck drinking out of a glass for right now. This was her last New Year's in New York City, and unbelievably, she was alone. She bet Justine wasn't alone. Most likely, she was screaming Lucas' name by now. Bitch. And she was really a bitch now. Who would have thought sweet little Justine would have tried to terrorize her like she had? Simone had to admit, she hadn't expected any retribution. She thought Justine would just cry into her pillow. Instead, Justine had shaken her enough that she purchased a gun for protection. Simone was pretty sure Justine hired someone to do it. After all, Justine would never do the dirty work herself. Still …

"Who thought she'd have the balls?" Simone asked herself. Another swig. She stood up unsteadily and turned to go to the bathroom. The phone rang. Her heart jumped into her mouth at the unexpected sound. It rang five times before it went to her machine.

"Hey, bitch! Happy New Year! I see you! Saw you earlier, too. You should be more careful. You could get hurt."

Simone rushed to the windows and closed the blinds. She was trembling. It was that same tinny voice. Those hadn't been shadows earlier, and maybe this wasn't Justine. Maybe it was Eric. She dialed star sixty-nine. Unknown number. Suddenly, something crashed through the pane of one of her French doors. Simone screamed and jerked around to see what it was. All she saw at first was glass. She dared to move a bit closer and then saw it. A hole in the wall. A bullet hole. Her hands flew over her mouth.

"Oh, shit! Oh — my — God!"

She ran into her bedroom and got the gun out of her nightstand with shaking hands. She drunkenly, or maybe conveniently, forgot all her previous thoughts about Eric being responsible. That was it. She'd had it. Justine was going to stop this shit tonight. She wasn't playing.

281

Karma

Chapter Fifty-Six

Lucas

Lucas couldn't get to Justine fast enough. His heart was pounding. He knew in his bones that something was horribly wrong. This was that bad feeling he'd been having, front and center. That sense of dread finally come to fruition, he could feel it. Noah rode beside him, deathly quiet. He and Noah were close. He knew that Noah had zeroed in on his feelings. He wore the same look of dread on his face that Lucas was wearing.

Lucas screeched to a stop in front of Justine's building, and they both jumped out of his double-parked car. They walked briskly into the lobby. Lucas glanced at the stairs. Noah shook his head.

"She lives on the 10th floor, bro. This is faster." He pushed the button for the elevator, and it dinged open instantly. They rode up in silence. When the doors opened, they hurried to her apartment and Lucas opened the door to a nightmare. Simone was astride Justine, choking her so hard and banging her head on the floor. The carpet behind Justine's head was wet with blood, and Justine was like a rag doll. Her eyes were closed, and she was totally limp. Lucas started screaming.

"What are you doing? What are you doing? Get off her! Get off!"

He and Noah reached the women at the same time, and they both pulled Simone off Justine. Noah wrestled Simone away as Lucas fell on his knees beside Justine. He gingerly put his hand behind her head to find the source of all the blood. He took his hand away quickly. It came back wet. She had a pretty bad head wound. Her skull actually felt soft. Lucas put his fingers to her throat, feeling for a pulse. He didn't find one. Oh, shit! Oh, Jesus! She killed her! He fought the anguish that threatened to drown him and immediately began CPR, praying he wasn't too late. Seconds later, he blew into her mouth and started chest compressions again.

"Oh, God, please. Please, baby, breathe. Come on." He worked on her frantically, only dimly aware of Noah trying to restrain Simone, who was fighting him like a wildcat. Justine wasn't responding. He worked harder and calmer. He didn't want to lose her because he couldn't control himself and stay cool. He swallowed the scream that worked itself into his throat. He distantly heard the jangle of Noah's handcuffs.

Karma

"Come on, baby, come on. Breathe. I love you. Breathe!" Lucas knew she couldn't stay this way without incurring irreparable damage. He was starting to lose hope when Justine hitched in air and started breathing, shallowly. What seemed like an eternity had really been under two minutes. He bent and kissed her forehead, weak with relief.

"Thank God." He touched her face and made the 911 call requesting an ambulance. He checked again to see if she was breathing on her own, then stood up. He could kill Simone with his bare hands. He looked at her with murder in his heart and started toward her. Noah had her on her feet with one hand cuffed, about to cuff the other. He was reading Simone her rights. They both saw the rage in Lucas' face.

"Whoa, Luke! Chill man!" Noah said. At that moment, Simone broke away from him and ran for her coat. Lucas was right on her. When he reached for her, she turned around holding a .32.

"Oh, shit!" Noah yelled. Lucas didn't have time to react. Simone pulled the trigger and shot him. He looked at her in shock as he felt the bullet crack his collar bone. The searing, burning pain only made him angrier. He kept coming for her, pulling out his own weapon and flicking off the safety. He heard Noah yelling again.

"Move, Lucas! Move!"

Simone squeezed her eyes shut and shot him again. This time, the bullet struck him between the ribs and he went down.

"You fuckin' bitch!" Noah screamed. Lucas heard three shots, and Simone fell on top of him. With fading strength, he pushed her body aside. She landed on her back and stared at him with lifeless eyes. She was dead, and he was glad. He tried to move as Noah phoned in an officer down. The ambulance would get here much quicker now. Lucas forced himself up on one elbow and pushed himself away from Simone. He didn't want to be anywhere near her. Fucking crazy bitch shot him! He couldn't believe this shit. Noah came and knelt over him. His face was scratched up.

"Justine's still breathing on her own. Stop movin' around. You don't know how bad she hurt you." Noah eased him back down. Lucas coughed a spray of blood. Noah looked horrified.

"Oh, shit, Luke! Get up, man. Get up. You can't lie on your back. I don't want you to drown. Oh, God. Oh no." He helped Lucas get to the sofa and let him down easy.

"Fucking bitch. I don't believe this shit. I don't believe it," Noah muttered.

Karma

Lucas heard sirens in the distance. He was finding it hard to breathe. He looked down at Justine. If it weren't for all the blood and the bruises on her neck, she looked as if she were sleeping. This shit was surreal. He coughed again with the same crimson spray. Noah looked terrified. Then he did something that was totally out of character for him. He held Lucas' hand and spoke very quietly.

"Listen to me. I have no idea how bad this shit is, but it ain't pretty, bro. You gotta hang in there, Luke. You can't leave me. You're my best friend. You're my brother. Oh, man, this is fucked up." He bowed his head. Lucas knew what he was doing. He was praying. While he was praying, everything went black.

ORDER FORM

Triple Crown Publications
PO Box 247378
Columbus, OH 43219
1-800-Book-Log

NAME	
ADDRESS	
CITY	
STATE	
ZIP	

TITLES	PRICE
A Hood Legend	$15.00
A Hustler's Son	$15.00
A Hustler's Wife	$15.00
A Project Chick	$15.00
Always A Queen	$15.00
Amongst Thieves	$15.00
Betrayed	$15.00
Bitch	$15.00
Bitch Reloaded	$15.00
Black	$15.00
Black and Ugly	$15.00
Blinded	$15.00
Buffie the Body 2009 Calendar	$20.00
Cash Money	$15.00
Chances	$15.00
Chyna Black	$15.00
Contagious	$15.00
Crack Head	$15.00
Cream	$15.00

SHIPPING/HANDLING
1-3 books $5.00
4-9 books $9.00
$1.95 for each add'l book

TOTAL $_____

FORMS OF ACCEPTED PAYMENTS:
Postage Stamps, Personal or Institutional Checks &
Money Orders.
All mail-in orders take 5-7 business days to be delivered.

ORDER FORM

Triple Crown Publications
PO Box 247378
Columbus, OH 43219
1-800-Book-Log

NAME	
ADDRESS	
CITY	
STATE	
ZIP	

TITLES	PRICE
Cut Throat	$15.00
Dangerous	$15.00
Dime Piece	$15.00
Dirty Red *Hardcover	$20.00
Dirty Red *Paperback	$15.00
Dirty South	$15.00
Diva	$15.00
Dollar Bill	$15.00
Down Chick	$15.00
Flipside of The Game	$15.00
For the Strength of You	$15.00
Game Over	$15.00
Gangsta	$15.00
Grimey	$15.00
Grindin' *Hardcover	$10.00
Hold U Down	$15.00
Hoodwinked	$15.00
How to Succeed in the Publishing Game	$20.00
In Cahootz	$15.00
Keisha	$15.00

SHIPPING/HANDLING
1-3 books $5.00
4-9 books $9.00
$1.95 for each add'l book

TOTAL $_____

FORMS OF ACCEPTED PAYMENTS:
Postage Stamps, Personal or Institutional Checks & Money Orders.
All mail-in orders take 5-7 business days to be delivered.

ORDER FORM

Triple Crown Publications
PO Box 247378
Columbus, OH 43219
1-800-Book-Log

NAME	
ADDRESS	
CITY	
STATE	
ZIP	

TITLES	PRICE
Larceny	$15.00
Let That Be the Reason	$15.00
Life	$15.00
Life's A Bitch	$15.00
Love & Loyalty	$15.00
Me & My Boyfriend	$15.00
Menage's Way	$15.00
Mina's Joint	$15.00
Mistress of the Game	$15.00
Queen	$15.00
Rage Times Fury	$15.00
Road Dawgz	$15.00
Sheisty	$15.00
Stacy	$15.00
Still Dirty *Hardcover	$20.00
Still Sheisty	$15.00
Street Love	$15.00
Sunshine & Rain	$15.00
The Bitch is Back	$15.00

SHIPPING/HANDLING
1-3 books $5.00
4-9 books $9.00
$1.95 for each add'l book

                                    TOTAL $_____

FORMS OF ACCEPTED PAYMENTS:
Postage Stamps, Personal or Institutional Checks &
Money Orders.
All mail-in orders take 5-7 business days to be delivered.

ORDER FORM
Triple Crown Publications
PO Box 247378
Columbus, OH 43219
1-800-Book-Log

NAME
ADDRESS
CITY
STATE
ZIP

TITLES	PRICE
The Hood Rats	$15.00
Betrayed	$15.00
The Pink Palace	$15.00
The Bitch is Back	$15.00
Life's A Bitch	$15.00
Still Dirty *Hardcover	$20.00
Always A Queen	$15.00

SHIPPING/HANDLING
1-3 books $5.00
4-9 books $9.00
$1.95 for each add'l book

TOTAL $_____

FORMS OF ACCEPTED PAYMENTS:
Postage Stamps, Institutional Checks & Money
Orders, All mail in orders take 5-7 Business
days to be delivered

31901050638743

Lucas. Those are his feelings, not mine. I'm in love with you, not Darius. I want to marry you. I want to have your children, not his. That relationship was over for quite awhile before I met you, Lucas. Please, honey, I don't know why he's even a subject we have to talk about. He has no place here. He's the past. You're my future."

Lucas studied her face. She seemed earnest enough. He did notice how she left out the details. It was probably just as well. He really had no desire whatsoever to know more than he already did. He took a deep breath and let it out slowly.

"I would be wrong not to say that you working so closely with him bothers me."

"I know, but there's nothing going on, Lucas, honestly. I mean, I can appreciate you being justifiably upset. You saw the same guy hugging me twice. I know I would have flipped if I saw some woman with her arms around you, too."

Lucas mind flashed quickly to Simone's head bobbing up and down, his hands wound roughly in her hair. Some woman had more than her arms wrapped around him. He felt a tremendous pang of guilt and decided to leave Justine alone. He closed the space between them.

Karma

"All right. Let's drop it. If I catch him with his hands on you again, that's his ass."

Justine put her arms around him. "All right." She tilted her head up, and he kissed her. He felt that same heady, giddy feeling she always gave him. He loved her. No question. Justine untied the belt to his robe and pushed it off his shoulders. She gracefully pulled her dress over her head and flung it across the room. She stood before him in nothing but a white thong. Lucas smiled; she smiled back coyly.

"I was hoping you'd be happy to see me."

He picked her up and threw her over his shoulder.

"Always," he said and carried her into the bedroom.